20p

ST[illegible]OOK 2

The clos[illegible] opened, and from the [illegible]ed woman. In her hand [illegible] which I had seen *the* [illegible] footstep. She turned r[illegible]ed the letters and seem[illegible] a livid face, the face as of a man long drowned – bloated, bleached – seaweed tangled in its dripping hair . . .

The Haunted and the Haunters by Lord Lytton is one of fourteen spine-chilling tales.

Also available in Star:

STAR BUMPER HORROR BOOK 1

STAR BUMPER HORROR BOOK 2

Edited by Kurt Singer

A STAR BOOK
published by
the Paperback Division of
W.H. ALLEN & Co. PLC

A Star Book
Published in 1986
by the Paperback Division of
W.H. Allen & Co. PLC
44 Hill Street, London W1X 8LB

First published in Great Britain by
Target Books as two separate volumes in 1985

These stories were first selected by Kurt Singer for inclusion in his anthologies *Tales from the Unknown, Ghouls and Ghosts, Satanic Omnibus, Gothic Horror Book* and *They are Possessed*
(W.H. Allen 1970, 1972, 1973, 1974, 1976)

Printed in Great Britain by
Hunt Barnard Ltd, Aylesbury, Bucks.

ISBN 0 352 31945 3

CONTENTS

A Terribly Strange Bed

WILKIE COLLINS

Shortly after my education at college was finished, I happened to be staying at Paris with an English friend. We were both young, and lived rather a wild life.

One night I said to my friend, 'Let us go somewhere where we can see a little genuine gambling, with no false glitter thrown over it. Let us get away from fashionable Frascati's to a house where they don't mind letting in a man with a ragged coat.'

'Very well,' said he, 'we needn't go out of the Palais Royal to find the sort of company you want. Here's the place just before us; as blackguard a place as you could possibly want to see.'

Entering the house, we went upstairs, left our hats and sticks with the doorkeeper and were admitted into the chief gambling room. We had come to see blackguards, but the people assembled there were something worse, and the quiet of the room was horrible. The thin, haggard, long-haired young man, whose sunken eyes fiercely watched the turning up of the cards, never spoke; the flabby fat-faced pimply player, who pricked his piece of pasteboard perseveringly, to register how often black won, and how often red—never spoke; the dirty, wrinkled, old man, with the vulture eyes and the darned greatcoat, who had lost his last sou, and still looked on desperately, after he could play no longer—never spoke. Even the voice of the croupier sounded as if it were dulled and thickened by the atmosphere of the room. I had entered the place to laugh, but I soon found it necessary to take refuge in excitement from the depression of spirits which began to steal on me.

I sought the nearest excitement by going to the table, and beginning to play. Unfortunately, as the event will show, I won—won prodigiously; won incredibly; won at such a rate that the regular players at the table crowded round me; and staring at my stakes with hungry, superstitious eyes, whispered to one another that the English stranger was going to break the bank.

The game was Rouge et Noir. I had played it in every city in Europe, but a gambler, in the strict sense of the word, I had never been. My gaming was a mere idle amusement. I never practised it so incessantly as to lose more than I could afford, or to gain more than I could pocket without being thrown off my balance by my good luck.

On this occasion it was very different—now, for the first time in my life I felt what the passion of play really was. My success first bewildered, and then intoxicated me. Incredible as it may appear, I only lost when I attempted to estimate chances, and played according to previous calculation. If I left everything to luck, and staked without any care or consideration, I was sure to win—to win in the face of every recognised probability in favour of the bank.

Time after time, I staked higher, and still won. The excitement in the room rose to fever pitch. The silence was interrupted by muttered oaths every time the gold was shovelled across to my side of the table—until the imperturbable croupier dashed his rake on the floor in a fury of astonishment at my success. Only one man present preserved his self-possession; and that man was my friend. He came to my side, and whispering in English, begged me to leave the place satisfied with what I had already gained. He repeated his warnings and entreaties several times; and only left me and went away after I had rejected his advice (for I was to all intents and purposes gambling drunk) in terms which rendered it impossible for him to address me again that night.

Shortly after he had gone, a hoarse voice behind me cried: 'Permit me, my dear sir! permit me to restore to their proper place two Napoleons which you have dropped. Wonderful luck, sir! I pledge you my word of honour as an old soldier, in the course of my long experience in this sort of thing, I never saw such luck as yours—never! Go on, sir. Sacré mille bombes! Go on boldly, and break the bank!'

Turning round I saw, nodding and smiling at me with inveterate civility, a tall man, dressed in a frogged and braided surtout. If I had been in my senses, I should have considered him as being rather a suspicious specimen of an old soldier. He had goggling blood-shot eyes, mangy mustachios, a broken nose, and the dirtiest pair of hands I ever saw—even in France. However, in the reckless triumph of that moment, I was ready to fraternise with anybody who encouraged me in my game. I accepted the old soldier's offered pinch of snuff; clapped him on the back, and swore he was the most glorious relic of the Grand Army that I had met.

'Go on,' cried my military friend, snapping his fingers in ecstasy—'Go on, and win! Break the bank. Mille tonnerres! My gallant English comrade, break the bank!'

And I did go on—went on at such a rate, that in another quarter of an hour the croupier called out: 'Gentlemen! The bank has discontinued for tonight.' All the notes, and all the gold in that 'bank' now lay in a heap under my hands.

'Tie up the money in your pocket-handkerchief, my worthy sir,' said the old soldier, as I plunged my hands into my heap of gold. 'Tie it up, as we used to tie up a bit of dinner in the Grand Army: your winnings are too heavy for any breeches pocket that ever was sewed. There, that's it!—shovel them in, notes and all! Crédie! what luck! Now then, sir—two tight double knots each way with your honourable permission, and the money's safe. Feel it! Feel it, fortunate sir! Hard and round as a cannon ball. Ah! Bah! if they had only fired such cannon balls at us at Austerlitz.

Nom d'une pipe . . . if they only had! And now as an ancient grenadier, what remains for me to do? Simply this: to entreat my valued English friend to drink a bottle of champagne with me, before we part.'

'Excellent! Champagne by all means!'

'Bravo! the Englishman; another glass. Ah! Bah!—the bottle is empty! Never mind! Vive le vin! I, the old soldier, order another bottle, and half a pound of bon-bons with it.'

'No, no, ex-brave; *your* bottle last time; my bottle this. Toast away! The French Army!—the great Napoleon!—the present company!'

By the time the second bottle of champagne was emptied, I felt as if I had been drinking liquid fire—my brain seemed all a-flame. 'Ex-brave of the French Army!' cried I, in a mad state of exhiliration, 'I am on fire! Let us have a third bottle of champagne to put the flame out!'

The old soldier placed his dirty forefinger by the side of his broken nose; and solemnly ejaculated, 'Coffee!'

'Listen, my dear sir, to an old soldier's advice. Coffee will help to rid you of your exaltation of spirits before going home. With all that money it is a sacred duty to yourself to have your wits about you. You are known to be a winner to an enormous extent by several gentlemen present tonight, who are in many ways worthy and excellent fellows; but they are mortal men, my dear sir, and they have their amiable weaknesses!'

As the ex-brave ended, the coffee came in, ready poured out in two cups. My attentive friend handed me one of the cups with a bow. I was parched with thirst, and drank it at a draught. Almost instantly afterwards, I was seized with a fit of giddiness, and felt more completely intoxicated than ever. I rose from my chair, holding on by the table to keep my balance; and stammered out that I felt unwell—so unwell that I did not know how I was to get home.

'My dear friend,' answered the old soldier, 'it would be madness to go home in your present state; you would be sure to lose your money; you might be robbed and murdered with the greatest ease. *I* am going to sleep here; do *you* sleep here, too—they make up capital beds in this house—take one; sleep off the effects of the wine, and go home safely with your winnings tomorrow—tomorrow in broad daylight.'

I had but two ideas left—one, that I must never let go of my handkerchief full of money; the other, that I must lie down somewhere immediately, and fall into a comfortable sleep. So I agreed to the proposal about the bed, and preceded by the croupier, we passed along some passages and up a flight of stairs into the bedroom which I was to occupy. The ex-brave shook me warmly by the hand; proposed that we should breakfast together, and then, followed by the croupier, left me for the night.

I ran to the washstand; drank some of the water in my jug; poured the rest out, plunged my face into it, then sat down in a chair and tried to compose myself. I soon felt better. The change for my lungs, from the foetid atmosphere of the gambling room to the cool air of the apartment I now occupied; the almost equally refreshing change for my eyes, from the glaring gas-lights of the 'Salon' to the dim, quiet flicker of one bedroom candle, aided wonderfully the restorative effects of cold water. The giddiness left me, and I began to feel more like a reasonable being. My first thought was the risk of sleeping all night in a gambling house; my second, of the still greater risk of trying to get out after the house was closed, and of going home alone at night, through the streets of Paris, with a large sum of money about me. I had slept in worse places than this on my travels, so I determined to lock my door, and take my chance till the next morning.

Accordingly I looked under the bed and into the cupboard; tried the fastening of the window; and then, satisfied that I had taken every proper precaution, pulled off my upper clothing, put my light, which was a dim one, on the hearth among a feathery litter of wood ashes, and got into bed with the handkerchief full of money under my pillow.

I soon felt not only that I could not go to sleep, but that I could not even close my eyes. I was wide awake and every one of my senses seemed to be preternaturally sharpened. I raised myself on my elbow, and looked about the room—which was brightened by a lovely moonlight pouring through the window—to see if it contained any pictures or ornaments that I could at all clearly distinguish. While my eyes wandered from wall to wall, a remembrance of Le Maistre's delightful little book *Voyage autour de ma Chambre*, occurred to me. I resolved to imitate the French author, and find occupation and amusement enough to beguile the tedium of my wakefulness, by making a mental inventory of every article of furniture I could see, and by following to their sources the multitude of associations which even a chair, a table, or a washstand may be able to call forth.

In the nervous, unsettled state of my mind at that moment, I found it much easier to make my inventory than to make my reflections and thereupon soon gave up all hope of thinking in Le Maistre's fanciful track—or, indeed, of thinking at all. I looked about the room at the different articles of furniture, and did nothing more.

There was, first, the bed I was lying in: a four-post bed, with the regular top lined with chintz—the regular fringed valance all round—the regular stifling unwholesome curtains, which I remembered having mechanically drawn back against the posts when I first got into the room. There was the marble-topped washstand, from which the water I had spilt, in my hurry to pour it out, was still dripping, slowly and more slowly, on to the brick floor. Then two small chairs, with my coat, waistcoat, and trousers flung on them. Then a large elbow chair, covered with dirty-white dimity, with my cravat and shirt collar thrown over the back. Then a chest of drawers with two of the brass handles off, and a tawdry, broken china inkstand placed on it by way of ornament. Then the dressing table, with a small looking-glass, and a large pincushion. Then the window—an unusually large window. Then a dark old picture, which the feeble candle dimly showed me. It was the picture of a fellow in a high Spanish hat, crowned with a plume of towering feathers. A swarthy, sinister ruffian, looking upward—it might be at some tall gallows on which he was going to be hanged. At any rate, he had the appearance of thoroughly deserving it.

This picture put a kind of constraint upon me to look upward too—at the top of the bed. It was a gloomy and not an interesting object, and I looked back at the picture. I counted the feathers in the man's hat— they stood out in relief—three white, two green. I observed the crown of his hat, which was of a conical shape, according to the fashion supposed to have been favoured by Guy Fawkes. I wondered what he could be looking up at. It must be the high gallows, and he was going to be hanged presently. Would the executioner come into possession of his conical crowned hat and plume of feathers? I counted the feathers again—three white and two green.

While I still lingered over this very improving and intellectual employment, my thoughts insensibly began to wander. I became absorbed in past scenes; but suddenly, in an instant, the thread on which my memories hung, snapped. My attention came back to present things more vividly than ever, and I found myself looking hard at the picture.

Looking at what?

Good God, the man had pulled his hat down on his brows! No!—the hat itself was gone! Where was the conical crown? Where the feathers—three white, two green? Not there! In the place of the hat and feathers, what dusky object was it that now hid his forehead, his eyes, his shading hand?

Was the bed moving?

I turned on my back and looked up. Was I mad? drunk? dreaming? giddy again? or was the top of the bed really moving down—sinking slowly, regularly, silently, horribly, right down throughout the whole of its length and breadth—right down upon me, as I lay underneath?

A deadly, paralysing coldness stole over me. I turned my head on the pillow, determined to test whether the bed-top was really moving or not, by keeping my eye on the man in the picture.

The next look in that direction was enough. The dull, black, frowsy outline of the valance above me was within an inch of being parallel with his waist. I still looked breathlessly. Steadily and slowly—very slowly—I saw the figure, and the line of frame below the figure, vanish, as the valance moved down before it.

I am, constitutionally, anything but timid. I have been on more than one occasion in peril of my life, and have not lost my self-possession for an instant; but when the conviction first settled on my mind that the bed-top was actually moving, was steadily and continuously sinking down upon me, I looked up shuddering, helpless, panic-stricken, beneath the hideous machinery for murder, which was advancing closer and closer, to suffocate me where I lay.

Motionless, speechless, breathless, I lay. The candle, fully spent, went out; but the moonlight still brightened the room. Down and down, without pausing and without a sound, came the bed-top, and still my panic terror seemed to bind me faster and faster to the mattress on which I lay—down and down it sank, till the dusty odour from the lining of the canopy came stealing into my nostrils.

At that final moment the instinct of self-preservation startled me out of my trance, and I moved. There was just room for me to roll myself sideways off the bed. As I dropped noiselessly to the floor, the edge of the murderous canopy touched me on the shoulder.

Without stopping to draw my breath, without wiping the cold sweat from my face, I rose instantly on my knees to watch the bed-top. I was literally spell-bound by it.

It descended—the whole canopy with the fringe round it, came down—down—close down; so close that there was not room now to squeeze my finger between the bed-top and the bed. I felt at the sides and discovered that what had appeared to me from beneath to be the ordinary light canopy of a four-post bed, was in reality a thick broad mattress, the substance of which was concealed by the valance and its fringe. I looked up and saw the four posts rising hideously bare. In the middle of the bed-top was a huge wooden screw that had evidently worked it down through a hole in the ceiling, in the way ordinary presses are worked down on to the substance selected for compression. The apparatus moved without making the faintest noise. There had been no creaking as it came down. Still, as I looked on it, I could not move, I could hardly breathe, but I began to recover the power of thinking, and in a moment had discovered in all its horror the murderous conspiracy framed against me.

My cup of coffee had been drugged, but—drugged too strongly. I had been saved from being smothered by having taken an overdose of some narcotic. How I had chafed and fretted at the fever-fit which had preserved my life by keeping me awake! How recklessly I had confided myself to the two wretches who had led me into this room, determined, for the sake of my winnings, to kill me in my sleep by the surest and most horrible contrivance for secretly accomplishing my destruction! How many men, winners like me, had slept, as I had proposed to sleep, in that bed, and had never been seen or heard of more?

Ere long, all thought was suspended by the sight of the murderous canopy moving once more. After it had remained on the bed—as nearly as I could guess—about ten minutes, it began to move up again. The villains who worked it from above evidently believed that their purpose was accomplished. Slowly and silently, as it had descended, that horrible bed-top rose towards its former place. When it reached the upper extremities of the four posts, it reached the ceiling too. Neither hole nor screw could be seen; the bed became in appearance an ordinary bed again—the canopy an ordinary canopy.

Now, for the first time I was able to move, to rise from my knees, to dress myself, and to consider how I should escape. If I betrayed by the smallest noise that the attempt to suffocate me had failed, I was certain to be murdered. Had I made any noise already? I listened intently, looking towards the door.

No! No footsteps in the passage outside—no sound of a tread light or heavy. In the room above—absolute silence.

Besides locking and bolting my door, I had moved an old wooden chest against it. To remove this chest—my blood ran cold as imagination suggested what might be its contents—without making some disturbance was impossible; and moreover, to think of escaping through the house, now barred up for the night, would be sheer insanity. One chance was left me—the window. I stole to it on tiptoe.

My bedroom was on the first floor, above an entresol, and looked into the back street. I raised my hand to open the window, knowing that on that action hung, by the merest hair's breadth, my chance of safety—for they keep vigilant watch in a House of Murder. If any part of the frame cracked, if the hinge creaked, I was a lost man! It must have occupied me at least five minutes, reckoning by time—five hours, reckoning by suspense—to open that window. I succeeded in doing it silently—in doing it with the dexterity of a house-breaker—and then looked down into the street. To leap the distance beneath me would be almost certain destruction. Next, I looked at the sides of the house. Down the left ran a thick water-pipe—it passed close to the outer edge of the window.

To some the means of escape which I had discovered might have seemed difficult—to me the prospect of slipping down the pipe into the street did not suggest even a thought of peril.

I had already got one leg over the sill, when I remembered the handkerchief, filled with money, under my pillow. I could well have afforded to leave it behind me, but I was determined that the miscreants of the gambling-house should miss their plunder as well as their victim. I went back to the bed therefore and tied the heavy handkerchief at my back by my cravat.

Just as I had made it tight and fixed in a comfortable place, I thought I heard a sound of breathing outside the door. The chill feeling of horror ran through me again as I listened. No! Dead silence still in the passage—I had only heard the night air blowing softly into the room. The next moment I was on the window-sill—and the next I had a firm grip on the water-pipe.

I slid down into the street easily and quietly, as I thought I should, and immediately set off at the top of my speed to a branch Prefecture of Police, which I knew was in the immediate neighbourhood. A Sub-prefect and several of his subordinates were up. But, when I began my story, in a breathless hurry and very bad French, I could see that the Sub-prefect suspected me of being a drunken Englishman who had been robbed. He soon altered his opinion, and before I had concluded, he shoved the papers before him into a drawer, put on his hat, supplied me with another (for I was bareheaded) and ordered a file of soldiers, desired his expert followers to get ready all sorts of tools for breaking open doors and ripping up brick flooring, and took my arm, in the most friendly and familiar manner possible, to lead me with him out of the house.

Sentinels were placed at the back and front of the house the moment we got to it; a tremendous battery of knocks was directed against the door; a light appeared at a window; I was told to conceal myself behind the police—then came more knocks, and a cry of 'Open in the name of the law!' At that terrible summons bolts and locks gave way before an invisible hand, and the moment after, the Sub-prefect was in the passage, confronting a waiter half-dressed and ghastly pale.

'We want to see the Englishman who is sleeping in this house.'

'He went away hours ago.'

'He did no such thing. His friend went away; he remained. Show us to his bedroom.'

'I swear to you, Monsieur Le Sous-préfet, he is not here! He—'

'I swear to you, Monsieur le Garcon, he is. He slept here—he didn't find your bed comfortable—he came to us to complain of it—he is here among my men—and here am I ready to look for a flea or two in his bedstead. Renaudin,' calling to one of his subordinates, and pointing to the waiter—'collar that man, and tie his hands behind him.

Now, then, gentlemen, let us walk upstairs!' Every man and woman in the house was secured—the 'Old Soldier' first. I identified the bed in which I had slept and we then went on to the room above.

No object that was at all extraordinary appeared in any part of it. The Sub-prefect looked round the place, commanded everybody be silent, stamped twice on the floor, called for a candle, looked attentively at the spot he had stamped on, and ordered the flooring there to be carefully taken up. This was done in no time. Lights were produced, and we saw a deep raftered cavity between the floor of this room and the ceiling of the room beneath. Through this cavity there ran perpendicularly a sort of case of iron thickly greased; and inside the case appeared the screw, which communicated with the bed-top below. Extra lengths of screw, freshly oiled; levers covered with felt, the complete upper works of a heavy press—constructed with infernal ingenuity to join the fixtures below, and when taken to pieces again to go into the smallest possible compass—were next discovered and pulled out on the floor. After some little difficulty the Sub-prefect succeeded in putting the machinery together, and leaving his men to work it, descended with me to the bedroom. The smothering canopy was then lowered, but not so noiselessly as I had seen it lowered. When I mentioned this to the Sub-prefect, his answer, simple as it was, was significant. 'My men,' said he, 'are working down the bed-top for the first time—the men whose money you won were in better practice.'

We left the house in the possession of two police agents—the inmates having been removed to prison. The Sub-prefect, after taking down my *procès-verbal* in his office, returned with me to my hotel to get my passport. 'Do you think,' I asked, as I gave it to him, 'that any men have really been smothered in that bed, as they tried to smother me?'

'I have seen dozens of drowned men laid out at the Morgue,' answered the Sub-prefect, 'in whose pocket-books were found letters, stating that they had committed suicide in the Seine, because they had lost everything at the gaming-table. Do I know how many of those men entered the same gaming-house that you entered? won as you won? took that bed as you took it? slept in it? were smothered in it? and were thrown into the river, with a letter of explanation written by the murderers and placed in their pocket-books? No man can say how many or how few have escaped the fate from which you have escaped.'

The rest of my story is soon told. I was examined; the gambling-house was searched from top to bottom; the prisoners were separately interrogated; and two of the less guilty made a confession. I discovered that the Old Soldier was the master of the gambling-house; justice discovered that he had been drummed out of the army as a vagabond years ago; that he had been guilty of all sorts of villainies since; that he was in possession of stolen property, which the owner identified; and that he, the croupier, another accomplice, and the woman who had made my coffee, were all in the secret of the bedstead. There appeared to be some doubt as to whether the servants attached to the house knew anything of the suffocating machinery; and they received the benefit of that doubt, by being treated simply as thieves and vagabonds. As for the Old Soldier and his two head myrmidons, they went to the galleys; the woman who had drugged my coffee was imprisoned for I forget how many years; the regular visitors to the gambling-house were considered 'suspicious', and placed under 'surveillance'; and I became for a week the 'lion' of Parisian society.

My adventure cured me of ever again trying Rouge et Noir as an amusement. The sight of a green cloth, with packs of cards and heaps of money on it, will henceforth be for ever associated in my mind with the sight of a bed-canopy descending to suffocate me in the silence and darkness of the night.

Psychic Alert Saved Film Star

FRANK STEVENS

In recent years, some of the best known public figures have shown a deep interest in the occult and in mystic phenomena, and some have been caught up in events related to the world of occult.

Jackie Kennedy's prediction of the assassination of her brother-in-law, Senator Robert Kennedy, is an example of the latter. The action of film director, Federico Fellini of *La Dolce Vita* fame, who abandoned a movie he had already started after being advised to do so by his astrologer, is another instance of the former.

Brigitte Bardot and her husband, Gunther Sachs, both consult astrologers before making important decisions in their lives. The late singer, Edith Piaf, was a firm believer in seers, mediums, and the possibility of contacting lost ones from beyond the grave. Singer Jane Morgan is convinced that her house in Kennebunkport, Maine, is inhabited by two irritable but harmless ghosts.

But of all the celebrities of our time who have good reason to believe in the reality of the forces of the occult, movie star Elke Sommer stands first.

Elke believes she has been saved from a horrible death twice in the past two years by the intervention of supernormal forces.

On March 13, 1967, Elke and her husband, writer and columnist Joe Hyams, escaped from a fire which caused extensive damage to their Hollywood house. Had not Elke been awakened by a 'spirit' which warned her of the danger, they would have been burned to death.

Two months earlier, a medium warned Elke to cancel a trip to her home town near Hamburg, Germany. Elke cancelled the trip—and escaped being kidnapped by an insane mass murderer named Klaus Gossman, who had already worked out detailed plans for kidnapping the actress and murdering her.

Elke, the long-limbed strawberry blonde from Germany who first gained fame by her appearance in the film *The Victors*, has not always been interested in psychic forces and the world of the occult.

In July, 1964, Elke and her husband, Joe Hyams, moved into a large house in Benedict Canyon, Los Angeles. The previous tenant hinted that the house was inhabited by a spirit—a man wearing a black jacket—but both Elke and Joe took the story as a joke.

Before a month passed, they no longer considered it funny. At night, lying in bed, they were bothered by the sounds of footsteps in the hall and downstairs, though no one else was in the house. Sounds of chairs scraping and scuffing against the floor in the dining room downstairs were also audible.

Doors and windows which had been firmly locked were found open an hour later though no one had touched them. Lights went on and off for no discoverable reason.

Finally, Elke, Joe and their guests got repeated glimpses of a stranger—a man in a black jacket—who disappeared minutes after they saw him and could be identified by no one who was nearby.

Hyams, disturbed and intrigued, looked at blueprints of the house to see if there might be a secret chamber somewhere, where an uninvited lodger might be staying. There was not.

He installed electronic sound detection and photographic equipment, and hired termite inspectors to search out every possible hidden nook and cranny in the structure of the house. Again, nothing was found.

By this time, many other people besides Elke and Joe had seen the 'ghost' or felt its presence. Mrs 'Red' Buttons came to inspect the house with a view to subletting it one summer. She walked up the steps, stopped, turned white, and refused to enter.

'This house has an evil aura,' she exclaimed. 'I've never felt this way about a place before.'

Harry Kantor, a businessman from New York City, actually did sublet the house in the summer of 1966. In the middle of a party he was giving, the lights went out and a heavy candelabra over the dining room table fell from the ceiling with a tremendous crash.

The lights were not controlled by a master switch—but by separate fuses. Investigation showed that the candelabra had been securely fastened.

Finally, Joe Hyams became so intrigued with the ghost in his house that he wrote a book about it. Before doing so, he called in the American Society for Psychical Research to document his claims that the place was inhabited by spirits.

With all this going on, it is no wonder that Elke became impressed by the possibility of unknown and mysterious psychic forces at work.

Because she did, she escaped death at the hands of Klaus Gossman, the infamous 'High Noon' killer.

Gossman, who became known in his native Germany as the 'High Noon Murderer' because all his killings were committed exactly at mid-day, was nabbed by police in Nuremberg, Germany in January, 1967, after murdering his seventh innocent victim.

It had been exactly 12 o'clock noon on a day in April, 1960, when he committed his first killing. He was then a student in a German university and considered brilliant. No one can understand why he started on the road to criminal insanity. But on that day he knocked on the door of an apartment in Nuremberg.

A young man and his attractive fiancée answered.

Gossman snapped out, 'Your money or your life, decide quickly.' Before they could answer, he shot them both dead. Then, without bothering to steal anything, he went home and calmly cleaned his pistol, hungrily eating four apples after his strenuous exercise.

He struck his next victim when he attempted to rob a bank and a timid clerk reached for his spectacles. Gossman, thinking he was reaching for a gun, shot him and made his escape without taking any cash.

His next murders were just as pointless. He killed a friend and his friend's old mother, after a trivial argument over a broken bottle. His sixth victim was a man on the street who jostled him.

It was right after Gossman's sixth killing that the well-known German seer and medium, Frau Rosa Bratter, was reading the explosive newspaper accounts of the 'High Noon' killer's crimes, and the frantic attempts of police to catch him.

As she turned over the page of the newspaper, Frau Bratter happened to glance at a photograph of Elke Sommer. Underneath the photo was a caption stating that the German born Elke was to make one of her periodic visits to her mother, who lives in a town about twenty miles away from Nuremberg.

'Suddenly,' Frau Bratter realtes, 'I felt the peculiar sensation of electric vibrancy which comes over me when my psychic powers take over my being.

'Something impelled me to turn the page back to the account of the 'High Noon' killer. As I did, I saw the photograph of Elke Sommer superimposed on the article about his crimes.

'There was an aura about the superimposed photograph, an aura of evil and horror. It seemed to have a dark glow.

'I felt a foreboding which I knew was not a casual hunch, but a genuine psychic premonition: Elke Sommer was in danger at the hands of the 'High Noon' killer, if she carried out her plans to visit her mother.'

Immediately, Frau Bratter sat down at her desk and wrote a short note to Elke Sommer. She told the actress that her psychic powers had warned her of mortal danger if she visited the area of Nuremberg, and urged Elke to cancel the trip.

Four days later, Elke, convinced of the reality of psychic phenomena through her own contact with them at home, did cancel her trip. She was never to regret it.

A week later, the 'High Noon' killer struck again, shooting a man who tried to stop him after he had snatched a woman's purse in a department store. This time, he was surrounded and captured.

When police broke into his apartment shortly after his capture, they found a diary recording his plans and criminal ideas.

On the last page of the blue leather diary was scribbled this notation in large block letters: '*Elke Sommer–kidnap her*!'

After intensive questioning by police, Gossman told them that he had read in a local newspaper that Elke was scheduled to visit her mother in the area soon. He had planned to kidnap the actress and ask a huge ransom for her return.

But the police did not believe him. They were convinced that Gossman intended to murder Elke after kidnapping her. In his apartment they discovered proof of this intention.

Among an armoury of weapons—including several rifles, a Sten gun, three hand grenades, four knives, a pistol with a silencer, and a .45 calibre revolver—was found a pistol clearly marked for Gossman's next murder.

On the butt was scratched clearly and deeply the words: X 'For Elke.'

Had Elke carried out her plan for a visit, in spite of the advice of Frau Bratter, Gossman would have made her his next victim, rather than the man in the department store.

Ironically, Gossman was later tried and after being found guilty, sentenced to the maximum punishment in West Germany, life imprisonment—with the judge handing down his sentence at exactly high noon.

Two years later, on March 13, 1967, a message from the spirit world once again saved Elke's life and that of her husband's also. This time, the message came from the spirit which haunted their Los Angeles home.

On March 20, 1966, Joe Hyams had contacted the well known psychic-sensitive Jacqueline Eastlund, and asked her to help solve the mystery of their haunted house. Joe had left the telephone on a table, and remained off the line while Mrs Eastlund listened to the aura of the house and collected her impressions.

She told Hyams 'I see this house in flames six months from now—be cautious—I also hear a sound like a lot of rain and a sort of tapping.'

It wasn't six months, but a year later that Elke woke around six a.m. with a feeling of vague unease. It was raining heavily. As she lay awake, Elke suddenly heard sounds—sounds from downstairs.

For a while she tried to pass them off as more pranks from their mischievous ghost. But this time she felt a sense of anxiety, dread and an inexplicable compulsion to move around.

Finally, she woke her husband. Just as she was telling him about the sounds downstairs and her feeling of dread, a new noise started.

A loud and frantic pounding sounded on their door, as if someone or something were desperately attempting to wake them.

Joe sprang to the door and opened it—to be met by a thick, hot cloud of black smoke. The house was in flames, and their access to the hall was cut off.

Quickly shutting the door again, Hyams called the fire department. Then he and Elke looked around for a means of escape.

Again, the sound of pounding came. This time it came from a window. When Elke ran to look out, she saw why. By climbing through this window she and Joe could drop a few feet to the roof of their garage, and from there easily drop to the ground and safety.

They did, and a quarter of an hour later they were helping the firemen. The fire caused damage estimated at 25,000 dollars.

If the mysterious sounds had not awakened Elke, and if there had been no pounding, Joe and Elke would have perished in the blaze.

Again, Elke had a psychic message to thank for saving her life, which served to reinforce her newly acquired belief in the reality of the world Beyond.

A few months after the fire, Elke happened to be dining in a restaurant in Rome when she was joined by friends. Among them was the beautiful Italian actress, Sophia Loren.

Sophia told the gathering she had just visited one of Europe's most famous mediums, the French seer, Rose Stoller, and that Madame Stoller, after reading a crystal ball, had warned her that someone was about to steal some of her most valuable jewels.

Sophia had ignored the advice. Now, she told her friends, she had just heard that thieves had broken into her Rome apartment and stolen jewels valued at 50,000 dollars.

By listening to and heeding the psychic messages she received, Elke had saved something far more valuable than her jewels—her life.

The Dark Star

G. G. PENDARVES

I

Alan Clova hid the winged exultant uprush of his emotion with habitual control. His face, thin to emaciation, dark and cleanly chiselled, was aloof and proud as a Pharaoh's. It was hard to believe he was only thirty. So much experience, so much hard-earned knowledge, so much resolution and critical cool judgement was in his eyes. Beneath straight black brows they gleamed, steady, brilliant and serene. Here was a man of action no less than a man of intellect. Breeding, dignity, pride of race had moulded the features, but they were instinct with a tense fighting awareness that was the New World's gift to the Old.

His cousin, David Wishart Clova, Earl of Glenhallion, narrowly observed his young kinsman. Hope stirred in him once more; hope he had thought was dead—dead and buried with his three sons beneath the sodden earth of Flanders. The words of the creed he had so often repeated in the little grey chapel on his estate, beat in his brain like the portentous opening bars of a tremendous symphony. '*I believe in the resurrection of the body and the life of the world to come.*' The words had never passed his lips since 1916, when his third and youngest son fell—1916, twenty years now.

Now, looking at Alan's six feet five inches of brawn and muscle, the beliefs he had forsworn flashed up again. Here in the flesh once more was an heir to the great name, the centuries of tradition, the wild splendour of Glenhallion estates. Here, under the roof of Gorm Castle, stood a man who might well have been one of his own sons grown older, stronger, more mature. Resurrection! . . . Yes, it seemed a resurrection indeed.

Alan stood at a great window looking out over Glenhallion estate, from walled grounds about the castle to meadow, forest, craggy hills, and far-distant sky whose April blue darkened to hazy greys and purples above the Kaims of Vorangowl. His absorbed gaze travelled from point to point, then came back to rest on a square grey tower within the grounds, ivy-hung and partly obscured by beech trees. He frowned at the sight of a man who was pacing round its battlements. His appearance, a great hulking figure in outlandish-looking grey clothes, stirred a sudden cold antipathy in Alan and he turned abruptly back to the room and its two occupants.

Lady Maisry, the Earl's only surviving child, sat by a log-fire. She had a fragile look and shivered now and then at the sound of the wind's bluster round the castle of Gorm. She looked, Alan thought, with her golden hair and green sheath dress, as if she had been transplanted from the daffodil-beds in the grounds below.

Some unfathomable instinct of protection for her made him hesitate to speak of the man on the tower roof. He strolled back to the window. Yes, the man was there still, pacing to and fro, to and fro, a long cloak flapping in the wind, hair and beard flaming red in the evening light. Such a fury of rage shook Alan that it was a minute before he could command his voice. Then he asked, 'Is that old tower a complete ruin? Or, do—do people live in it?'

Earl Glenhallion came over to the window. 'Birds, bats, spiders! That's all you'll find living in the old Keep. Fine old stronghold, all that's left of the original castle; the rest was burned down about two hundred years ago. No, you'd not find man, woman, or child who'd go inside that tower for five minutes.'

'I'm going.'

Alan's remark had the effect of a pistol-shot on Lady Maisry. She got to her feet and moving quickly across to him, put a pleading hand on his arm.

'No—no—no! You mustn't! It's dangerous, very dangerous. There's something . . . there's someone . . . you never know if—it skips some generations! My father thinks it all nonsense, but . . .'

Alan almost promised never to set foot in the tower if it worried her. The distress in her grey eyes, the frightened pallor of her cheeks shook him. She interested and gripped his imagination profoundly. Yesterday's first impressions of her were strengthened by today's. Her clear ivory-pale skin, wide grey eyes, gold thick shining hair, gentle slow ease of every movement, and above all to his critical sensitive ear, her low deliberate exquisite voice, immensely charmed him. Beyond these things, though, rare as he had found such physical perfection, he was deeply aware of a mind fully as alive and equipped as his own, of a nature as exacting, and a will as inflexible. But there was something about her that puzzled him; he had the impression of a deeply hidden preoccupation which she dreaded might be discovered.

'She looks as substantial as a dragonfly, but I believe she's made of steel covered with white velvet,' he reflected. 'I know that fragile-looking type of thoroughbred. She'd live through famine and earthquake—if she felt like living! I know horses and I know dogs, and that gives me a line on humans. She's letting go for some reason, and I'm going to know that reason.'

All the same he found it difficult to remember she wouldn't die easily as he met her panic-stricken eyes. A grim thought struck him. Was that man on the battlements her lover?—was she hiding him there from the Earl?

'Why do you feel like that about the tower?' he asked.

Her father drew her to him, an arm about her shoulders. 'She's had a queer life here in this old castle. You must forgive her fancies, Alan! The legend about that old Keep dies hard. Everyone on the estate swears by it. Maisry believes it, too.'

'Just what is the legend?'

'A-a-ah!! Hrumph!' The older man stalked over to the window and glowered at the grey Keep. 'They say it's haunted by an ancestor of ours, who lived some two hundred years ago. He was known as the Red Earl of Glenhallion, or Red Alastair, because of his flaming red beard.'

Alan felt his heart jump as if a mine had exploded under the polished flooring under foot. He tried to keep his glance from the old tower, and failed. He must look again; perhaps the setting sun had dazzled him, given a false illusion. He joined the Earl; his keen gaze followed the other's look.

A clear shaft of light struck across the glen from over the high moorland of Vorangowl and picked out the tower like a searchlight; every ivy leaf stood out like carved metal, every irregularity of weathered stone showed up, discolorations of dripping rain from the roof, the gold patina of lichen, the rusty brown of winter leaves lodged in iron-barred windows—all was mercilessly clear.

And, on the breast-high battlemented wall that ran round the roof, a man leaned with face directly turned to Alan and the castle window at which he stood. The man's hair and beard flamed red as torchlight.

'The story of Red Alastair does us no credit,' went on the Earl. 'He was a wild, dissolute, savage man, from all the records. You can read him up in the library if you're interested. But as to haunting the Keep—that's nonsense, the talk of ignorant peasants, the sort of story that people like to invent about any old ruin.'

'So no one lives there, no one climbs up to the roof to look round, not for any reason?' Alan's voice was harsh.

'No one. It stands there as you see it now—deserted! I've been up, of course. Jamie has the key—the only key. When I succeeded to Glenhallion there were constant scandals and wild tales because visitors were allowed to go over the Keep and explore it. I locked up the place, and since then there've been no more tales of ghosts and people being pushed off battlements or crushed behind doors and all the rest of it. I've not been inside for a year or more, and certainly no one else has. A good specimen of Tenth Century architecture it is, and that's all. If you see Red Alastair when you go over it, let me know. I rule here now; he's had his turn and made a very bad job of it, by all accounts.'

The two men turned back to the fire, the Earl chuckling, Alan feeling more angry, more stupidly bewildered than he'd ever felt in his whole vigorous sane existence. He believed in ghosts no more than he believed in the Divine Right of kings; and he connected both beliefs with forgotten centuries when people had no bath-rooms, enjoyed heretic burnings in place of cinemas and night-clubs, and fought for 'the Glory of God' or some other such unpractical cause.

He thrust the whole thing out of his mind for future cogitation. Maisry was watching him with painful anxiety, as if she divined his inner discomfort. He was determined to share it with no one, and made up his mind to investigate the Keep before he slept that night.

In order to get the legend as it was bandied about the countryside before reading up a literary account, he tried to extract information from the close-mouthed Jamie, who valetted him as he dressed for dinner. Jamie shied away from the subject like a nervous horse from a white flapping sheet.

'It's not good to talk of *him*, not about this time of year, my lord.' The man spoke the broad Scots of the countryside, and became almost unintelligible as his agitation and embarrassment increased.

Alan turned to the big swinging mirror on his dressing-table, pretending to examine his chin. He saw the reflected Jamie glance over his shoulder.

'Why at this time of year, especially?'

'Eh, my lord?—you that'll be next Earl of Glenhallion to be asking that!'

The thin dark face turned from the mirror with a smile, so pleasant and friendly a smile that the old servant relaxed to it with: 'It's not you I'll be blaming, my lord; it's those that brought you up so far from your own land and kinsmen. You that were born to all this!'

'But I wasn't! When I was born, exactly seven other heirs came before me.'

'It's the Earl will be telling you all the family history, him and her Ladyship. It's not for me to be havering of the gentry.'

'Tell me at least why April's a bad time to discuss Red Alastair? Must a ghost be in season like grouse or blackcock?'

'Wheest, wheest for pity's sake, my lord! You can't tell what's abroad these evenings. The master hasn't "the sight"; he could go up into the Keep this very night and not see a thing to fright him. But there's others can—aye, there's others can see! And I tell you this, my lord: the Dark Star is up over the Kaims of Vorangowl again.'

'You mean the high moors at the head of the glen?'

'No. Not the moors you've seen. The star's in the Picture, the cursed thing *he* left in the Keep. Aye, the Picture I'm meaning of the moors and the cliff where the bride he stole from another man jumped to her death.'

A deep sonorous booming distracted Jamie from his confidences.

'That's the dinner gong, my lord. I'll not weary you with my tales now. It's all writ in black and white, and every word's true, for all the master's fleeing at the legend.'

When he made his way down to the lofty, shadow-filled dining-hall, exasperation had rubbed Alan's temper rather raw.

'Am I crazy—or am I crazy?' he demanded of himself, one hand lightly sliding over the broad baluster rail for the sensuous pleasure of touching the lovely seasoned wood, undesecrated by varnish, worn by time. His reason was floundering and plunging in heavy seas of unfamiliar and unpalatable sensations, ideas and thoughts.

'And, so far, there's nothing in the facts to justify my going up in the air like this,' he complained to himself. 'Even if I did see—and most certainly I did—a red-bearded man, what of it? They exist—especially here in Scotland; it's almost the hallmark of a Scot. Maybe porridge produces red beards! Jamie's daft about his old legend. Now there's a picture to reckon with, and a dark star, and a lady friend of Red Alastair's! Can you beat it? Even a Hollywood director couldn't think up this one. But the man—the man on the tower. . .'

A fighting look came into his dark eyes. 'Revolting sight! Don't quite know why—but somehow—filthy! Reminded me of that fat one in Paris, sitting like a blotchy swollen spider in his den, waiting for his doped girls to be brought along—bah! I'll get Red Beard! Hunt the hairy brute right off the map.'

Dinner rather took his mind off his troubles. There were guests he liked. One, an MP for one of the Border counties, met him more than halfway on the question of road development. Over some fine old brandy from the cellars of Gorm, the two men built bridges and tunnels and roads over Scotland; opened up Northern China; decided on the best type of car for use in desert country; and were passionately reclaiming, for Holland, vast new tracts of submerged country when their host brought them back to the social duties of the moment.

Alan, however, was himself again, perfectly confident of being able to deal with life and its problems in his rational systematic way. The old tower and the man on its battlements no longer seemed ominous.

'Liver, I suppose,' he told himself. 'Never knew I had one before, though. I'll satisfy myself that beggar's not about before I go to bed, though. Might set fire to the trees with his flaming red beard.'

In the big drawing-room, where lamps and fires made shadows dance on moulded ceilings and white panelled walls, on the faded coral of brocaded curtains that shut out sky and stars and wind-torn clouds, the Lady Maisry sang to them; of love, of death, of ecstasy, of bitter longing—ballads of olden times. She sang with the last perfect simplicity of a genuine artist, and with smiles, with tears, the listeners paid tribute to her gift.

As the last note echoed in the quiet, spellbound room, Alan knew! He knew he was in love, exquisitely, irrevocably, passionately.

A few hours later, when the guests were gone and the old Earl sleeping in his room, he and Maisry sat and talked together. Her low, shaken voice confided in him the horror that had thrust itself into her life, and he listened with a mounting love and pity and fear for her that carried him like a tidal wave far, far beyond every intellectual boundary his mind had ever recognized.

He wanted to think that she was ill, that her nerves were playing tricks, that the old castle of Gorm with its memories and legends had worked on her, that change of scene would cure her, that she must marry him and come away and live and laugh in the sun and forget. His sane logical mind clamoured for each solution of her secret. But below the rational protests of his disciplined clear mind, deeper understanding stirred and apprehended.

The woman he loved looked at him; her haunted eyes besought him. He must make a decision. Now!

He got to his feet, bent down and drew her up beside him, her hands in his strong clasp. He did not kiss her—no, not even the slim, cold hands that trembled in his own. But in the silence his very soul spoke to her, gave lasting deep assurance of his passion.

'I believe you,' he said at last. 'Every word you've told me. And I'm going to follow this up. It had never occurred to me that things like—like Red Alastair and his Picture could exist. You've convinced me.'

'But Alan! Alan!' her low voice broke in fear. 'I've told you only because your love for me gives you a right to know my secret, because I want you to see how useless it is to love me. It is hopeless, most dangerous to interfere. This is my fate. All these years, these centuries, he has waited, growing stronger. Perhaps, at first, he might have been sent back—back to his own place. Now it's too late. He's learned the trick of leaving his awful painted moorland and getting into our world.'

She shivered at the fierce fighting light of battle her words brought to the dark eyes looking down into her own.

'Alan! It is fatal—quite fatal to oppose him. You must never put foot inside the Keep. Oh, can't you see, have I not explained it all? It is hopeless. I told my secret to prevent your interfering, running into hideous peril. To stop you going, Alan! Not you—not *you*. . . .'

His grip of her hands slackened. He stooped; his eyes sought hers in sudden overwhelming wonder.

'D'you mean that you—that you care, too? Maisry! Maisry! If you do, nothing can separate us. No dream or ghost! Now I know the facts, I am prepared. You have armed me against surprise. I'm ready for Red Alastair. Do you think—do you think I'd let man or devil take you from me—now?'

II

One. Two. Three.

The strokes tolled out from a church-tower of some nearby village as Alan left the castle and made his way to the old grey Keep. The chimes brought a flash of self-mockery into his face.

'If the old crowd at home could see me now—trotting off in the moonlight at three a.m. to meet a fellow who died two hundred years ago! Mack's waistcoat buttons would shoot clear across Lake Huron with the laugh he'd get out of it!'

The wild clear sky, glittering stars and stinging wind were beginning to put a different complexion on the past few hours at Gorm—vast shadow-filled firelit romantic old castle that it was. Here, striding across the turf, trees tossing and creaking, clouds driving, the shrill mad pipe of the wind in his ears. Alan's body exulted in the challenge to his senses; his physical rather than psychical powers were called upon.

It was extraordinarily difficult for a man of his type to sustain the vision that Maisry's story had called up. With every step, old habits of reasoning took hold more firmly. When he reached the huge, barred, iron-studded door of the Keep he had once more put the Red Alastair legend into the realm of fantasy. He wondered at himself for accepting it at Maisry's valuation even for an hour. He recalled a bit of doggerel he'd chanced on that day, or, rather, the previous day:

Love, love, love, love,
Love it is a dizziness!
It winna let a puir body
Gang aboot his bizziness!

'And that explains me to myself.' He fitted a big oiled key into the lock and gave a half-shamed laugh at his own expense. 'What odds, though! If Maisry wants me to make a fool of myself in this particular way—I'm for it. Anyhow, I intended to see the ugly, hairy beggar off the premises. Might as well take a look at the Picture too, while I'm here. There aren't many back home can beat me at sightseeing, I'll say!'

He confided these conclusions to the inner side of the door as he closed and locked it behind him, in order to trap any vagrant lurking inside the tower. He switched on his torch, a large, powerful one with a new battery, and began his strangely timed visit.

'Better check up on the plan again.'

He patted the wide pockets of his overcoat, drew out a folded piece of semi-transparent tough paper familiar to architects, opened out the worn crackling sheet and examined once more the scale-drawing and faded cramped letter press.

'H-m-m! Ground floor. This was where soldiers were lodged.'

He forced back a narrow door on its rusted creaking hinges and went in. Silence and darkness. The nine-foot thick walls were cut to north and south exposures, forming huge window-seats, broad and cold as tombstones. The windows were small, narrow, and heavily barred by iron grilles as thick as a man's wrist. A yawning fireplace like a roofless cupboard showed stained and blackened floor and a pair of massive iron dogs.

He stood on the hearth and peered up. A vast chimney gaped to the sky; he could see a pale moon with torn rags of cloud across her face.

Sound of a shuffling, heavy footstep somewhere above took him to the foot of the stairway; he craned his head to listen. The spiral stairs were steep and a bare two feet in breadth; his shoulders rubbed the outer wall as he climbed. He reached the next level and flashed his torch into the thick, absorbent darkness of another hollow room. The door of it stood wide. He moved cautiously across the threshold; the brilliant spotlight of his torch showed no one there.

This was the dining-hall and a higher ceiling, more windows, a smoother flooring, and less rough-hewn fireplace distinguished it from the room below. Above the hearth, with its hollowed, blackened stones and battered mantelpiece, a startling, vivid thing brought Alan's travelling torch to an abrupt halt.

'For heaven's sake! Is that the Picture?'

His dark lean face regarded it with a positive glare of incredulous belief—unwilling furious belief.

'Land of Moses! Just a fake! It's as new as—as the Chrysler Building! The paint's as fresh as a ship's just out of dry dock.'

In the shock of discovery, he forgot the footsteps. He strode across the dusty floor, trained his torch full on the painted scene.

'Damn—and damn—and damn again!' he glowered, swearing in soft whispered fury, eyes narrowed under black impatient brows. 'Maisry was dead right about its infernal technique. It's more like Vorangowl than it's like itself. It's damnable!'

It was. The thing confronted him, exquisitely improbable, perfect beyond human hand or brain to conceive and execute. Some six feet square of the rough wall that formed the chimney-breast had been smoothed down and prepared to a surface even and fine as asphalt. Far-reaching miles of country were compressed within that six-foot bit of wall, the whole of Glenhallion estates from castle grounds to the Kaims of Vorangowl—high, brooding, eagle-haunted plateau of moor and rock and fir-woods that was the western limit. It was the view that stretched before the windows of the library at Gorm castle where he had watched yesterday's sun go down behind the same craggy ridge of rock portrayed on the painted horizon before him; the view he'd been watching before his eyes dropped to the Keep and that abominable tramp that lounged there on its battlements.

Stranger, newcomer he might be, but he knew that view very thoroughly indeed, and his trained, falcon-keen eye recognized and acknowledged the astounding reproduction of one landmark after another.

'It's like looking through a window at the thing. If it weren't three a.m. and this wall facing due east instead of west, I'd take my oath that I was staring through a sheet of plate-glass at Vorangowl itself as it looked yesterday about five o'clock! The same effect to the last detail—the same feathery cloud-shape over the pointed hill—and blue haze over the patch of wood to the north. It's not just an April evening, it's the identical evening I watched yesterday.'

He started, frowned, looked more intently at the Picture on the wall.

'This cursed torch . . . if it were only daylight! The infernal thing—why—it looks like mist rolling up over the road—actually rolling up before my eyes!'

And then his whole mind and body, every faculty and sense were suddenly sharpened to amazing perception. His breath came in deep sighs as though he were toiling up-hill with a weight to carry; his face hollowed and lost colour; sweat stood in great beads on his forehead.

The faint far-off figure of a man on the painted road—a stony track flung down across the heights—was coming nearer, nearer, nearer. . . . A figure that had been a vague shadow in the mist, when Alan first looked at the Picture, whose minuteness had served to emphasize the deserted aching loneliness of the moors. Now, the figure was moving forward, swiftly, swiftly over the stony endless road—past miles of dark woods, down the steep drop to the glen until it was swallowed up in the trees and shrubberies of Gorm which formed the foreground of the Picture.

A corner of the Keep itself showed in this same foreground, a bit of the grey weathered battlements.

Alan stared, waiting with pulses beating heavy and slow, watching for the man to reappear. Abruptly he came. He was there on the battlemented roof of the Keep, his great red head and fiery beard sharply defined. He turned to look at Alan, flung up a great arm in menace or derisive greeting.

In that instant a sound of high hooting wind filled the Keep, shrieked through the barred windows, roared down the hollow shaft of the stairway. Alan whipped about, torch in hand, to see the door slam in his face. The wind dropped as he flung himself forward to pull and tug with mad violence at the clumsy ring of iron that formed a handle. As he vainly struggled, there was a sound of heavy footsteps coming from above, halting outside his door, moving on downward and out of hearing.

Silence, heavy and sightless as a grave's, closed down on the Keep and its prisoner.

The shock of it roused Alan like a blow in the face. He'd stood bemused, dreaming, hypnotized by a bit of painted wall and let himself be trapped. Tricked! Some bit of ancient conjuring, some ingenious contraption in the chimney-flue had caused the illusion.

And the uproar of the wild and sudden wind? He shrugged that problem off. Whoever worked the Picture fake could take care of that too!

He flashed his light up the chimney but could see nothing beyond bare, grimed old stones rising in rough crumbling perpendicular. He examined the rooms opening off the dining-hall; they were merely cells, unlighted, full of dust and rubble. He returned to the main room and looked up at the windows with careful, calculating eye; they were narrow, strongly barred, set high on the walls so that no arrow, glancing through, should strike a human target. No faintest hope from them, even could he climb like a fly or were possessed of the sharpest of files. Only an explosive could burst open his prison bars.

And now that cursed red-bearded man was at large while he was trapped and helpless here. What was the game? Robbery—the old plate at Gorm? Or jewels—would the beast go near Maisry, frighten her, hurt her? What had he plotted and planned as he hid here all those hours?

Not even hidden, though, Alan reflected. The creature had brazened it out on the battlements in full light. How was it no one but himself had seen him? The Earl had been standing beside him when. . . Hastily averting his mind's eye from the thought that leaped out of ambush to answer his question, Alan said aloud in clearest, concisest tones:

'That's an easy one! The old man's sight is failing!' and this in spite of knowing that only twelve months ago the Earl had once more carried off the Forfarshire trophy for target shooting at the annual sports. 'And, after all, it's not likely that people who live here go poking about and staring as I've been doing. It's *perfectly* simple that I happened to be the only one to see that infernal tramp.'

Other explanations buzzed in his brain and he beat them back like a cloud of noisome flies. There was no other explanation.

Maisry's words sounded in his memory. 'Only some have *the sight*. Father hasn't got it, and that's why he's never seen Red Alastair and doesn't believe in the legend—but it's fact and no legend at all. I have *the sight*. And you have it too, Alan. I knew at once; I always recognize this wonderful, this terrible power in anyone else. You will see Red Alastair—most certainly you will see him—and that is why I can explain to you about his Picture that he lives in.'

For some time Alan closed his eyes, recalled deliberately scenes and images and places he had left behind in America. He wanted to shake off illusion, to steady his swirling thoughts, to forget the dark disturbance that swelled and rose and battered at his sanity.

He thought of a holiday he had spent loafing in the sun and warm salt water in Florida. He remembered a day in the woods near a logging-camp when an angry she-bear had chased him as he made off with her cub. He saw himself rocking and smoking and yarning on the broad-screened porches of his aunt's country-house in the White Mountains; flashed through the hours of last Christmas day, spent with old Friedland in New York . . . the fires and friends and brilliant dinner-table. . .

He opened his eyes on the Picture, and had the sensation of dropping from heaven to hell. On the road—returning, retreating to the misty Kaims of Vorangowl—the man was back again. But this time, and Alan watched with all his soul although he denied the thing he watched, a faint shadowy second figure followed after the man. Beyond a rocky cliff-face far up on the Kaims the red-haired figure halted, turned about to beckon the weary shadow that toiled after him, a shadow that grew clearer with every step it took. Suddenly Alan knew it.

'Maisry! Maisry! Maisry! Come back—come back to me!'

His full-throated anguished cry beat and echoed against the high cold walls of his prison. Again, again he called. He must bring her back, he *must*, before she set foot on that high narrow trail skirting the precipice.

That meant death to her, lasting, damnable, eternal death. He was conscious of a single overmastering passion of determination to bring her back—back from the cliff-face where she would slip to darkness, where he would lose her in this world and the next.

With a new shock, he recognized that his will was locked with the will of the red-haired man who waited for Maisry beyond the cliff path. The Picture darkened. Mist rolled grey and baffling down from the heights, and in the leaden skies a dark star shone, a star of evil copper-red that changed the green woods and April grass to sombre purples.

Old Jamie's warning darted across his memory: 'The Dark Star is up over the Kaims of Vorangowl.'

He saw Maisry move forward, saw Red Alastair beckon with insistent hand. Deathless love. Deathless hate. The twin fires leaped up, all his conscious being focused to a single point—to conquer Red Alastair.

He knew his antagonist, acknowledged him at last. He knew his own weapon too. His only weapon. The Will. A clean strong sword that all hell tried to tear from his grasp.

And now Maisry was coming back, back to him from the dark cliff, from engulfing mists, from Red Alastair, slowly, moving wraith-like past wood and glen and through the unfolding trees in the grounds at last. As she vanished, she turned to smile at him.

His torch fell from his nerveless hand. He sagged to the ground, huddled with head on knees; he felt old and worn and done. His next recollection was of light at the windows. Dawn, and the high sweet note of skylarks on the wing.

And the Picture showed a fresh and verdant April evening, an empty road wound up over far-distant heights, a clear tender sky shone above all. It was a magic tender exquisite study of a northern spring. Alan looked and experienced emotions he had never dreamed of possessing.

'And that was her dream! That child caught—held—dragged to hell!

'Maisry!' he addressed the Picture as if she were still on the road before his eyes. 'Forgive me. My faithlessness, my stupidity. You shall never tread that road again. It is my fight now. It is between me and Red Alastair. *And —I—will—win.*'

The last words fell with slow, deadly emphasis, a vow abruptly extinguished the echo of the last word torn from his lips by an inferno of wind. The Keep rocked in its fury, vibrating ominously to its high tremendous shriek.

He turned to the door, prepared for assault, and was faced by a new shock of surprise. The door stood wide open. Cool morning air, bearing a tang of pine and freshness of young wet leaves and grass, met him as he ran to the lower floor, to find the outer door unlocked and opened to the misty morning.

Soberly, slowly, thankfully he returned to Gorm, deeply aware that the Keep was solitary now; no need to search. Its demon was not there. For the moment there was no enemy, no battlefield.

There was only Maisry, and he must go to her.

III

'And Maisry?' Alan looked at the breakfast table laid for two and his eyes lost their eagerness. 'Not joining us, Cousin David?'

'No. Her maid says she had a bad night. I don't know what to make of it; these last weeks she's altered beyond recognition. I've tried to persuade her to go away for a change. Our local man, Doctor Shields, says she's well enough but makes no effort; he thinks there's something on her mind.'

Alan regarded the fish on his plate with a stern frown. He'd been doing some hard, intensive thinking and saw a gleam of light on the very dark horizon of his thoughts.

'I met a chap on the ship coming over. Lives in Stirling. Several people on board knew him well. Seems he's made a great reputation as a nerve specialist. Broome, Eliot Broome's his name.'

The Earl's unhappy face lightened.

'Ah, that's a household word in Scotland, and in other countries too. A nerve-man, yes! I didn't think of him for Maisry. D'you suppose she. . . .'

'It's hard to do anything but guess. This fellow Broome impressed me more than anyone I've met in years. Got to know him fairly well—y'know how it is on board ship. We yarned several nights away together. Made a good team for discussions, as he always took a diametrically opposite viewpoint from mine. I'm for fact, the proven fact.'

His voice weakened as he proclaimed his lifelong standard. How foolishly short it fell of measuring up with last night's phenomenon!

'Maisry might be upset, imagine there was something seriously wrong if I called in Broome.'

'Let me go to Stirling and talk to him. I could bring him back as a friend, not introduce him professionally. Let him see Maisry off guard.'

It was quickly arranged. By ten o'clock, Alan was speeding along the road south, a great relief in his mind that there was someone likely to listen to his fantastic, improbable story and discuss it without prejudice. So far as he knew Eliot Broome, the impossible and fantastic interested him profoundly. If only he'd come, and at once! Maisry must not endure last night's horror again.

He found Broome at home, and the specialist listened with immense concentration.

'Yes, I can come, and now!' he said. 'I returned by an earlier ship than I had intended—meant to finish off some laboratory experiments before seeing patients. A few days in retreat, y'know. But this won't wait an hour; we'll talk on the drive back.'

After lunch, at which Maisry did not appear, the Earl took the two younger men into his study. The father's idea was that Maisry needed a change of scene, that she was moping here at Gorm; and it was evident he knew nothing of her dream, or the fear that shadowed her life. He would strongly have resented the idea of his daughter sharing the vulgar superstitions of the countryside; he appreciated Red Alastair as a picturesque legend but not as an existent contemporary.

After their conference, Alan took his ally over to the Keep.

'God! It's altered again!'

Alan, who had made straight for the Picture, regarded it with angry incredulity.

'It was a clear late afternoon scene when I left it. There was no figure. Just bare spring landscape. Now the man's back in it again! He was right up in the mist when I first saw this infernal thing; I thought it a clever dodge of the painter—that solitary tiny figure emphasized the vast desolate moor. Now—look at that, will you!'

The two stared. On the road, not a mile from the entrance-gate to Gorm, and facing toward it, a man's figure was painted. Insolently, he seemed to dominate the lovely, lonely Glen, and his uncovered head burned red as fire under leaden skies.

Alan's face set like a mask. With loathing, he noted the changed aspect of the Picture, its gloom and shadow and brooding horror; a scene from Dante's purgatory rather than the living, burgeoning earth.

'Even the star is in it again,' he muttered. 'The Dark Star.'

His companion looked long at the blood-red portent over Vorangowl.

'The star is Red Alastair's signal, then! A sort of challenge.'

In striking contrast with Alan's quicksilver energy, Broome stood regarding the Picture; his massive proportions, leonine head, and slow deliberate movements typical of the man. Alan was all speed and movement and quick fiery courage, lean and swift and dangerous in anger as a black panther. Broome's was a slow, deadly, precise strength that makes no mistakes, that waits to strike and never misses; superbly master of himself, he was a man to seek as desert-travellers turn to the shelter of a rock.

'You consider this,' Broome's quiet voice began, 'the work of a man, some tremendous work of genius?'

The other looked at him, his lean face, his black eyes cold, furious, implacable.

'It's a trick, a damnable hellish trick—to put the wind up—to unnerve me. Why not? He's had two hundred years to learn, to practise his infernal game.'

The specialist regarded him with pity, with comprehension.

'I was prepared to accept your theory, that Red Alastair was a miracle-man, a marvel who had discovered the secret of perpetuating life. The secret could—it will—be discovered! *But this Picture is not the work of a man.* It proves that Red Alastair died—in the flesh.'

Alan turned an impatient eye on his companion. 'What proves it?' he demanded.

'He couldn't accomplish that,' Broome's eyes narrowed on the Picture, 'while he was still bound by human limitations in his body. He had to say good-bye to that body before journeying to the hell where such magic was learned.

Red Alastair is dead. The Picture is an open door by which he comes and goes to that far hell of his.'

Alan flung a defiant look at the painted moors. 'If there's a way to open a door, there must be a way to close it.'

'Undoubtedly! As we saw in the records, though, a door of this nature can't be manipulated in any obvious way.'

The other nodded gloomy assent. 'They seem to have tried everything. Painting it out—cutting it out—every sort of destruction. . . .'

'And each failure gave new advantage to the enemy.'

'How's that?'

'Because,' Broome answered, 'they actively acknowledged Red Alastair's power. Without defence or understanding, they offered combat and he won. His existence in our world depended, and still depends, on such victories.'

The Picture gleamed sullen, threatening, unchanged upon the wall. Unchanged! Not quite. The man's face was lifted, flung back, its eyes green as a storm-wave in the lightning's glare.

Alan's eyes met them unflinching; he gave back look for look, he seemed to project his very soul to thrust back the power in that painted evil face. Broome, acutely aware of the sudden impact of will against will, stood like stone: he bent the whole weight of his strong, disciplined mind to Alan's need. Then, like the snapping of a twig, it was over. The strain, the tension, the unbearable pressure ceased. Alan's breath was expelled in a long quivering sigh, he leaned his weight on Broome's shoulder, turned a grey face and sunken eyes.

'Let's get out—away from this.'

With eloquent gesture he turned and left the tower, his companion close behind. They walked across the intervening space in silence, stood at the castle entrance to look back at the grey, ominous Keep.

'I was wrong!' Alan's voice was hoarse. 'Reason—fact—logic—all wrong! It's neither genius nor science behind Red Alastair's devilish Picture. It's black magic, it's from hell.'

'Don't blame yourself; no sane man would accept the

true explanation without proof—the sort of proof you've had.' Broome put a hand on Alan's shoulder. 'Can you arrange for us to see Lady Maisry now, and be undisturbed for the next hour? There's only a bare margin of safety for her; she must never, as you said, follow *him* on that road again; she'd not survive it.'

'If she went away, now, at once, within the hour! Out of the country! She could fly across to. . . .'

Alan stopped at the other's decisive gesture.

'Physical distance is a factor that does not count. The man, the devil she follows on that moorland road can summon her at will—from across the world. It is the soul, the ego, the flame within the lamp of clay that is subject to Red Alastair; the body is a thing apart, governed by different laws and limitations."

IV

They went upstairs and were admitted by a maid to Lady Maisry's apartments. Alan sent a message.

The girl quickly returned. 'Yes, my lord, at once! And this gentleman, also. Will you come to her sitting-room please?'

The two waited in a room that hung like a nest high up in the south-west wing of Gorm castle. Its window thrust out in a semi-circular sweep over a bit of wild uncultivated ground below—long grass and daffodils tossed together, and bushy willow-stumps flashed in sun and wind beside a shallow stream whose soft chuckle sounded in the room through widely opened windows.

How like Maisry, how like her strange lovely self, this room! Straight from the devil-haunted tower, it seemed to Alan as velvet-sweet and fresh as a copse of wood-violets.

She came in to them at once. Her eyes, their cloud-grey beauty repeated in the chiffons of her dress, showed immense fatigue—dark pools no fresh quick source could stir, no sun touch to happy life again. Her face was pale as ivory; she moved across the room slowly, with trained habitual grace, but could not hide her deathly weariness.

Eliot Broome made up his mind at once. Here was one who deserved no less than truth. She was a fighter, strong, and able to endure. He explained himself without preamble, begged her to let him put what knowledge and resources he had at her disposal. She met him with equal directness.

'It is good of you—quite extraordinarily kind—to have come so quickly. Everyone knows your fame, your skill. Tell me one thing, first, and I want the absolute truth, please, Mr Broome. Alan has told you about my dream?'

The specialist nodded.

'And that I connect it with Red Alastair and his Picture?'

Again he gave grave assent.

'You know, then, that I consider myself to be haunted by this ancestor of mine; and, knowing this, do you believe that I am unbalanced, my nerves deranged, my brain affected?'

'Dear Lady Maisry, I believe you to be as sane as I am, very sane and unusually well-balanced. That is the reason you can bear to hear the truth from me.'

She grew very white. 'I understand. I am in danger—in deadly peril?'

'Yes,' he agreed. 'In more than mortal peril; yet, courageous as you are. I would not confess this if I did not know you could be rescued.'

Light flashed, died out again in her eyes, grey as lake-water at dawn. She shook her golden head.

'Please, not that! I dare not, dare not think along those lines. I am one of the ill-fated of my line. In life, in death, *he* cannot be defeated.'

Broome rose to his feet, took her two hands, and drew her up to face him. His eyes, his voice, were stern.

'Listen to me, Lady Maisry. That is a piece of unwisdom I had not dreamed you could say, or believe. It is just such unquestioning belief in Red Alastair that has enabled him to remain earthbound, expanding his mad-rapacious ego to colossal dimensions. *His existence depends utterly on people's faith and fear.*'

She stood rigid in his grasp, her face fixed in tense abstracted thought. 'But he—he is more than man! He is a devil—served by devils. It is not one human soul against another, it never has been that. You do not know Red Alastair's history, nor does Alan; there has been so little time.'

'No. We have only glanced at the records. Is there any special reason why you are haunted? Are all the women of your family tormented?'

'No. I am the first; the first woman that has had '*the sight*'. And the reason why he—why he calls me, draws me after him, is this. . . .'

She took up a small shabby leather case from a table at her side and opened it to show an oval miniature set in pale gold with rim of pearls. The two men looked at it and at her.

'A lovely portrait of you,' Alan said.

'No—not of me. That was painted in 1700. It is a portrait of an ancestor of mine on my mother's side—Lady Jean Haugh. Red Alastair stole her on her wedding-day, snatched her from the bridegroom's side as the pair stood before the priest, and rode off with her. To escape him, she flung herself off the cliff-path on the Kaims of Vorangowl. He was riding recklessly, as always, and no doubt his grasp of her loosened as he held up his frightened horse. This is all in the records, and there were many witnesses to this particular crime; for it was April and shepherds were all out on the moors tending the ewes and lambs.'

'Then Lady Jean Haugh did actually defeat him for once!'

'Not finally. She merely postponed his victory. He has waited some two hundred years for her. And now—here am I.'

'Exactly. Here are you. And you are not the Lady Jean Haugh.'

'Physically I am, to the last gold hair; and more than that Red Alastair would not recognize. There is no time now to tell you more fully of his life; one year was like another to him, blood and battle, riding and fighting. But chiefly women—the records are black with their names—their unspeakable fate.'

Eliot Broome watched the girl narrowly. His next question made Alan start and lean forward with hands suddenly cold and shaking, the pulses throbbing at his temples.

'And you? You have not thought of escaping as Lady Jean escaped?'

Maisry did not shrink. The idea was evidently a familiar one. 'My unwisdom, as you call it, is not so great as that. Nor do I count suicide escape—from anything.'

Broome's square rugged face lightened. 'Ah, now you are wise, indeed. If you will continue to think with such intelligence and courage, I repeat—Red Alastair can be defeated.'

Again she shook her head. 'You scarcely know how truly monstrous he is, and was from the beginning. Oh, they are not old wives' tales, the records of his birth and life and death. They come from varying sources, perfectly sound and authentic, and all agree that he was monstrous, devil-possessed from birth.'

'And his death? What is recorded of that?'

'It was never recorded as proved fact. He lived alone at Gorm after Lady Jean's death; entirely, mysteriously alone, cut off from every human being. No one took food to the castle, no one saw him outside its walls. But at night the Keep would blaze with light—and books say "ringed about with most infernal fire", and thin high pipings and whistlings echoed to the hills. It was a terror in the countryside for three years.'

'And then?'

'The old castle of Gorm was burned to the ground. It blazed and smouldered for nights and days. No one would go near it. Only the Keep was left standing.'

'And the Picture? Is it mentioned in the early records?'

Alan, listening, strained forward to hear her reply.

'Yes.' Loathing dawned in her eyes. 'Duncan, tenth Earl of Glenhallion, inherited after Gorm was burned. Red Alastair had vanished, although his bones were never found, and the popular belief was that he had not died in the fire. Duncan rebuilt the castle as it stands now, and attempted to destroy what was recorded in those days as "a most strange and foule magick". Instead, he was himself destroyed, his body found on the battlements with a broken back.'

Alan frowned, turned to Broome.

'At least, Alastair was living then! He must have been responsible for that murder.'

'But many have died like that,' Maisry went on. 'Many have tried to destroy the Picture. For almost two hundred years men have tried, and failed, and died most horribly.'

'Opposing the psychical with the physical.' Broome's massive head was hunched between his shoulders, his abstracted gaze bent on the carpet. 'Red Alastair died. He exists in another state of being. He must be met, opposed, conquered in that other state.'

Alan's words came slow and weighted. 'I would not acknowledge that before. I've been bluffing myself. I knew he was something—not human—when first I saw him on the battlements. I dared not admit it. It seemed too difficult too dangerous. I was afraid.'

Tears came to Maisry's eyes. Broome's smile, however, was a benediction. 'Now you've come to grips with yourself. Of course you're afraid. What do you expect? You're human, not a devil like Red Alastair.

'What I mean, more precisely,' Alan continued in the same slow painful way, 'is that I recognize at last what must be done—and I'm prepared to do it. I know in the main, that is; I shall leave details to you.'

'I can give you protection. I can prepare you for the journey. Beyond that none can help.'

'What journey? What are you both talking about?' Maisry broke in with quick breathless words. 'Alan! You mustn't—you're not dreaming of. . . .'

He took her hand, kissed the fingers that clung to his. She turned to Broome, her hand still holding fast to Alan's.

'Tell me! Tell me! What are you going to let him do?

Protection, you said. Oh, what are you going to do?—where is Alan going?'

'Don't break now, my dearest.' Alan rose and stood before her. 'I need your help, all you can give.'

'All you can give,' echoed Broome, and his tone touched her to profound stillness. 'You have a capacity for faith. It is a two-edged quality. You brought Red Alastair into the compass of your existence by your faith in him and his power to do you harm. You can transfer that faith to Alan and his power to conquer Red Alastair. You must choose. There can be no compromise. Do you believe in Alan's power to defeat your enemy, or do you not?'

Her look turned to Alan's straight, tall figure. He was changed, much changed since his surrender to the deep-hidden unconscious self he had so long ignored. His dark Pharaoh look of impenetrable command and dignity added a decade to his years.

As she watched him, amazement swamped her fear. It was not possible to conceive defeat for this regal-looking man. 'I fight for you, Alan, I believe in you.'

He looked long into her eyes, saw all that lay behind her spoken words, and took her hand as if to seal a compact. 'Then we're ready now for the fight—for the victory.'

He turned to Broome. 'We are of one mind now, one resolve, utterly and completely one.'

V

Two great seven-branched candelabra, on massive stands, reached tall as young trees on either side of the fireplace. Their candles showed the Picture in warm golden light. Through the barred, unglassed windows, night air drifted mild and sweet with scent of hawthorn, mingling with tang of wood and leaves that glowed and sizzled in a brazier upon the hearth.

A truckle-bed showed dimly in a corner of the dining-hall; two light garden seats and a great pile of wood and many thick white candles were also visible.

'You are sure, you swear, that Maisry is safe? To wait here while she, perhaps, is—'

Broome interrupted him. 'I know she is safe. For *her* I can absolutely vouch. For you, it is different; I can only protect you up to a point; the issue depends entirely on yourself after that. Your will against his. You are taking the most fantastic risk, as I warned you. If you lose, if your endurance and courage are mastered by him for an instant, you are mastered for all time. You will become what he is—a devil; you will work for him, yes, even if it means helping to bait the Lady Maisry to hell!'

'Never!' There was none of Alan's wonted fire and scorn in his voice; emotion was stripped from him, human attributes consumed by divine unbending will. 'You are sure, then? She is tired, ill, she may fall asleep. And in sleep Red Alastair calls her.'

'You don't know the laws that govern other states of being, but, believe me, Red Alastair is restricted in his activities as we are ourselves. Laws of gravity, of magnetism, of attraction and repulsion, of growth and decay, of tides and winds and electricity—all the myriad laws that govern us and our objective world have their parallels in other worlds.'

'Who makes them?'

'Who makes ours?' was the quiet response. 'Fire burns you; a fall from a height will break you in pieces! Why?'

'Because we're made of human stuff, perishable matter.'

'And do you imagine that, free of your body, you cannot suffer or perish? Red Alastair, I repeat, has no power to pass the barriers that protect Lady Maisry for this one night.'

'And after that?'

'Her protection will be in your power.'

Broome turned abruptly to the wall. 'Watch! Watch the Picture, on your life! He mustn't see you first. He mustn't call you to him. The attack must be from you.'

The two men stood shoulder to shoulder, their gaze sternly set upon the Picture. A faint copper tinge darkened its evening sky, grey haze began to cloud the heights, shadows fell across the wide moors, the woods, and glen; the long road seemed a net flung down—a trap—a sinister living thing that coiled and waited for its prey.

Mist thickened and spread upon the heights, and Broome's hand went to his breast pocket. He drew out a small phial and unstoppered it, pressed it into Alan's hand.

'Keep your eyes on the mist, on the mist above Vorangowl. He is coming. Drink this, *on the instant*, when his figure appears. He must not catch you in the body.'

The coppery gleam deepened in the sky, focused, concentrated to a centre. The Dark Star shone out over the broad estate of Glenhallion; and, on the far horizon of the Picture, mist rose, wreathed, and crept across the sullen moors . . . blind herald of doom.

Alan stood with the phial to his lips, breathing slowly, evenly. The hand that held the little clouded glass was steady, his dark brows met in a frown of concentration over eyes black as a deep tarn in winter, and as cold. The fine bones of his face showed under taut muscles and sunken cheeks.

On the heights of Vorangowl, on a craggy spur of rock above the fatal gorge and dizzy cliff-path, the mists grew thin . . . parted . . . swirled aside. A figure, a mere black speck, but infinitely menacing, was visible.

Swift as a bird's flash, Alan drank. The phial slipped, crashed to the stone floor.

Broome's strong arms were about him instantly, supporting him, lifting him to the truckle-bed in the corner. Blind, deaf, an empty shell, his body lay there as Broome turned quickly back to the Picture.

Watching it, his heart seemed to turn over in his breast. The dread he had concealed from Alan racked him now.

'Gone. Beyond all help, all knowledge now. Fighting alone, unaided. Following—following that devil—even to hell.'

Then, in the Picture, he saw Alan signal from the Keep across the gulf of time and space the painted surface bridged; signal from the battlements. Next moment, Broome saw his tall light figure running through the grounds, through the gates, along the road that led to Vorangowl. Swiftly, swiftly Alan's feet carried him, borne by the impetus of his strong will.

Now the glen lay behind him; the wooded Kaims closed about him jealously. On, on he went, past threat of glooming trees, past barren reaches of the upper glen.

Broome watched, his heart going as if he himself ran across the fatal spellbound moors. He could see Red Alastair fighting his way downward—restrained by Alan's stronger impetus—taken unawares. Ah, Red Alastair was gaining ground now! If he reached the cliff-path, if he crossed it first, then Alan must suffer terribly. It was clear the fact was apprehended by both adversaries.

All Red Alastair's unbridled longing, his mad unappeasable desire, had focused on the scene of his defeated lust. For two hundred years his restless, terrible ghost had wandered there, watching, waiting. The cliff and rocky narrow trail were deep imprinted with his torment, his deathless hate.

Swifter, swifter Alan ran, up the steeps, over heather and stony tracts, on—on—on. And, from the mists, Red Alastair loomed larger; the balefire of hair and beard gleamed. From either end, the two antagonists approached the fatal wall of rock.

Broome leaned forward, his whole consciousness centred on Alan's last tremendous effort. 'He's done it! He's there first!'

The quiet thankful voice rang in the still room and the candles flared in answer, showing every detail on the painted wall.

On the dizzy edge of space. Alan took the path lightly, easily; and, on its further side. Red Alastair bulked gigantic, the mist recoiling—leaving him in space—alone—waiting. . . .

Alan had crossed, flashed upon his enemy—closer, closer, until to Broome's sight there scarcely seemed a yard between them. Then, for a long moment of torture, both figures were motionless. Broome well understood the meaning of that titanic pause. Will battled with will. One must retreat, one pursue.

The Picture suddenly assumed the look of some vast amphitheatre: hollow curving mountain ranges, their crested heads upreared, closed in upon the combatants. Beyond them, screened by vaporous mist, Broome was aware of watchers, felt the pressure of their blind malevolence.

'So,' he whispered, 'Red Alastair is not come alone!'

A knife seemed to twist in his heart as he watched; every moment was a year of horror; every instant of the grim rigid contest meant unspeakable effort to Alan.

The mist rolled blindingly, it wrapped about Red Alastair, drew him back, back to the heights. And Alan followed on.

Broome was aware that he followed with sure and steady purpose, more and more slowly, growing smaller, dimmer at every step. The Kaims of Vorangowl were being blotted out. Mist rose on every side. The hills, the glen, the woods were only smears of vague colour. Now the foreground and the corner of the old Keep vanished. Only the Dark Star shone with metallic copper glow and showed Alan's tiny, toiling figure going upward—upward. It reached the farthest peak, showed for a flashing second, black, tiny, remote; then it was lost.

Broome's eyes ached; he closed them, opened them again. No it was really over now. The Picture on the wall was only a grey dull blur of moving swirling mist. Not a stone, not a leaf, not a blade of grass was visible. Even the Dark Star had sunk, its blood-red gloom wiped out. Mist—impenetrable, blinding, moving mist hid everything.

VI

Two long days dragged to evening. The weary terrifying hours of a third night closed on Gorm. Maisry, sleepless and worn, went at midnight to share Broome's vigil.

Nothing was changed. The candles, burning in a windless

night, showed nothing more—only grey surging clouds of mist in ceaseless movement. The Picture was like the crater of a volcano where smoke eddied and swung in the void before the destroying fire burst up from its depths.

The watchers saw no change in Alan's face except, perhaps, a deeper shadow of repose. It was a sign, Broome knew, that he was farther and farther away with every passing hour—following—following through space—on and on to dim uncertain, perilous horizons where the finite mind can no longer function.

Broome faced his thought steadily, though it was overwhelming in its horror. Had Red Alastair the power to lead on to voids no mortal spirit can endure? His straining eyes grew more intent.

'Something is moving behind the mist,' he said.

A rift showed at the top of the Picture; a glimpse of pale sky, a tooth of jagged rock appeared. Thin whispy trails floated across the rift. Gradually, as if rent and shredded by a furious wind, the whole horizon cleared to show a colourless cloudless sky and moorland heights, below which a sea of mist whirled and eddied to and fro.

But no figure was visible. Until long past dawn the two kept watch, their eyes red-rimmed and aching, but a cold pale sky and desolate peaks of Vorangowl mocked them with their emptiness.

Broome had watched narrowly in all the long hours for some change in Alan, too; but it did not come. The day passed and the fourth night passed. Dawn of the fifth day approached. Broome and Maisry once more shared the vigil, for he had warned her it was the most pregnant of the twenty-four hours.

The Picture showed the same chill breadth of sky and sharp-toothed crags. The rest was veiled. It was in Alan's face that Broome read indication of a crisis. Its indescribable look of sphinx-like, age-old remoteness was softened. The eyelids no longer gave the impression of carven lids that covered sightless eyes; they seemed merely to have drooped in sleep. A warmer, fuller outline curved cheek and jaw and temples.

'Alan! Alan!'

'No.' Broome curtly stopped her. 'It is the Picture you must watch. It is the door he must pass through to his body.'

Round a tall spur of rock they saw a dark speck moving. Slowly—oh, very slowly—it came on. Impossible to see its face, its outline, or any distinguishing mark at all, but both knew at once who struggled there up on the heights of Vorangowl.

'Bring him back! Bring him back with all your will.' Broome spoke to the trembling girl beside him but kept his eyes on the Picture. 'He's done! You and I must give him strength—his is spent, and overspent.'

They watched the efforts of the far-off lonely figure and tried to fight back their own despair. The road stretched so endlessly—so endlessly. . . Would that halting, stumbling traveller, so miraculously returning—would he ever reach his bourn?

Now it was full dawn in the green leafy actual world outside the Keep. Birds shook the spell of silence into sound. Long rosy fingers of sunlight thrust through an east window and touched the dusty floor. The candles, paling ghostly sentries, burned on.

Dawn too, it seemed, in the changing Picture. Behind Alan the sky grew light, throwing sun and shadow on the heights he had passed. But in front of him the road wound into mist and shadows—shadows that fell blackest and most impenetrably into the deep gorge which the cliff-path skirted.

Once more that haunted cliff-path must be crossed. Could Alan traverse it? Could he control his swooning weariness on its sharp edge?

'Good, ah, good! His will holds firm.'

Broome's voice sank to a deep exultant note as they saw Alan drop on hands and knees to crawl along the path. Maisry watched with pain too overpowering for tears. She spoke to him as if he were close beside her, as if she trod the path before him.

'Dear—it is halfway now. We will rest on the other side.

Follow, follow me—a little more—a little more. Ah, you will not let me go alone—Alan! Alan! Come with me . . . come. . . .'

Broome marvelled at her. And Alan's face lifted as if he saw her on the path before him; now and again he put out a hand as if to touch her own. It was full noon when at last he reached the end of the path and lay on the heather slopes beyond.

Until sunset, Maisry coaxed and pleaded and besought the figure on the painted Picture. With Broome beside her, aiding her strength, her wisdom, she fought for Alan, bringing him mile after weary mile along the dark glen road, bringing him back across the cursed painted miles from hell, back to the warmth and beauty of his own green earth, to her and to her love.

The sun sank low, and lower. And still Alan was outside the gates of Gorm. Candlelight showed him on the endless road, swaying and lurching with weariness beyond control. More than once he fell, but rose and stumbled on in answer to Maisry's low entreating words of love. Then at last he fell and did not rise; he seemed deaf to her voice, her pleadings, her tenderness.

Behind him, the long road was clear of mist and shadow, but the foreground he had not yet passed still lay obscure and dark.

Maisry turned imperiously to her companion. 'A chair! Put one close that I may touch him, help him up again.'

He saw her climb and lean close until her hands could touch the exhausted broken figure lying on the road. Close, close to the painted wall, her moving tender hands seemed to raise, to lift him to his feet. Once more, miraculously, he dragged himself forward—on—on to the gates of Gorm. He reached them, passed through and was swallowed up in velvet darkness of the trees.

No shred of mist remained in all the Picture. In its foreground, the grey Keep abruptly thrust up, grim, boding, expectant.

Dimly in the starlight, someone bulked faintly,

uncertainly upon the battlements. Broome's lips formed a word: 'Alan!'

The name died on a sudden breath of horror. It was not Alan who so monstrously obscured the stars. It was a heavier figure. It moved, turned, thrust forward a great head. Ah, that demon's face, that flaming beard and hair!

Broome leaped to Maisry's side, to draw her away, to interpose himself between her—leaning forward, her golden head and lovely face not a foot from the painted Keep—and the peering lustful mask. But she resisted him, thrust back his hands, turned a changed face and eyes that flashed like swords full on Red Alastair. She was a golden flame of anger.

'Go back!' her voice rang in the echoing room like bugles blown for war. 'Dead, cursed thing—go back to your own hell! Dead—defeated—forgotten ghost! I am not afraid! Back—back to hell!'

The thing upon the tower roof shrank, wavered, dwindled in the starlight. Maisry's eyes pierced it, followed it, tortured it. The monstrous bulk grew vaporous, insubstantial as a web, a dusty cobweb flung on the massive wall. The web, caught by a breath of wind, was torn from its last slight moorings—tossed from the Keep—drifted from sight. . .

As it vanished, the Picture cracked across and across. Its painted scene faded, dissolving, disintegrating, obliterated by the all-pervading dust of centuries. In a moment, nothing remained of outline or of colour. Above the hearth, a cracked and mouldering wall showed in the golden candlelight.

Maisry sprang down, caught Broome's arm. 'Now he can come to me! Now I am free! Alan! Alan! Alan!'

She knelt beside the truckle-bed. Alan lay still. He seemed to sleep, to dream. A faint smile curved his lips, and his heavy eyelids quivered. Maisry kissed the curving lips, the fluttering eyelids, until the dark eyes opened wide. His voice was a faint exhausted whisper.

'You came for me. You brought me home. I could not

have won back—alone. Your voice—dearest—I followed it—your voice—your little hands. . .'

His eyes closed in weakness, then opened once again.

'I tried to warn you, to tell you he was coming, too. It was forbidden—I was not allowed! If you had been afraid—he would have had power—to stay. We had to fight—together, my beloved—together. . .'

He sank back to deep oblivion and sleep. Maisry, crouched beside him, let her head fall on the hands that clasped his own. Sleep folded her too, softly, suddenly.

Portrait in Moonlight

CARL JACOBI

The Trinidad offices of Holworth and Company, Importers and Exporters, in Weightson Road near the Port-of-Spain waterfront, were under the capable, if unprogressive, managership of Rupert Clarkson. Clarkson, in his forty-sixth year, was a widower and a rather moody individual, with a tall, loose-jointed frame, narrow shoulders, and lonely eyes. He lived in Queen's Park West, quite a distance from the Holworth offices, but he always chose to walk, claiming that he needed the exercise.

As a matter of fact, there were a number of things Clarkson felt he needed. He was in a word growing old, and none realized it more than he. There were lines and crow's feet about his eyes. He had developed a slight stoop, probably from bending for long hours over a desk, and his hair was greying rapidly.

Psychologically, Clarkson knew that he should accept these changes as a matter of course, but somehow he couldn't do that. He was still young in spirit, and the knowledge that his material body was showing some signs of wear, however slight, greatly concerned him. The bureau in his bedroom was littered with bottles of restorers, dyes, and other masculine cosmetics, all of which he had given a trial and then discarded as either worthless or too obvious in their effect.

'It's this infernal sticky heat,' he said on more than one occasion. 'It ages one. Trinidad is no place for a white man.'

Fearful of getting into a rut, Clarkson varied the course of his walk to work each day. But he always stopped at the corner of Dundonald Street and Tragarete Road to watch an aged Negro stand before an improvised easel on the sidewalk and paint pictures of local scenes.

The old fellow was quite good, Clarkson thought. He used a dried palm leaf for a palette, and his colours apparently were made from crushed berries and roots which only a West Indian black would know where to obtain. One time he painted The Three Sisters, the trio of mountain peaks for which Trinidad was famous. Again it was a scene of the harbour with the many vessels at anchor there.

While interested, Clarkson had never been tempted to buy one of these paintings until one blazing afternoon in August. Then he watched the Negro add the finishing touches to a picture smaller in size than usual. In rudely lettered Spanish, it bore the title *Youth*. Curiously, it presented the likeness of a middle-aged man with a gaunt, lined face, thin lips, and eyes set wide apart. But the moment Clarkson gazed upon that face, a responsive chord was touched in his brain. The picture cost him six and threepence.

Later in his room he debated with himself as to where he should hang the painting, if indeed he should hang it at all. It was then that he noticed the five words printed in pencil on the back of the canvas. The words read:

Put me in the moonlight.

Clarkson frowned. Picture in the moonlight. It didn't make sense. But then so many things didn't make sense here in the islands. In the end he hung the picture high up on the east wall, opposite the two French windows, and forgot about it.

For a week thereafter Clarkson was forced to forego his

daily walks because of inclement weather. The rain came down in torrents, and the offices of Holworth and Company were damp and gloomy. The gloominess made him irritable, and when he was told that Stephen Tarpan requested an interview, Clarkson lost his temper. Stephen was the Negro who formerly had been in the employ of the company as a messenger. His duties had included delivering last-minute notes to ship captains, the customs office, and other simple missions. In his spare time he had done a little dusting and cleaning.

'So you're here again,' Clarkson said as the black shuffled into the office. 'How many times do I have to tell you your services are no longer needed.'

Stephen rolled a faded cap back and forth in his hands nervously.

'Please, sar,' he said, 'give Stephen 'nother chance. I work ver hard, sar. I tek care of letters and t'ings very rapidly.'

'No.' Clarkson shook his head in quiet decision. 'That's just your trouble. That's why I had to let you go. You loiter, Stephen.' Then he added brutally. 'You might as well realize it, you're getting old, and this company is no home for the aged.'

Clarkson went home that night in worse spirits than usual. Port-of-Spain was getting to be a hopelessly dull place. It seemed that all the unattached women in his club circles were either too old or too young. People no longer enjoyed good times any more. He wondered what had become of that lovely Baret girl with whom he had had such wonderful times the summer of . . . Good Lord, that had been the summer of '29, eighteen years ago. It seemed incredible.

He reached his home at length, a modest 'villa' set well back from the street in a grove of palmistes, and went directly to his bedroom, intending to lie down for a while before dinner. But the first thing that caught his eye as he crossed the threshold was the picture he had bought from the Negro street artist. It was a picture no longer, merely a blurred mass of run-together colours.

Clarkson went up to it and studied it for some moments. Vaguely, he could discern the outlines of the former painting: the eyes, the lips, the jaw, but that was all. He swore softly. That's what came from patronizing these blacks. They were a worthless lot, all of them.

Nevertheless, Clarkson made it a point to stop the next morning at the intersection of Dundonald Street and Tragarete Road. The Negro artist was there, his easel propped up on a shady spot of sidewalk. Without wasting words, Clarkson explained what had happened.

The black smiled. 'You hang him in de sunlight,' he said. 'Thas de trouble. You must hang him in de moonlight.'

'But that doesn't do me any good now,' Clarkson said. 'The picture's ruined.'

Again the Negro smiled. He opened a little tin box from among his assortment of brushes, rolled canvases and paints and drew forth a long slender stick of bamboo. At the end of it was fitted a small cap of yellowish transparent material that looked not unlike amber.

'Tek this stick, sar. Rub him all over de picture. Then he will come back.'

Clarkson accepted the bamboo doubtfully. It occurred to him as he lingered there that there was something strangely familiar about the Negro's face. Then he remembered Stephen Tarpan; of course, the artist and his former messenger must be related. He was about to ask if this were true, but for some reason his query died unspoken.

The weather turned clear that day, and early in the evening a full moon came up. Clarkson carefully massaged his face with a new kind of cleansing clay he had sent for from the States and retired early. He awoke in the middle of the night with the moon shining through his open window. It was also shining on the faded painting on the wall, and he remembered suddenly the artist's instructions as to how to restore it. He got out of bed, took up the bamboo stick from the bureau and began to run the capped end slowly back and forth over the blurred canvas. For a moment he was conscious of an electric thrill, like a faint vibration, passing from the bamboo stick up his wrist into his arm. Then the sensation passed, only to be followed by a vague impression that the faded lips in the painting had curved upward and were smiling at him. Clarkson rubbed his eyes sleepily and went back to bed.

He did not sleep well the rest of the night. The skin about his cheeks and lower jaw and across his abdomen seemed to have become tight and drawn. He was conscious, too, of his heart beating more rapidly than usual. Shortly before dawn he fell into a heavy slumber and dreamed a gloomy unpleasant dream that he was a boy again but that all his friends were old men and old women.

When he awoke, the first thing that focused into his eyes was the picture. He sat bolt upright, staring. The painting was completely restored! Gazing back at him from the depths of brilliant pigment was the face of the middle-aged man with the wide-apart eyes. But the face could hardly be called middle-aged now. There was an indefinable freshness to it that changed its appearance entirely. It was as if ten years of time had been removed from it.

Clarkson got his second start when he went into the bathroom to shave. The reflection that looked back at him from the mirror was different from yesterday morning or even a morning a year ago. The crow's feet above his eyes were still there, but they had thinned perceptibly. The bald spot over the left temple was covered with a nice growth of hair. And his hair! It was a rich, shiny black with only the faintest trace of grey.

It couldn't be that cleansing clay, Clarkson told himself; but what then was responsible for the change? After a moment it came to him that perhaps the signs of age he thought he had detected before had existed only in his imagination. He broke out in a cheery whistle as he pursued this line of reasoning, took particular pains with his dress that morning and headed for work in a fine fettle.

That day was a memorable one in Clarkson's life. From the moment he first entered the Holworth offices and was greeted by his stenographer to the time he met Inspector Bainley of the Trinidad Constabulary on his way home, the hours presented one steady round of complimentary remarks about his youthful appearance. Bainley was even more enthusiastic than the others.

'What the devil have you done, Clarkson,' the inspector said, 'found your own private fountain of youth? You look positively juvenile today.'

Only one circumstance in fact marred the day's routine. Late in the afternoon Stephen Tarpan approached Clarkson again, asking for a return to his job. The whining insistence of the black broke the manager's patience. He marched Stephen to the door, and then when the Negro still hesitated, he gave him a forceful push down the stairs. Stephen pitched headlong, rolling over and over to the bottom. He lay there motionless a long time while Clarkson suffered a pang of dismay. Then with a low moan he got painfully to his feet and hobbled off.

That night was almost a repetition of the one before. Some time in the small hours Clarkson awoke to find a shaft of brilliant moonlight shining into the room and illuminating the portrait on the wall. The face in the painting seemed to be smiling even more broadly now. Yet Clarkson got the impression that there was no mirth in the smile, but rather that the lips were parted in a kind of hideous mockery. Again he slept badly during the remaining hours, and again he felt that same drawing sensation in the skin of his face, abdomen, and to a lesser extent, his legs. When he began to dream, it was a wild fantastic dream, without sense or meaning.

He was walking along a broad highway that ran straight as a crayon line to the horizon. Flanking the highway on either side were the brown stumps of chopped-down trees, and upon each stump stood the black-garbed figure of a very old man, leaning on a long cane. As Clarkson strode past these figures, he looked at their faces, and he saw that each was the face of some acquaintance he had known or met in the past. And with each step he took he felt the years sloughing off him, felt himself growing incredibly younger.

The next morning Clarkson was amazed at what he saw

in the glass. He beheld a man of scarcely thirty. The crow's feet had entirely disappeared. There was not a thread of grey in his hair, and his complexion was clear and alive with the freshness of youth.

So great was the change that he had some misgivings about what his fellow workers at the office would say. Accordingly, with a little smile of satisfaction, he dusted a little talcum over his temples. Whatever miracle he had stumbled upon—and it must be a miracle—it would not do to let his friends become curious all at once.

No easel or Negro artist met his gaze at the street corner that morning. Mildly curious, Clarkson was prompted to enter the tobacconist's shop in front of which the black had always done his painting and inquire as to his whereabouts.

'I don't know where he is,' the tobacconist said. 'He left here in a hurry yesterday, saying that his brother had been injured in a fall down a flight of stairs.'

Arriving at the Holworth and Company offices, Clarkson found an important letter waiting for him. The letter required his presence at Fort de France, Martinique, immediately. The *Compagnie de Français*, an import concern with which the Holworth branch had had dealings, was aroused over what it claimed to be false representation of merchandise. Clarkson might have entrusted his reply to the post or the wireless, but the *Compagnie de Français* was a big account, and he preferred to arrange matters in person.

There was just time to catch the *Island Queen*. He left word that he would be gone for a week and hurried home to pack a few necessities.

The instant he entered his room he was aware that a prowler had been there. One of his bureau drawers was partially open, and the bamboo stick given him by the Negro artist lay on the floor, not on the table where he had left it. A faint spicy odour lingered in the air. A quick search, however, failed to reveal any stolen valuables. Clarkson made sure his door was locked before he left.

Two days later he walked down the gangplank of the

Island Queen and entered Fort de France. It was ten years since he had been in Martinique, and the island seemed strange to him. Historic Fort Louis with its massive walls and battlements brooded over the harbour, and in the background Mont Pele towered, quiet now since its earth-shattering eruption of 1902. Only the *Savane*, the open park in the centre of the town, studded with royal palms, looked cool and inviting under the tropical sun.

No more than an hour was required for Clarkson to convince the French company manager that an error had been made, and the Holworth import man found himself faced with two full days and nights before he could return to Trinidad.

He took a room at the Hotel de la Paix, drank an aperitif, and ate his luncheon. It was while he sat enjoying a cigar in the hotel dining room that he suddenly became aware of the young woman at a table some distance away. He was on his feet in a moment, striding across to her.

'Mona Albrey,' he greeted. 'How are you? What on earth are you doing here?'

The woman's face broke into a smile of surprise and recognition as she looked up. 'Why, hello, Rupert!' she said. 'Don't tell me you've exchanged Trinidad for Martinique in your old age?'

'No, I'm still living in Port-of-Spain,' Clarkson replied. 'I'm here on business.' And added, 'Do I look older?'

She was a handsome brunette in her early forties, dressed in a cool linen suit, with a pert green hat to match her jade earrings. She gazed across the table with eyes filled with admiration.

'Not a bit of it,' she said. 'In fact, you look so boyish I hardly would have recognized you.'

They sat there, chatting of old times and idle gossip. At length Mona Albrey reached for her purse. She was doing an article for an American magazine on native costumes, she explained. She had all her material, but as a final wind-up she wanted to take in a Martinican festival scheduled for that afternoon in a village near St. Pierre.

'Want to come along?' she asked. 'It's only about forty kilometres, and I have a rented car outside.'

Clarkson replied that nothing would please him more. They drove north out of Fort de France, crossed the fashionable residential Plateau Didier, and then followed the highway through the villages of Balata and Absalon. Here Mona Albrey turned off into a wretched side road that climbed steadily into the highlands. As he sat beside her, Clarkson began to experience a feeling of unease. The drawing and tightening sensation about his skin was there again, though latent, and he knew that that feeling presaged a change again in his appearance. How long, he wondered, would this retrogressive action on the part of his age continue. It seemed he could feel a fresh vitality rippling through his body with each passing hour. Right now, in fact, he felt like leaping from the car and racing it on foot up the hill.

Mona Albrey shifted her hands on the wheel.

'You know, Rupert, the air in these latitudes must agree with you. I declare, you positively look as if you were still in your twenties.

Clarkson thought of the portrait back in his room in Port-of-Spain and the strange series of events that had so changed his life since he had obtained it. Did that painting exert a power upon him? Was it his imagination or was he growing younger even as the man in the portrait grew younger?

Then all at once he had other things to occupy his mind.

The car missed firing, slowly, and stopped. Mona jiggled the controls on the dashboard, pressed the starter repeatedly without results. She turned helplessly.

'I'll fix it,' Clarkson said. 'I'm rather good at this sort of thing.'

But the hours dragged past, and still he laboured with greasy hands under the car's bonnet. When at length he stepped back with a sigh, and the motor roared into life once more, shadows had begun to lengthen across the road and a golden moon was rising above the tree-tops.

And simultaneously with the appearance of that moon, Clarkson felt the drawing and tightening increase about his body a hundredfold. His complacent satisfaction was gone now. In its place a dull horror began to creep upon him. For he realized that with each passing minute he was slowly but irresistibly growing younger.

It was now, of course, too late to attend the festival. Mona drove rapidly back toward town, her hands playing nervously with the wheel. From time to time she cast an uneasy glance at the man beside her. Yet as the miles passed, they saw no sign of the highway.

'I'm certain we should have turned left at that last fork,' Clarkson said. 'This stretch of road doesn't seem familiar at all.'

The countryside appeared to be growing wilder and more rugged. They crossed deep valleys over narrow ramshackle bridges that threatened to plunge them into the roaring streams below. Jungle took the place of open savannah. Tall bearded cabbage palms towered up into a blue-black sky, and in the moonlight massive ferns loomed like so many phantoms crouching on either side of the road.

They were crossing a narrow plateau when abruptly a low sound reached their ears over the hum of the car's motor. It was the sound of drums, and it grew steadily louder as they advanced. The road made a sudden turn. Before them a small glade was revealed in the flanking wall of trees, and in its centre a large fire blazed luridly. Around that fire a group of shadowy figures paced slowly to the tempo of muted tom-toms.

Mona stopped the car and watched them for some minutes in silence.

'A voodoo dance,' she said at length. 'Come on. I want to see this.'

With misgivings, Clarkson followed her out of the car. Keeping carefully in the shadows, they entered the rank undergrowth and made their way forward until they reached a point twenty yards from the fire.

Clarkson saw then that there were about twenty Negroes in the group. All were in poor nondescript costume save a very old black woman who wore a full skirt of flowered silk with a gaudy fichu about her throat and a flaming red *madras* over her head. Heavy gold earrings glittered in the firelight.

Other details came into focus then as the Trinidad manager's eyes accustomed themselves in the gloom. Tied to a stake at the far side of the glade and bleating tremulously was a young goat. Beside the fire stood an upturned tree stump like a rude altar, on the top of which rested an earthen cup and a brass crucifix. And suspended from vine lashings above hung the squirming and twisting body of a captive *fer-de-lance*.

These were the physical details. But as Clarkson looked into the faces of the blacks, as he saw the unbridled fanaticism in their eyes, a wave of loathing swept through him.

The ceremony began with a multiple-voiced shout. The *mamaloi* in the crimson turban seized a long hooked knife and with a cry plunged it into the throat of the goat. An instant later the earthen cup was filled with the spurting blood from the dying animal. The frenzied blacks dipped hands into the crimson cup and leaped and danced to the wild rhythm of the tom-toms. Then suddenly the drums fell silent, and an ancient black man hobbled into the light of the fire.

The *mamaloi* approached him, carrying a long narrow wooden box. She opened its cover and drew out a length of bamboo, capped at one end with an amber-like substance. She dipped the capped end into the blood cup and began to rub it over the body of the aged black. Horror blanketed Clarkson. The stick was the same kind of bamboo given him by the Negro street artist in Port-of-Spain.

And then as he watched he saw the old black before him rapidly change in physical appearance. The flesh on his wrinkled face sloughed away; his body became erect, thinner and smaller. Now he was a callow youth of fifteen, now a young boy, and finally as the wasting-away process continued, a squalling infant that squirmed on the ground helplessly. It was all vague and indistinct with the light from the fire flickering uncertainly.

The *mamaloi* seized the knife and approached the child.

But Clarkson had seen enough. He seized Mona's arm and led her stumbling back to the car.

They spoke no words during the remainder of the drive. Miraculously, a few miles beyond, the road branched into the main highway, and presently they were back in Fort de France. Clarkson said goodnight and goodbye to Mona Albrey and climbed the stairs to his room. There he threw himself on the bed, covered his eyes and moaned aloud.

In heaven's name, what was happening to him? How long would this change continue? What was the cause of it? Lying there in the darkness, he strove to throttle the horror that was engulfing him and apply logic and reasoning to the enigma. But it was all a wild chaotic dream without reason or motive.

Only one fact was clear to him. In some incredible way his life was tied up with that portrait on the wall in his room in Port-of-Spain. When the moonlight shone upon it, as it must be doing tonight, he grew steadily younger. When the moonlight passed, time for him moved on again.

He must get back to Trinidad and tear that painting from the wall!

But there was still another day and night to be spent in Fort de France before the boat would leave. Morning, and Clarkson deliberately avoided looking at himself in the mirror. He ate his breakfast in the dining room, and he thought the waiter looked at him oddly several times. He went out on the street and began to walk in long brisk strides, heading towards the *Savane*. Beside the statue of Empress Josephine he paused a moment. A youth scarcely out of his teens approached and addressed him in French.

'Pardon, M'sieu, am I early or have the others gone already?'

Clarkson regarded him curiously. 'There must be some mistake,' he said. And added inanely, 'I'm a stranger here, you know.'

'Of course,' said the other, covering his embarrassment, 'it was stupid of me. But I was told all the young people who were going to Mademoiselle Chauson's country drive would meet here, and when I saw you, I thought that . . . Ah, here they are now.'

A group of rollicking young people approached down the street, followed by three old-fashioned horse-drawn phaetons. Quickly the youth joined them, and the procession moved to the far side of the square. Clarkson ran a hand slowly over his beardless jaw. *None of the group was more than nineteen or twenty years old!*

Was it possible he now looked so young the boy had mistaken him for one of his companions?

Deep in thought, Clarkson began to walk again, moving aimlessly down Rue Schoelcher, emerging at length into Place Barre. A small sign announced a book shop some distance ahead, and he stumbled towards it like a man seeking a sanctuary.

A bell jangled as he entered. Inside was dust and a bald-pated proprietor with pince-nez glasses. Clarkson moved down the row of shelves, seeing neither titles nor authors' names. He pulled down books at random and returned them after absently rifling their pages. In this manner he read the opening pages of a half dozen long out-of-date novels and travel books. But suddenly his eyes focused on the volume in his hands. It was a well-worn copy of *Voodooism in the West Indies* by Rene Callott, and with unsteady hands he opened it.

For half an hour he stood there in the half light, reading descriptions of the black practices, followed in the name of superstition in the islands. Rites which had their origin in West Africa and imported to the Caribbean during 'black-birding' or slave-trade days. He was about to replace the book when a passage caught his gaze:

> One rite which the author has never witnessed, but which the authorities, McCullough and Brissac, have both reported to be practised not infrequently by blacks of Trinidad and Martinique, is the ceremony of the bamboo *tevail* or Damballah stick. This is a variation of serpent worship and probably has its source somewhere in the Niger river country. The *tevail* is formed from a length

of bamboo cut by the *mamaloi* and capped at one end by a transparent substance. (McCullough calls this substance *lessadum* and states that it is formed from the serum and digestive juices of the *fer-de-lance*, to which has been added the crushed seeds of the *daatura*-plant.)

According to the superstition, the *tevail*, when rubbed upon a person's body, causes a retrogression of age. Another belief associated with the *tevail*, but even less founded upon fact, is that when used upon some possession of the person, which in turn is placed in the moonlight, the reversal to youth will continue as long as that object is left in the moonlight . . . *until life itself is gone*.

Clarkson read that passage three times. Carefully, with an unsteady finger, he traced that last sentence word for word. Then with a short cry he flung the book to the floor and rushed madly from the shop. . . .

He was on the ship at last. The door to his cabin was closed and locked. The two ports were shut tight, and the electric lights were turned out. In utter darkness Clarkson lay on the bed, body bathed in cold perspiration.

It was midnight, and up on deck the ship was swathed in moonlight. Moonlight, too, Clarkson knew, was shining over Port-of-Spain, Trinidad, was shining through the windows into his room and upon the portrait on the wall. He could sense it, could feel it with every fibre of his body. As if he were encased in a steel net, the skin about his chest, his abdomen, his legs, arms, and face grew steadily tighter.

Clarkson knew that he had shrunk in stature by more than half. His body was now that of a small boy. And as he lay there and Time flowed backward, he looked through the darkness at the far wall. Was he quite mad, or did he see that portrait there shining with an evil luminosity, the face growing steadily younger. . . .

. . . he was flying his kite on the high knoll back on his Connecticut farm home. The wind was cool on his face, and he could hear his mother calling him. He turned and began to run towards the house, but halfway his little legs fell as he tried to climb the steps. . . . His mother gathered him in her arms and placed him in his crib, crooning to him softly. . . . The white milk felt warm and good in his throat . . . and he closed his eyes as the blackness of infinity slowly gathered about him.

Inspector Bainley of the Trinidad Constabulary had given the room a thorough search without result.

'It looks like a closed case as far as our end is concerned,' he told the Warrant Officer. 'This chap, Clarkson, left for Martinique on Tuesday noon. He was due back here the following Wednesday at the latest, according to ship schedules. We know that he registered at the Hotel de la Paix in Fort de France and that he embarked for the return trip to Trinidad.'

'He seems to have left nothing behind in his room,' the Warrant Officer said, 'nothing that would show he was despondent or that he feared foul play.'

Bainley nodded, frowning. 'The facts are tight at every point. Clarkson complained of feeling ill, declared that he would stay in his cabin and said that he did not want to be disturbed. The steward had instructions to leave his trays outside the cabin door. No one saw Clarkson after he boarded the vessel at Fort de France. Yet when it docked at Port-of-Spain, Clarkson had disappeared. Vanished utterly! And his cabin was locked from the inside. . . . What the devil are you staring at?'

The Warrant Officer's eyes were wide with incredulity.

'This picture on the wall, sir,' he said. 'I could have sworn that it was the portrait of a very young baby when I first entered the room. Now, as you can see, sir, it's a blank canvas.'

The Ghost Ship

RICHARD MIDDLETON

Fairfield is a little village lying near the Portsmouth Road about halfway between London and the sea. Strangers who find it by accident now and then, call it a pretty, old-fashioned place; we who live in it and call it home don't find anything very pretty about it, but we should be sorry to live anywhere else. Our minds have taken the shape of the inn and the church and the green, I suppose. At all events, we never feel comfortable out of Fairfield.

Of course the Cockneys, with their vasty houses and noise-ridden streets, can call us rustics if they choose, but for all that Fairfield is a better place to live in than London. Doctor says that when he goes to London his mind is bruised with the weight of the houses, and he was a Cockney born. He had to live there himself when he was a little chap, but he knows better now. You gentlemen may laugh—perhaps some of you come from London way—but it seems to me that a witness like that is worth a gallon of arguments.

Dull? Well, you might find it dull, but I assure you that I've listened to all the London yarns you have spun tonight, and they're absolutely nothing to the things that happen at Fairfield. It's because of our way of thinking and minding our own business. If one of your Londoners were set down on the green of a Saturday night when the ghosts of the lads who died in the war keep tryst with the lasses who lie in the churchyard, he couldn't help being curious and interfering, and then the ghosts would go somewhere where it was quieter. But we just let them come and go and don't make any fuss, and in consequence Fairfield is the ghostliest place in all England. Why, I've seen a headless man sitting on the edge of the well in broad daylight, and the children playing about his feet as if he were their father. Take my word for it, spirits know when they are well off as much as human beings.

Still, I must admit that the thing I'm going to tell you about was queer even for our part of the world, where three packs of ghost-hounds hunt regularly during the season, and blacksmith's great-grandfather is busy all night shoeing the dead gentlemen's horses. Now that's a thing that wouldn't happen in London, because of their interfering ways, but blacksmith he lies up aloft and sleeps as quiet as a lamb. Once when he had a bad head he shouted down to them not to make so much noise, and in the morning he found an old guinea left on the anvil as an apology. He wears it on his watch chain now. But I must get on with my story; if I start telling you about the queer happenings at Fairfield I'll never stop.

It all came of the great storm in the spring of '97, the year that we had two great storms. This was the first one, and I remember it very well, because I found in the morning that it had lifted the thatch of my pigsty into the widow's garden as clean as a boy's kite. When I looked over the hedge, widow—Tom Lamport's widow that was—was prodding for her nasturtiums with a daisy-grubber. After I had watched her for a little I went down to the Fox and Grapes to tell landlord what she had said to me. Landlord he laughed, being a married man and at ease with the sex. 'Come to that,' he said, 'the tempest has blowed something into my field. A kind of a ship I think it would be.'

I was surprised at that until he explained that it was only a ghost ship and would do no hurt to the turnips. We argued that it had been blown up from the sea at Portsmouth, and then we talked of something else. There were two slates down at the parsonage and a big tree in Lumley's meadow. It was a rare storm.

I reckon the wind had blown our ghosts all over England. They were coming back for days afterwards with foundered horses and as footsore as possible, and they were so glad to get back to Fairfield that some of them walked up the street crying like little children. Squire said that his great-grandfather's great-grandfather hadn't looked so dead-beat since the Battle of Naseby, and he's an educated man.

What with one thing and another, I should think it was a week before we got straight again, and then one afternoon I met the landlord on the green and he had a worried face. 'I wish you'd come and have a look at that ship in my field,' he said to me, 'it seems to me it's leaning real hard on the turnips. I can't bear thinking what the missus will say when she sees it.'

I walked down the lane with him, and sure enough there was a ship in the middle of his field, but such a ship as no man had seen on the water for three hundred years, let alone in the middle of a turnip field. It was all painted black and covered with carvings, and there was a great bay window in the stern for all the world like the Squire's drawing-room. There was a crowd of little black cannon on deck and looking out of her portholes, and she was anchored at each end to the hard ground. I have seen the wonders of the world on picture-postcards, but I have never seen anything to equal that.

'She seems very solid for a ghost ship,' I said, seeing the landlord was bothered.

'I should say it's a betwixt and between,' he answered, puzzling it over, 'but it's going to spoil a matter of fifty turnips, and missus she'll want it moved.' We went up to her and touched the side, and it was as hard as a real ship. 'Now there's folks in England would call that very curious,' he said.

Now I don't know much about ships, but I should think that that ghost ship weighed a solid two hundred tons, and it seemed to me that she had come to stay, so that I felt sorry for the landlord, who was a married man. 'All the horses in Fairfield won't move her out of my turnips,' he said, frowning at her.

Just then we heard a noise on her deck, and we looked up and saw that a man had come out of her front cabin and was looking down at us very peaceably. He was dressed in a black uniform set out with rusty gold lace, and he had a great cutlass by his side in a brass sheath. 'I'm Captain Bartholomew Roberts,' he said, in a gentleman's voice, 'put in for recruits. I seem to have brought her rather far up the harbour.'

'Harbour!' cried landlord; 'why, you're fifty miles from the sea.'

Captain Roberts, didn't turn a hair. 'So much as that, is it?' he said coolly. 'Well, it's of no consequence.'

Landlord was a bit upset at this. 'I don't want to be unneighbourly,' he said, 'but I wish you hadn't brought your ship into my field. You see, my wife sets great store on these turnips.'

The captain took a pinch of snuff out of a fine gold box that he pulled out of his pocket, and dusted his fingers with a silk handkerchief in a very genteel fashion. 'I'm only here for a few months,' he said; 'but if a testimony of my esteem would pacify your good lady I should be content,' and with the words he loosed a great gold brooch from the neck of his coat and tossed it down to landlord.

Landlord blushed as red as a strawberry. 'I'm not denying she's fond of jewellery,' he said, 'but it's too much for half a sackful of turnips.' And indeed it was a handsome brooch.

The captain laughed. 'Tut, man,' he said, 'it's a forced sale, and you deserve a good price. Say no more about it.' And nodding good-day to us, he turned on his heel and went into the cabin. Landlord walked back up the lane like a man with a weight off his mind. 'That tempest has blowed me a bit of luck,' he said; 'the missus will be main pleased with that brooch. It's better than blacksmith's guinea, any day.'

Ninety-seven was Jubilee year, the year of the second Jubilee, you remember, and we had great doings at

Fairfield, so that we hadn't much time to bother about the ghost ship, though anyhow it isn't our way to meddle in things that don't concern us. Landlord, he saw his tenant once or twice when he was hoeing his turnips and passed the time of day, and landlord's wife wore her new brooch to church every Sunday. But we didn't mix much with the ghosts at any time, all except an idiot lad there was in the village, and he didn't know the difference between a man and a ghost, poor innocent! On Jubilee Day, however, somebody told Captain Roberts why the church bells were ringing, and he hoisted a flag and fired off his guns like a loyal Englishman. 'Tis true the guns were shotted, and one of the round shot knocked a hole in Farmer Johnstone's barn, but nobody thought much of that in such a season of rejoicing.

It wasn't till our celebrations were over that we noticed that anything was wrong in Fairfield. 'Twas shoemaker who told me first about it one morning at the Fox and Grapes. 'You know my great great-uncle?' he said to me.

'You mean Joshua, the quiet lad,' I answered, knowing him well.

'Quiet!' said shoemaker indignantly. 'Quiet you call him, coming home at three o'clock every morning as drunk as a magistrate and waking up the whole house with his noise.'

'Why, it can't be Joshua!' I said, for I knew him for one of the most respectable young ghosts in the village.

'Joshua it is,' said shoemaker, 'and one of these nights he'll find himself out in the street if he isn't careful.'

This kind of talk shocked me, I can tell you, for I don't like to hear a man abusing his own family, and I could hardly believe that a steady youngster like Joshua had taken to drink. But just then in came butcher Aylwin in such a temper that he could hardly drink his beer. 'The young puppy! the young puppy!' he kept on saying; and it was some time before shoemaker and I found out that he was talking about his ancestor that fell at Senlac.

'Drink?' said shoemaker hopefully, for we all like company in our misfortunes, and butcher nodded grimly.

'The young noodle,' he said emptying his tankard.

Well, after that I kept my ears open, and it was the same story all over the village. There was hardly a young man among all the ghosts of Fairfield who didn't roll home in the small hours of the morning the worse for liquor. I used to wake up in the night and hear them stumble past my house, singing outrageous songs. The worst of it was that we couldn't keep the scandal to ourselves, and the folk of Greenhill began to talk of 'sodden Fairfield', and taught their children to sing a song about us:

'Sodden Fairfield, sodden Fairfield, has no use for bread-and-butter;
Rum for breakfast, rum for dinner, rum for tea, and rum for supper!'

We are easy-going in our village, but we didn't like that.

Of course we soon found out where the young fellows went to get the drink, and landlord was terribly cut up that his tenant should have turned out so badly, but his wife wouldn't hear of parting with the brooch, so that he couldn't give the Captain notice to quit. But as time went on, things grew from bad to worse, and at all hours of the day you would see those young reprobates sleeping it off on the village green. Nearly every afternoon a ghost wagon used to jolt down to the ship with a lading of rum, and though the older ghosts seemed inclined to give the Captain's hospitality the go-by, the youngsters were neither to hold nor to bind.

So one afternoon when I was taking my nap I heard a knock at the door, and there was parson looking very serious, like a man with a job before him that he didn't altogether relish. 'I'm going down to talk to the Captain about all this drunkenness in the village, and I want you to come with me,' he said straight out.

I can't say that I fancied the visit much myself, and I tried to hint to parson that as, after all, they were only a lot of ghosts, it didn't very much matter.

'Dead or alive, I'm responsible for their good conduct,' he said, 'and I'm going to do my duty and put a stop to this continued disorder. And you are coming with me, John

Simmons.' So I went, parson being a persuasive kind of man.

We went down to the ship, and as we approached her I could see the Captain tasting the air on deck. When he saw parson he took off his hat very politely, and I can tell you that I was relieved to find that he had a proper respect for the cloth. Parson acknowledged his salute and spoke out stoutly enough. 'Sir, I should be glad to have a word with you.'

'Come on board, sir; come on board,' said the Captain, and I could tell by his voice that he knew why we were there. Parson and I climbed up an uneasy kind of ladder, and the Captain took us into the great cabin at the back of the ship, where the bay window was. It was the most wonderful place you ever saw in your life, all full of gold and silver plate, swords with jewelled scabbards, carved oak chairs, and great chests that looked as though they were bursting with guineas. Even parson was surprised, and he did not shake his head very hard when the Captain took down some silver cups and poured us out a drink of rum. I tasted mine, and I don't mind saying that it changed my view of things entirely. There was nothing betwixt and between about that rum, and I felt that it was ridiculous to blame the lads for drinking too much of stuff like that. It seemed to fill my veins with honey and fire.

Parson put the case squarely to the Captain, but I didn't listen much to what he said; I was busy sipping my drink and looking through the window at the fishes swimming to and fro over landlord's turnips. Just then it seemed the most natural thing in the world that they should be there, though afterwards, of course, I could see that that proved it was a ghost ship.

But even then I thought it was queer when I saw a drowned sailor float by in the thin air with his hair and beard all full of bubbles. It was the first time I had seen anything quite like that at Fairfield.

All the time I was regarding the wonders of the deep, parson was telling Captain Roberts how there was no peace or rest in the village owing to the curse of drunkenness, and what a bad example the youngsters were setting to the older ghosts. The Captain listened very attentively, and only put in a word now and then about boys being boys and young men sowing their wild oats. But when parson had finished his speech he filled up our silver cups and said to parson, with a flourish, 'I should be sorry to cause trouble anywhere where I have been made welcome, and you will be glad to hear that I put to sea tomorrow night. And now you must drink me a prosperous voyage.' So we all stood up and drank the toast with honour, and that noble rum was like hot oil in my veins.

After that Captain showed us some of the curiosities he had brought back from foreign parts, and we were greatly amazed, though afterwards I couldn't clearly remember what they were. And then I found myself walking across the turnips with parson, and I was telling him of the glories of the deep that I had seen through the window of the ship. He turned on me severely. 'If I were you, John Simmons,' he said, 'I should go straight home to bed.' He has a way of putting things that wouldn't occur to an ordinary man, has parson, and I did as he told me.

Well, next day it came on to blow, and it blew harder and harder, till about eight o'clock at night I heard a noise and looked out into the garden. I dare say you won't believe me, it seems a bit tall even to me, but the wind had lifted the thatch of my pigsty into the widow's garden a second time. I thought I wouldn't wait to hear what widow had to say about it, so I went across the green to the Fox and Grapes, and the wind was so strong that I danced along on tiptoe like a girl at the fair. When I got to the inn landlord had to help me shut the door; it seemed as though a dozen goats were pushing against it to come in out of the storm.

'It's a powerful tempest,' he said, drawing the beer. 'I hear there's a chimney down at Dickory End.'

'It's a funny thing how these sailors know about the weather,' I answered. 'When Captain said he was going tonight, I was thinking it would take a capful of wind to carry the ship back to sea, but now here's more than a capful.'

'Ah, yes,' said landlord, 'it's tonight he goes true enough, and, mind you, though he treated me handsome over the rent, I'm not sure it's a loss to the village. I don't hold with gentry who fetch their drink from London instead of helping local traders to get their living.'

'But you haven't got any rum like his,' I said, to draw him out.

His neck grew red above his collar, and I was afraid I'd gone too far; but after a while he got his breath with a grunt.

'John Simmons,' he said, 'if you've come down here this windy night to talk a lot of fool's talk, you've wasted a journey.'

Well, of course, then I had to smooth him down with praising his rum, and Heaven forgive me for swearing it was better than Captain's. For the like of that rum no living lips have tasted save mine and parson's. But somehow or other I brought landlord round, and presently we must have a glass of his best to prove its quality.

'Beat that if you can!' he cried, and we both raised our glasses to our mouths, only to stop halfway and look at each other in amazement. For the wind that had been howling outside like an outrageous dog had all of a sudden turned as melodious as the carol-boys of a Christmas Eve.

'Surely that's not my Martha,' whispered landlord; Martha being his great-aunt that lived in the loft overhead.

We went to the door, and the wind burst it open so that the handle was driven clean into the plaster of the wall. But we didn't think about that at the time; for over our heads, sailing very comfortably through the windy stars, was the ship that had passed the summer in landlord's field. Her portholes and her bay window were blazing with lights, and there was a noise of singing and fiddling on her decks. 'He's gone,' shouted landlord above the storm, 'and he's taken half the village with him!' I could only nod in answer, not having lungs like bellows of leather.

In the morning we were able to measure the strength of the storm, and over and above my pigsty there was damage enough wrought in the village to keep us busy. True it is that the children had to break down no branches for the firing that autumn, since the wind had strewn the woods with more than they could carry away. Many of our ghosts were scattered abroad, but this time very few came back, all the young men having sailed with Captain; and not only ghosts, for a poor half-witted lad was missing, and we reckoned that he had stowed himself away or perhaps shipped as cabin-boy, not knowing any better.

What with the lamentations of the ghost-girls and the grumblings of families who had lost an ancestor, the village was upset for a while, and the funny thing was that it was the folk who had complained most of the carryings-on of the youngsters, who made most noise now that they were gone. I hadn't any sympathy with shoemaker or butcher, who ran about saying how much they had missed their lads, but it made me grieve to hear the poor bereaved girls calling their lovers by name on the village green at nightfall. It didn't seem fair to me that they should have lost their men a second time, after giving up life in order to join them, as like as not. Still, not even a spirit can be sorry for ever, and after a few months we made up our mind that the folk who had sailed in the ship were never coming back, and we didn't talk about it any more.

And then one day, I dare say it would be a couple of years after, when the whole business was quite forgotten, who should come trapesing along the road from Portsmouth but the daft lad who had gone away with the ship, without waiting till he was dead to become a ghost. You never saw such a boy as that in all your life. He had a great rusty cutlass hanging to a string at his waist, and he was tattooed all over in fine colours, so that even his face looked like a girl's sampler. He had a handkerchief in his hand full of foreign shells and old-fashioned pieces of small money, very curious, and he walked up to the well outside his mother's house and drew himself a drink as if he had been nowhere in particular.

The worst of it was that he had come back as soft-headed as he went, and try as we might we couldn't get anything reasonable out of him. He talked a lot of gibberish about keel-hauling and walking the plank and crimson murders—things which a decent sailor should know nothing about, so that it seemed to me that for all his manners Captain had been more of a pirate than a gentleman mariner. But to draw sense out of that boy was as hard as picking cherries off a crab-tree. One silly tale he had that he kept on drifting back to, and to hear him you would have thought that it was the only thing that happened to him in his life. 'We was at anchor,' he would say, 'off an island called the Basket of Flowers, and the sailors had caught a lot of parrots and we were teaching them to swear. Up and down the decks, up and down the decks, and the language they used was dreadful. Then we looked up and saw the masts of the Spanish ship outside the harbour. Outside the harbour they were, so we threw the parrots into the sea and sailed out to fight. And all the parrots were drowned in the sea and the language they used was dreadful.' That's the sort of boy he was, nothing but silly talk of parrots when we asked him about the fighting. And we never had a chance of teaching him better, for two days after he ran away again, and hasn't been seen since.

That's my story, and I assure you that things like that are happening at Fairfield all the time. The ship has never come back, but somehow as people grow older they seem to think that one of these windy nights she'll come sailing in over the hedges with all the lost ghosts on board. Well, when she comes, she'll be welcome. There's one ghost-lass that has never grown tired of waiting for her lad to return. Every night you'll see her out on the green, straining her poor eyes with looking for the mast-lights among the stars. A faithful lass you'd call her, and I'm thinking you'd be right.

Landlord's field wasn't a penny the worse for the visit, but they do say that since then the turnips that have been grown in it have tasted of rum.

I Am A Psychic Detective

HORACE LEAF

If you don't believe in ghosts—and of course you don't—I cannot expect you to believe in ghost laying, and I can hardly expect you to believe the amazing things I am about to tell you.

I shall not try to convert you. There was a time when I didn't accept such things, either.

All I ask you to believe is that I, Horace Leaf, Fellow of the Royal Geographic Society, earn my living by ghost laying, and that, in the process, I have actually had the experiences set down here.

If you will go that far with me, I think you will not regret it.

First, lest you think me utterly crazy, I should explain that this ghost-laying business was not my idea—that it was, as a matter of fact, forced upon me.

My friend the late Sir Arthur Conan Doyle was the one who first introduced me to the subject, although I had read, as you undoubtedly have, of the so-called occultists of the Middle Ages who claimed to be able to banish troublesome spirits by tracing circles or interlacing triangles on the floor of the 'haunted' room.

Sir Arthur's ghost laying was of a more scientific nature, and was undertaken by him simply as part of his long experimentation with psychic phenomena. He had come to believe that what we call spirits were actually departed spirits who, for some reason, were chained to this earth, and that, once this spiritual chain was broken, they could cease to trouble either themselves or others.

It was not difficult for me to accept this theory. I had had the common experience of feeling that certain friends who had died under unusual or violent circumstances were frequently close to me. More difficult to believe was that a living person could get through to these restless spirits, talk to them, and free them from their bonds. Well, I did not have to wait long for a demonstration on this point.

You may have read in the papers of Conan Doyle's attempts to lay the ghost of Lenin. Some people living in a house in London where the Marxist dictator had once lived, found themselves—or, as you would say, *thought* they found themselves—haunted by his ghost.

Sir Arthur visited the house, and took with him the Rev Vale Owen, a well known clergyman, and myself, both of whom he had found useful as instrumentalities in his psychical experiments.

No one was more surprised than I was when—quite contrary to my own intentions at the time—*I* laid the ghost of Lenin. At least I got the credit for doing so—and that credit, vouched for by Sir Arthur Conan Doyle, changed the whole course of my life.

I had never known there were so many people who were troubled with ghosts—beg pardon, who thought they were. Requests came in from all over the world, asking me to perform a service similar to that which I had apparently performed for those harassed Londoners.

At first I laughed at these epistles, and at myself. A ghost layer! That was good. But the number of them and the sincerity of them finally wore me down. I began experimenting with this alleged power of mine, and found that I could voluntarily give myself up to some other self whose gifts were quite different from my own.

I cannot explain what happens to me as clearly as I could wish, because I do not know much about it myself. But I am told by those who have listened to me under these conditions that I speak without a trace of the British accent normally mine, and in a mellow voice of distinctly Oriental quality, and that I use the terms 'sahib' and 'memsahib' instead of 'sir' and 'madam'.

Make what you will of that!

The point is that year after year my reputation as a ghost layer has steadily increased, and that it has taken me all over the world.

I was not surprised, therefore, to find myself, in the late summer of 1931, in New Orleans, a guest in an eighteenth-century house which boasted, among other attractions, the loveliest ghost I have ever known.

The house itself was almost as beautiful as the beautiful girl who haunted it. It was situated in the picturesque Old French Quarter of the city. Its exterior was enriched by semicircular verandas with elaborate iron railings wrought by slaves. Its interior featured a noble marble staircase.

'I have dismissed my servants for the night,' said my white-haired host, as he led me to a door which gave on a courtyard. 'We shall not be interrupted.'

'At least, not by living things,' I said.

He laughed uneasily and switched off the electric lights. The great house was apparently in total darkness except for a flickering candle. Holding this high above his head, he bade me precede him into the courtyard.

It was a moonless, starless night. I was vaguely aware of vegetation, of leaves shimmering in the candlelight. Then all was still again, and black.

'I think,' said my host, 'that I owe you an explanation of the happenings which preceded the manifestations you are to observe tonight. My ancestors on my father's side came to what is now Louisiana with Ferrier. My mother's people arrived with Don Antonio de Ulloa in 1764. Some years later the man who built this house, a great-great-uncle of mine named Simon de Rouvroy, came over from Santo Domingo, and brought slaves.

'Among the slaves were a half-caste mother with two sons and a daughter. The father had been half Negro and half

Spaniard; the mother was a mixture of Negro and French. The daughter, however, showed no signs of her African blood. Judging by her ghost, she was very beautiful. At sixteen she bore my uncle a child which he afterwards brutally murdered.

'The crime deranged the young mother and she soon died insane. There is every reason to believe that Simon had her strangled by a big slave called Julius in the room to which I am leading you.'

'Is that where the manifestations occur?'

'You shall see. Come!'

I followed gropingly to a long row of former slave quarters. A door yielded to the turn of old Mr de Rouvroy's key and disclosed an inner row of small rooms like cells, which had no windows—or, so far as I could see, any other ventilation.

'This little room,' said my host, standing aside and bidding me enter the narrowest and darkest of them, 'is where Juanita met her death.'

'Juanita was the beautiful slave girl?'

'Yes. Her two brothers died here too.'

'Of strangulation?'

'No. Simon didn't bother. He just chained them up and left them to suffocate. They haunt the place too. And so does Julius. We'll meet them all tonight. We'll see The Hand, too, or its work.'

'The Hand?'

'Yes. One of Uncle Simon's favourite forms of torture was gradual mutilation of his victims.'

By the faint light of the candle I observed that two chairs had been placed side by side in the centre of the narrow room, and that a handsome Japanese screen had been set up in one corner, with a gap between it and the wall wide enough for one person to pass through.

Now, frankly, I didn't like that screen. It savoured too much of magic and sleight of hand. My host must have sensed that I was a bit disturbed by it, for he told me that I would soon see the reason for it. Further to avoid suspicion, he handed me an ordinary writing pad and pencil, and asked me to place them behind the screen.

'The Hand,' he said, 'may wish to write.'

Of course I used this opportunity to make a thorough examination of the wall. It was, you may take my word for it, unpleasantly solid. I was satisfied that the door through which we had come—and which, by the way, Mr de Rouvroy had shut and locked after us—was the only entrance to the room.

Motioning me to one of the chairs, and seating himself in the other, he blew out his candle.

I do not know how long we waited in the darkness, but after what seemed like an interminable time, there was a noise as of people moving.

'They are here,' my host remarked laconically.

He had barely uttered the words when from behind the screen there stepped one of the most beautiful women I have ever seen—slender, graceful, with a mass of lovely black hair which contrasted with her ivory skin. She was as white as the White Lady of Avenel. Her body had the allure of Aphrodite. If it is possible for a man of flesh and blood to fall in love with a ghost—and I am not at all sure that it isn't!—he might perhaps have lost his heart that night in Simon de Rouvroy's death cell.

I had a feeling the old Creole gentleman beside me was watching closely to see the effect on me.

'This is Juanita,' he said pleasantly. 'Juanita, let Mr Leaf feel the texture of your hair.'

To my amazement, the phantom form walked slowly up to me and, lifting a few strands of her hair, let them fall on my hand. Then, raising her long slender fingers, she threw me a kiss and receded behind the screen.

'Is that all we get of Juanita?' I asked.

I again had the feeling that my host was watching me closely and with a not too friendly eye. Could it be possible that he, old man though he was, had already fallen in love with the beautiful half-caste? But when he answered my question, it was with the usual disarming casualness.

'Don't worry, my dear sir. We shall see quite enough of

her before the night is over. This is the anniversary of my uncle's crime—and there is always the devil to pay here on anniversaries. Perhaps—'

He stopped abruptly. Emerging from behind the screen was a giant Negro with the arms and hands of an ape. In a stride he had crossed the cell to where I sat, and was glowering threateningly down at me.

'This is Julius, the strangler,' explained my host; and as he spoke, the figure—to my great relief—sank out of sight through the floor.

My attention was now attracted by a faint scraping behind the screen, as if someone was scribbling, not with a pencil but with a bad pen. My thoughts went at once to The Hand. A sheet of paper came fluttering over the screen and fell close to my feet. Mr de Rouvroy relit his candle. I picked up the paper and tried to read the ill-formed Spanish words written on it. I could not, and my host again snuffed his candle.

As he did so, the cathedral clock struck eleven; and as the last throb died away, I heard weeping and moaning. Every now and then I also caught the faint jangle of chains, accompanied by sighs and groans.

'The brothers,' he whispered. 'It doesn't look as if they are going to get through tonight.'

The more attentively I listened, the more distinct these sounds became. They seemed distant, or to come through a wall, but with a persistency that was most horrible, inured though I was to ghostly phenomena.

Whether this unearthly experience caused my imagination to run riot, I cannot be sure, but I could have sworn that I saw walking about the room a stoutish Spaniard with a fine-cut beard and fierce moustaches. In one hand he carried a whip and in the other a small knife. His eyes were preternaturally bright. The whole expression of his face was terribly malignant.

Mr de Rouvroy said he did not see this apparition at all. When, however, I described it to him, he assured me that it coincided with his great-great-uncle.

For professional reasons, I should have liked to stay

longer in the death cell. It was probable, I thought, that if I succeeded in laying the old butcher's ghost first, I should have no trouble laying the others.

His great-great-nephew, however, was now as impatient as if he had an appointment he must keep. Perhaps he had! Anyhow, he insisted almost crossly that it was time to go to bed. And indeed it was, for as we groped our way back across the courtyard, the clock in the cathedral tolled out midnight.

Once again in the main house, Mr de Rouvroy offered me a Scotch-and-soda, which I declined. I had thinking to do, and I needed a clear head. The old gentleman did not press me. He seemed tired.

But as we approached the beautiful marble staircase, all his casualness dropped from him. His body became tense, rigid. With his free hand he clutched me to save himself from falling. Then, pulling himself together, he turned once again to the staircase. It was no use. He could not bring himself to set foot on those marble steps.

Finally I drew from him the reason. It was on this staircase, a hundred years ago that very night, that Simon de Rouvroy had snatched from the arms of his favourite slave girl their newborn son, dashed out its brains, and tossed its body to the floor below.

The telling of the story seemed to give him strength. Without further ado, he started to ascend the staircase. A little more than halfway up, he stopped and pointed to the broad rail. 'It was here,' he said in a hoarse voice, 'that my uncle brained the baby.'

As he bade me a rather stiff good night at the head of the stairs, he remarked with a quizzical smile:

'We shall see what we shall see.'

I was in no mood for sleep. Several things had puzzled me. Mr de Rouvroy had been at great trouble and some expense to bring me from London to Louisiana to rid his home of these restless spirits. Yet he seemed unmistakably to enjoy their presence and to be on the friendliest terms with them. Juanita had obeyed him implicitly. Even Julius, the strangler, had melted away at his first word. . . .

Suddenly there were terrific noises in the room adjoining mine. For a moment I wondered if my host, who seemed to have lost his taste for my company, was taking this odd way of unnerving me and driving me from his house. I did him an injustice. When I opened the door and ran out on the landing, he was already there, obviously as alarmed as I was.

'Even on anniversary nights there never—' He didn't finish that sentence.

Juanita—her face distorted with grief and fright her arms holding the bleeding body of her child—was ascending the stairs.

Her body was so transparent that we could see through it the stairs and balustrade. She passed so close to me that I could have touched her—but my arms hung helpless at my sides.

Unseeing, she glided across the landing and disappeared into the room whence the sounds had been issuing.

'My uncle's bedroom,' the old gentleman managed to say, then tottered towards the stairs.

I think he would have fallen their length if I had not caught him firmly by the shoulders. He was very limp. His whole body seemed to have been drained of every bit of energy it possessed. Suddenly I knew what I should have known the moment that first spectre had appeared from behind the death-cell screen.

The nephew of Simon de Rouvroy was—without knowing it—a materializing medium!

Of course, if you don't believe in ghosts, you don't in mediums; but at least you know that there are people in this world who have the gift of making spectres *seem* to appear before the eyes of sensible people like yourself. You may rest assured that Mr de Rouvroy was one of these people, and that—if you insist—he 'fooled' me and 'fooled' himself as I have described.

Personally, I believe, too, that this elderly aristocrat used his mediumistic powers—unconsciously of course—to bring these spirits out of their hiding places to make for him a ghostly holiday.

But that is neither here nor there.

If he had a sufficiently good reason for wishing to rid his property of these phantoms, he would be quite willing to stay away and give me a free chance to labour with them.

Fortunately, he did have a very good reason for desiring to render his estate ghostless. He wished to sell his property, so that he might go to France to live in the land of his ancestors—a goal which, I am happy to say, I was able to help him achieve.

I'll wager, though, that he sometimes thinks fondly, perhaps regretfully, of the beautiful Juanita!

The Old Lady of Battersea

I suppose it will surprise you that one supernaturally gifted as a ghost layer—I can hear you laughing!—should need to go to a dentist.

But it happens that I cut two quite normal sets of teeth before I discovered that, under certain circumstances, I could 'see things' that most other people could not see, and found myself—much to my surprise—earning my living by doing so.

It was while Basil Trencher, my dentist of many years' standing, was giving the second of those sets their semi-annual going over that he told me of the 'haunted' house he owned in the Battersea section of London.

'You know, Leaf,' he said, 'that I am not a fussy man.'

He had two hands, a mirror, and a pair of pliers in my mouth at the moment, so I said nothing.

'I shouldn't have minded a couple of well behaved ghosts in the old house,' he continued, in a tone which showed that he didn't believe in ghosts any more than you do. 'It was to be expected, I suppose, that a building so old, so sombre, and so sparsely occupied should be a prey to its past.'

He laughed gaily.

'But, you see,' he said, 'I had a sort of branch office there, and what I objected to was having my patients continually falling downstairs—and then claiming that someone had pushed them!'

It was bad enough, he explained, when two angry females maintained that he himself had done the pushing. But the crisis arrived when a testy old gentleman, who had suffered a dislocated thigh, threatened to sue on the ground that he had been shoved by 'an unseen hand.'

At this point, Basil Trencher, who was a man of peace, decided to abandon the old three-storey house on Queen's Road, and confine his practice to his principal office, in the fashionable region near Hyde Park.

Financially, the closing of the Queen's Road establishment meant little to the distinguished dental surgeon. Professionally, however, he had valued the wider experience it afforded him. Sentimentally, too, the place had a claim on him. The Trenchers had lived in the old house for generations, and a beloved uncle had left it to him.

There was also the practical problem of what to do with the property. It wouldn't have been readily leasable, anyhow, because of the Queen's Road traffic and the proximity of the railroad. But now, with the reputation it had acquired for accidents and bad luck generally, there was nothing that could be done with it in an income-producing way.

In fact, no one could be persuaded to live in it on any terms, except a faithful caretaker, who occupied the top floor.

'There is an atmosphere about the place,' continued Trencher, 'an eerie something which seems to hang like a cloud around it. I can't describe that exactly. It is something that is felt rather than seen.'

This detail interested me more than anything else he had told me—'clouds' being among the most dependable signs of ghosts.

'You feel this cloud yourself?'

'I do. In fact, now that I have cut my daily ties with the place, I have become increasingly unwilling to enter the house. Perhaps you had better go out yourself, Leaf, and try your spells on it.'

Spells! I am no more of a spell caster than you are, my doubting reader. Perhaps not so much, for you may be a salesman or a musician or a writer for the cinema or an actor or a poet, whereas I am just a plain student of psychical research, who couldn't cast a spell if he wished to—and wouldn't if he could.

The only difference between my relations with so-called ghosts and some other people's is that I get along better with them. Ghosts behave very well for me! The reason, I have always thought, is that I do not think of them as hideous creatures stalking around in sheets, but as restless spirits prevented, for some unknown reason from getting away from this earth.

Far from casting spells over these poor distracted creatures, I try to reach them and talk to them and comfort them just as if they were living beings in distress, and help them, if I can, to break the unnatural bonds which tie them to a life in which they no longer have a place.

It was in this spirit that I continued my inquiry into the weird doings in the house in Battersea.

'And your old caretaker?' I asked. 'Has she had any unfortunate experiences?'

'More than anyone else. This evening, if it is convenient for you, I will run you out to Queen's Road, and you can question her.'

Shortly after ten he called for me at my rooms in a rakish high-powered sports roadster which he drove through the traffic with an abandon which was much more frightening to me than a hundred ghosts. Yet, when we pulled up at the old Queen's Road house, this man, who had just risked death a dozen times, was obviously afraid to enter the door of his own property.

'Mrs Toms,' he said to the stoutish middle-aged caretaker who answered the bell, 'this is my friend Mr Leaf, and he is to do anything he wishes.'

With this wholesale certification, he was gone. And I must say that for a few moments after the door swung to, leaving the silent woman and myself in the darkness of the lower hall, the 'cloud' to which Trencher had referred seemed thick enough to cut. I could see nothing. All I could hear was the caretaker groping in the shadows behind me.

At length she struck a match. The flame made little headway against the almost impenetrable gloom, but it apparently enabled Mrs Toms' more accustomed eyes to locate two candles on a small table. She lit both of these, handed me one and took one herself.

'Have you no electricity or gas?' I managed to say.

'Only candles and lamps,' she replied.

She seemed so taciturn that I thought it wise to break the ice with a thorough inspection of the premises before embarking on any campaign of inquiry.

The house was high-ceilinged, marble-floored, heavy-moulded, like many another in south London. The basement was given over to dining room and kitchen, now unused. The first-floor front had been the dentist's waiting room. Everything was as he had left it.

The first-floor rear was empty. Trencher had not used it. He preferred, so Mrs Toms said, the better light of the second-floor rear, which was reached by the stairway that had caused so much trouble.

This staircase was somewhat more twisted than is customary today, but in no sense treacherous in itself. I examined it carefully by the light of my candle—creeping up slowly from one step to another. The treads were worn by many footsteps into an uneveness that should have retarded rather than accelerated a fall.

The second-floor front was a bedroom, now, of course, unused. Mrs Toms made no move to show it to me.

The second-floor back was where Trencher had done his dentistry. It was from this room that his patients had emerged on to the landing whence, according to their testimony, they had been given the shoves which had sent them hurtling down the twisting staircase.

'It won't be necessary for me to intrude on your privacy right now, Mrs Toms, so if you care to leave me alone for a while—'

The good lady needed no further hint, but bolted upstairs

to her own quarters. I could hear a door slam and a key turn. Except for the flickering flame of my candle, I was alone in the darkness.

Now it was inevitable that my curiosity should centre on the one room which Mrs Toms had not offered to show me—the second-floor front.

Here was the very spot where Basil Trencher's patients claimed to have been pushed.

There was a closed door.

Was it possible that the person who did the pushing, whether living or dead, was hidden behind that door?

I groped my way along the wall by my candle's uncertain light. As I opened that door, it failed me altogether.

I didn't bother to relight it. There was enough light from the street to show me the room's contents—a high wooden bed stripped to the mattress, two straight chairs, an over-stuffed chair, a worn carpet, and a huge dark-coloured tallboy, either walnut or mahogany, which stood like a gloomy sentinel opposite the windows.

On the tallboy, supported by a twisted metal holder, was a large unframed photograph of a very disagreeable-looking old woman—without doubt, a former occupant of the room. In spite of the malignant expression, there was a distinct structural resemblance to the features of my friend Trencher.

Having satisfied myself on this point, I replaced the photograph, drew the blinds tight, pulled a chair to the centre of the room, and sat down to wait.

I may have waited half an hour. It seemed much longer. I tried to keep my mind on trivial things unrelated to the night's experience. It was natural, though, that my eyes should wander in the direction of that photograph, and that I should be acutely conscious that those sinister features were staring down upon me.

It was not natural, however—and I was quite unprepared for it—that the portrait, whose outlines I could just make out in the semidarkness, should suddenly rise in the air and fall with a thud on the top of the tallboy.

I had scarcely recovered from the shock of this

bewildering occurrence when I perceived a cloud revolving slowly around the prostrate portrait, which forthwith rose to a vertical position and—well, of course, you won't believe me, but I must tell this as I saw it—and *seemed* to come to life.

I rubbed my eyes, to see if I was dreaming; then covered and uncovered them to make sure that the vision I saw was objective. I shall never forget the sneer on that old woman's face, the curl of the lips when they moved as if trying to speak.

'What is it you wish to say?' I asked.

Then clearly came these words:

'Get out of my house!'

Next moment the portrait fell at my feet.

Taking due account of the possibility of some illusion, I considered the strictly physical factors. My chair was a good ten feet away from the tallboy. It was hardly conceivable that the photograph, supposing that it had been simply shaken from its perch by a tremor caused by passing traffic, could have traversed that distance. When I again replaced it, I noticed that the top of the tallboy was covered with a thick coat of dust. The picture itself, and the arms of the chair in which I sat, had been in the same condition. The rest of the house, on the other hand, even to the steps of the stairs, had been scrupulously clean.

Mrs Toms, I thought, does not open this door for herself any more than she does for me.

So I went up to her quarters.

'Have you a family living with you, Mrs Toms?'

'I did have,' she answered reluctantly.

It took time, but cautious inquiry elicited from her the information that she had spent eighteen years in this house as Trencher's caretaker. The first thirteen years were uneventful, even happy. Her husband remained healthy and steadily employed. Her two children, a boy and a girl, completed their schooling and became self-supporting. She herself waxed comfortably buxom. Then, suddenly, everything began to go wrong.

Her husband, who had never known a sick day in his

life, contracted an incurable lung trouble of which he was even now dying in a near-by nursing home. Although this misfortune was in no way attributable to the ghost on the staircase or to the talking photograph, it was while the husband and father was being removed from the house on a stretcher the ghostly manifestations began. The boy, George, fell down the twisting staircase and broke his thigh. He still walks with a pronounced limp. The daughter, Gracie, fell down it just six months later, and has never since had the proper use of her left arm.

Both young people refused to live there any longer. For their mother's sake, however, they refrained for some time from suggesting that the house was haunted. It was only after a visiting friend of the family had tumbled down the same flight of stairs, and swore that she had been ruthlessly pushed by an invisible presence, that the daughter broke down and admitted that she, too, had been pushed.

Since then, Mrs Toms said, no less than sixteen people had fallen down these stairs, and she herself had been saved by the narrowest of margins.

'Did you, too, feel that you were pushed?' I asked.

'I did.'

'Why didn't you move away?'

'It was a good job here.'

'Do you know of any tragedy that occurred in this house *before* all these mishaps began?'

'No, sir. The Trenchers were very quiet people—not only Mr Basil, sir, but his aunt—'

We had come down now, and were again on the fateful second-floor landing. Although I could not see her face, I distinctly felt that Mrs Toms had just caught herself up sharply, as if she regretted her mention of Basil Trencher's relative.

'This aunt you speak of—was she a Miss Trencher?'

'Yes.'

'Does she live here?'

'She doesn't live anywhere. She's dead. About five years ago, she *was* run over, crossing the road outside the house.'

'Five years, you say? Was that before or after your husband's first illness?'

'Before—but why do you ask all these questions? Miss Trencher was a nice old lady. She couldn't have anything to do with the hauntings. She *couldn't*!'

I ignored her protest. 'In which room did she sleep?'

I could feel rather than see her eyes turn involuntarily towards the closed door to the second-floor front.

'Shall we go in?' I said, just to test her.

She made no reply, and no move. Holding my candle well above my head, I advanced alone towards the door. As I was about to take hold of the knob she shrieked:

'Don't do it! Don't go into that room! You don't know what might happen! She's a fiend, that old woman!'

Fiend? Old woman?

Not a 'nice old lady' after all!

Good Mrs Toms had evidently been restrained by a combination of household loyalty to her Mr Basil and desire not to stir up the ghostly occupant of the second-floor front. Now, however, the dam was down. Hate, fear, and candour flowed from her like a torrent.

Old Miss Trencher, in whose room I had had my extraordinary experience, had been an evil termagant, hated by all, especially by those who knew her best. Her habits were intolerably dirty, her behaviour indicative of heavy secret drinking. At her worst, her temper waxed so violent that no one dared approach her.

Chief anathema to her hate-distorted mind was nephew Basil. Up to the time of her death she had held her hatred somewhat in check, presumably because she was totally dependent on his charity. After death, she had seemed still to be somehow in awe of him, for she had made no direct attack on him.

Apparently, though, she had made up her mind to drive him and all other occupants from the building—and was jolly well succeeding in doing so.

By now I was thoroughly convinced that I had found the ghost that must be laid. All that remained for me to do was to win the confidence of that malevolent old woman in the talking photograph.

The task proved far simpler than I had hoped.

From the old lady's own lips I learned that she was unable to find peace because she had died with a grievance. Slightly mad, she had felt that the Queen's Road house, law or no law, belonged to her and not to her nephew, and she was determined that he should never live in it or otherwise enjoy it.

When I convinced her that he thought so little of it that he had no intention of ever crossing its threshold again, she threw me a look of intense relief and straightway disintegrated.

I know you will not believe that I actually talked with this evil ghost, or that such a ghost ever existed. But the fact remains that all those people did fall downstairs, and that all of them claimed they were shoved by a hand they could not see—and that after I had finished with the occupant of the second-floor front no further falls occurred!

A Full House

My acquaintance with Mr Godfrey Kent went back over many years, but always, until he walked into my office in London to consult me, we had met only between the pages of his delightful books, which are as well known on your side of the Atlantic as on mine.

'Just how do you go about laying a ghost?' he asked as he settled himself in one of my office chairs.

'My work,' I said, 'doesn't describe very well. I would much rather demonstrate it.'

'I appreciate the difficulty,' he replied. 'But do you work as a magician or as a normal human being?'

I did my best to keep back a smile.

'Not a magician, surely—and not always, I suppose, as what you would call a normal human being. Sometimes the normal senses are enough. Many gentle apparitions, for instance, I can talk to—'

'You talk to them?'

'Why, yes. That's all there is to ghost laying, really: talking to these poor souls, finding out from them just what is binding them against their wills to this earth.'

'You talk to them as you are talking to me?'

'That's the point. Sometimes, as I was saying, I can make myself understood in my own personality. Sometimes I have to have the help of a second personality working through me. You believe, don't you, that we all have two personalities, the one we normally use and the one which we could use if we had the power—as I seem to have—to summon it?'

'I know something of that theory,' he said. 'My old friend Conan Doyle used to talk to me about it.'

'You had a good teacher. He was my friend, too.'

'I know. That's why I am here. That's why I am asking you to come down to Hertfordshire with me.'

In a quarter of an hour we were weaving our way in his big car through the streets of Greater London.

It was as I had thought. Life was being made intolerable for the author and his entire household by noises which they had tried in vain to account for.

As is usual in such cases, the servants were at first suspected. In fact, the most persistent of the disturbances had been traced from the room in which they habitually originated along a passageway and up to the servants' quarters on the next floor. Several people had heard footsteps ascend the stairs to the door of the butler's room, and had distinctly heard the latch rattle.

Far from denying the testimony of these persons, the butler acknowledged that he too had heard the footsteps, seen the latch move, and on one occasion actually observed the door swing open. He hadn't mentioned the matter at the time, for fear of losing his position. Now, however, the poor man had begged and received permission to sleep in the village. But during his absence the disturbance had continued.

That was as much as my host had told me when we

rolled up to the Elizabethan mansion which the Kents had recently purchased.

'Please take me at once to the room,' I said.

'Mrs Kent's sewing room and study,' he informed me, throwing open a door at the end of the main hall.

Both that night and the next I spent alone in that room. During neither was there anything to see or hear. But I have learned to be patient.

With me on the third evening was my friend the Reverend Mr Vale Owen, who accompanied Sir Arthur Conan Doyle and me when he laid the ghost of Lenin, and who is himself possessed of recognized psychic powers.

We had no sooner drawn the blinds, put out the lights, and settled ourselves in easy chairs than we began to have 'goose flesh'. A damp chilliness gradually pervaded the room. Owen felt only the lowering of the temperature and the eeriness which naturally accompanies strange supernormal phenomena; but my limbs slowly stiffened until I had to take care not to pass into a state of complete catalepsy.

Presently we heard a number of faint taps, which seemed to come from a bookcase standing opposite the window. The taps became distinct knockings. I went to the door. There was no one there. So I went back to my chair, and tried to visualize the sort of person who was making these weird noises.

What followed was a complete surprise to me. As we sat there silently in the darkness, we were soon aware of a dim phosphorescent light shining halfway between us, which grew gradually brighter until it illumined the whole room. Out of this light there stepped a charming old lady of seventy or seventy-five, dressed in the ultra-feminine costume of the first half of the eighteenth century. Her snow-white hair was partially covered by a cap of the most delicate lace. From her eyes and lips came the gentlest of smiles.

'Who are you, madam?' my companion asked.

'A former inhabitant of this house.'

'What brings you here?'

'Oh, I always visit here when I wish to.'

'It must be you, then,' I interjected, 'who walks along the passage outside and up the stairs to the corner room on the next floor.'

'I always go that way,' she said. 'This room was my bedroom, and the room upstairs was the nursery.'

With that, she vanished. Soon, however, we again heard her voice. This time she mentioned her name, Lady Matilda Dudley, and reiterated that she had during her lifetime tenanted the house—a statement which we subsequently found to be true.

I asked her to promise never to visit Mr Kent's house again. If ever there was an indignant ghost, it was that old lady!

'I shall do nothing of the sort,' she retorted. 'I owned this house before he did, and I shall come here when I like. If any one is to get out, it must be he.'

'I am sure,' I said, 'that he would have no objection to your coming here whenever you wished, Lady Matilda, if it makes you happy to do so. What he wishes to be spared is the noise of your nightly progress from this room along the passage and up the stairs.'

Her manner changed instantly from anger to concern. As I had suspected, she had not been aware she was causing any uneasiness. She promised that her future visits would be noiseless.

I made no further effort to lay this gentle ghost. Somehow, I felt—and my feeling, I am glad to say, was justified by subsequent events—that Matilda Dudley was the kind of ghost that would keep her word.

We sought our host to receive his congratulations.

He looked sceptical. 'A woman, you say?'

'Yes; and she has promised not to—'

I never finished that sentence.

A shriek like that of a dying man rent the atmosphere. More shrieks followed, and groans; they came apparently from a cellar under the main stairway.

'That must be Curtayne!' exclaimed Mr Kent.

'Curtayne? Have you more than one ghost here?'

'I didn't think so. But, frankly, the ghost I was expecting you to find was a man.'

These cries we had just heard, he said, did not occur so frequently as the sound of steps in the corridor, and had been accepted as simply another manifestation of the same troubled spirit. The story he now told us will doubtless seem to you unbelievable. When finally convinced against his will that the disturbances which were driving him and his household to desperation were supernormal, he had sought out the well known medium Mr Vout Peters. He had told Peters nothing. He had even concealed the whereabouts of the estate by a night motor ride from London. Then, still basically sceptical, he had awaited results.

The famous psychic did not succeed in laying the ghosts. That isn't his business. But he did tell Kent that his fine old mansion had played an important part in the Civil War of the seventeenth century which resulted in the beheading of Charles I. On one occasion, Peters insisted, a young Cavalier of King Charles' army had been tracked to the cellar under the main stairway and brutally slaughtered by the Roundheads.

Furthermore, the medium declared that the body of the murdered man had been buried close to an old wall bordering the estate, but that this wall had since been knocked down and all trace of the grave lost.

The last statement impressed Kent, as he already knew from old plans of the property that there had been such a wall. Further research disclosed that the medium had also been right about the murder of the young Cavalier, Rupert Curtayne by name.

'Is there an entrance to that cellar from this floor?' I asked.

'Yes. Under the stairs.'

He led me to it, and I descended, with my candle, through a trap door into the dungeonlike hole from which the shrieks were again issuing. From the odour that assailed my nostrils, I could well believe that the dead man's remains were still rotting there. However, I encountered nothing more terrifying than his astral body—which appeared almost immediately, garbed in the torn but still gay costume of the Cavaliers.

There was nothing vindictive about this spiritual manifestation, either. The owners of the mansion in Curtayne's time had given him sanctuary. He bore no grudge against the present occupants of the house. He was simply chained, presumably by the brutal circumstances of his death, to the scene of it. In short, Rupert Curtayne's gentle ghost was as desirous of getting away as I was to have him. Therefore I had no difficulty at all in laying it to the satisfaction of Kent—whose relief and that of his household was touching.

'Thanks to you,' he said, 'my family and I are to have our first good night's sleep in months.'

The words had scarcely passed his lips when there came from the drawing room on the right of the main hall a sharp explosion, like the report of a pistol.

Still another ghost in this historic country house?

'Have you heard that before?' I asked.

'Many times—but never in the same evening that I heard the cries from the cellar. Naturally, I thought it was the same ghoulish creature manifesting himself in different ways. Is it possible, Mr Leaf, that the laying of one ghost might—what shall we say?—automatically release another?'

I told him that, according to psychical research, it was distinctly possible.

'What are you going to do about it?' Mr Owen asked.

'I am going to interview the one in the drawing room.'

Whereupon I persuaded my companions to go to bed as they had planned, and disposed myself to await developments. None came that night. But on the next night I was rewarded by a most startling experience.

Without warning, there stepped straight out of the table in the centre of that stately room a handsome young dandy dressed in frilled habiliments. My candle had long since gone out. There was, however, enough moonlight in the room to illumine his eyes, which gleamed maliciously at some unseen foe.

The young man was very angry. His lips moved rapidly but gave forth no words. He was evidently defending himself against the accusations of invisible accusers. I got the impression that he had been cheating at some game and had been caught at it.

For several moments I could not make out any of the persons with whom he was arguing. Then two of them came into view. One, a big florid man who bore a strong resemblance to the young dandy, was talking as fast as he. The other was a small timid-looking old fellow who seemed to be trying to reconcile the two.

The peacemaker might have succeeded if the dandy hadn't raised his hand to his sword's hilt. The big man thereupon whipped out a long pistol and shot him dead.

On the sound of the shot, the scene faded out.

Later inquiry disclosed that the death of the young dandy had actually occurred in that room in precisely that manner. He had quarrelled over a game of cards with his own father, William John Ransome, and the older man had shot him in self-defence.

Meanwhile I had a feeling that the ghost would reappear. It did—but not in objective form. The young gambler did not stand before my eyes. Believe it or not—and you probably won't—his spirit entered my body. It spoke through my lips. Foul blasphemy, oaths that I had never heard poured through them as I vowed vengeance on him who had shot me. Through no will of my own, I was participating in an incident which must have happened in the last half of the seventeenth century.

Then, as suddenly and inexplicably as it had come, the spirit which possessed me took its departure. I was once more plain, unfrilly, unprofane Horace Leaf of the twentieth century, engaged—albeit, at the moment, none too successfully—in my business of ghost laying.

What had happened was nothing unusual. Students of the psychical are convinced that ghosts frequently take possession of the body and mind of the person who is trying to master them.

In this instance, as soon as I had dispossessed myself of

the spirit, I was able to rid the drawing room of hauntings as completely as I had the cellar.

It was a more difficult job, however, because this young gambler was a very difficult ghost!

The Incubus

Of all a professional ghost layer's critics, none is so severe as the average doctor.

Imagine my surprise, therefore, when a note came to me from my old schoolfellow, Dr Stanley Thwaites, the famous Harley Street nerve specialist:

> With this I am sending you my patient, Major C Eversleigh Calthrop, V.C., O.B.E., late of the 7th Fusiliers. I have been treating him for delusions, but the incisions in his flesh are—well, I do not know what to think they are. Perhaps he is more in your line than he is in mine. Anyhow, better have a look at him.
>
> Yours sceptically,
>
> Stanley Thwaites.

'Show the Major in,' I said.

I confess I was surprised. For Eversleigh Calthrop was not the type one would suspect of thinking he saw ghosts. Tall, erect, broad-shouldered, India-tanned, he was the picture of all that a retired military man of fifty-five should look and be.

'Thwaites is the one who is having delusions,' I thought to myself.

On closer inspection, however, the Major betrayed unmistakable signs of severe nervous strain. There was no doubt about it: this once doughty soldier, who had acquitted himself with distinction in the guerrilla warfare of the Far East and who had won his Victoria Cross in the dark days on the western front, was badly frightened.

He had lived since his retirement at Richmond on Thames, in a quiet respectable inn. Life had moved serenely for him and for its other occupants, gentlefolk like himself, until the previous year, when they had been joined by a new lodger, very rich, very ignorant, very old, and so dirty and malodorous that they finally served notice on the proprietor that the newcomer must go.

The old man went, but not without vowing vengeace on Major Calthrop, whom he had singled out, probably with justice, as the ringleader of the movement against him. A few days later, the angry old man committed suicide. That was seven months before this visit.

Of those months, the Major now told me his story. He would no sooner turn out the light, he said, and get into bed than he would be aware of a great staring evil eye peering insolently down at him out of the darkness. Each night it grew bigger, more malicious; yet always it was the eye of the dirty old man. At first, if he closed his eyes, he shut it out. Later on he seemed to see it whether he closed his eyes or not. He could not escape.

One night, lying there in a cold sweat with his evil eye upon him, he thought he observed an eerie white mist revolving rapidly close to his chest. At the same moment he felt a curious drawing sensation about his heart, as if energy were being sucked out of him.

'Every night after that,' he whispered, 'the cloud appeared. Then suddenly, one night, the cloud burst, and out of it peered the head of a human ape.'

He covered his eyes with his hands.

'Was there any resemblance,' I prompted, 'to the former lodger?'

'That's it, Mr Leaf, that's it!' he almost shouted. 'It was an ape—but it was the old man!'

One night he woke to find, to his horror, that the creature was in bed with him. With the strength of desperation, he pummelled and kicked it until it seemed to fade away into nothingness. But night after night it returned. Finally it brought along a sickly white animal resembling a small bear, which seemed to have no body, only a head and a large mouth.

In my professional experience I had heard many weird tales, but none which so taxed credulity as this. The man's obvious sincerity, however, as well as his reputation as an officer and a gentleman, precluded the possibility that he was trying to hoax the doctor and me. There seemed, therefore, to be only one plausible explanation: Major Calthrop was insane.

He must have read my thoughts, for he hastily bared his neck and chest and revealed the small red marks which had so puzzled Thwaites. There was no doubt that they had been caused by sharp teeth.

Was it possible that I had to deal, not with a mere ghost, but with some ghostly vampire?

'Any other evidence of this character?' I asked.

'Yes, but not here. I should be glad to show you footprints, if you care to come to the inn.'

'At what hour do these apparitions appear?'

'About eleven o'clock.'

'I will come tonight before eleven,' I assured him.

The situation was alarmingly complicated by my doubt as to the Major's sanity. To be sure, he had not dreamed those marks on his neck and shoulders; but he might have acquired them in some way not at all connected with such apparitions as he described. I did not fear ghosts, even human apes with hair all over their faces and bodiless white bears, half so much as I did a crazy man who might leap at me in the dark and destroy me in his mad frenzy.

Altogether, my ride to Richmond in a taxicab was attended with forebodings. Major Calthrop was waiting for me on the steps of the inn. In the dim light of the porch lamps, the ravages of fear and despair were deeply written on his twitching face.

The house itself, however, was unexpectedly reassuring, entirely matter-of-fact. There was nothing unusual, either, about the stairway up which the Major led me. His room was not exactly cheerful, but its stiff spick-and-spanness was no setting for horrendous doings.

My doubt of the man's sanity was growing at every step. Then my eyes caught the ghostly imprints of which he had spoken. They were very faint. A casual glance would not have distinguished them from the pattern of the wallpaper. But there were literally hundreds of these pawlike marks, with distinct five-toe impressions. They were especially numerous on the wall at the head of his bed. Several of them, apparently the most recently made, were covered with a dark red substance which I was able to scratch off with my fingers.

'My blood,' the Major said simply.

'Do these creatures attack you only in bed?' I asked.

'At first that was so. Now they follow me all over the room.'

That being the case, Major, I will ask you to sit here.'

I drew a straight-backed chair to the centre of the floor. Then I drew from my briefcase several ordinary Chinese joss sticks. Two of these I lighted and handed to my host, who had silently taken his position as instructed.

'You will please hold one in each hand,' I said.

Without question he obeyed. Whereupon I pulled the heavy window drapes and plunged the room into darkness. Then I groped my way to a seat against the wall near the electric-light switch.

The joss sticks were for defence against the Major, not against ghosts. If he was indeed a madman, he might attack me in the dark. So long as he held the lighted sticks in his hands, I would be sure of his whereabouts. If he dropped them, I could turn on the light.

For a long time we sat thus. Then he whispered:

'Do you see anything?'

'No,' I said.

'You will. I feel that sensation I told you about.'

You will have to take my word for it that everything else I tell from now on is exactly as I saw and heard and experienced it. A dim phosphorescent cloud seemed to form between us. At first it was small and swirling and near the Major's breast, but it rapidly grew larger.

'You see that?'

I did not have time to answer. Even as he spoke, the cloud swung suddenly around and I saw distinctly the dark hairy head he had described to me.

The joss sticks in the Major's hands, were trembling now. Suddenly he dropped them and sprang to his feet with a blood-chilling shriek.

Next moment he was upon me. I thought he had lost his reason and was attacking me. Then I saw all too clearly the cause of his distress. Towering over us was the figure of a stout man. One coarse dirty hand was clenched in a gesture of hatred. The other brandished a thick walking stick. The face—and this was the most terrifying thing of all—was the face of the giant ape that had sprung from the cloud.

'Save me! Save me! This time he will kill me!'

As the Major spoke, the horrific creature deliberately raised its cudgel and brought it down in the direction of his head. I turned on the light.

The threat seemed so real, the peril so imminent, that I expected to hear the crash of the club on the Major's skull, but I heard nothing; and if he felt anything, he gave no sign. He made no effort to move from the position into which he had flung himself. His arms were rigid around my neck, his body a dead weight. He was whimpering like a frightened baby.

Finally I roused him. The apparition had disappeared with the turning on of the electric light, but it was evidently still in the room. We both heard dull thuds like the thumping of a heavy stick on the floor.

In spite of these portentous sounds, however, the soldier in Eversleigh Calthrop soon reasserted himself. We picked up our joss sticks and prepared for our second vigil.

This was to be brief. I had no sooner switched off the light than I felt something soft brush against my left leg, and heard what seemed like a small soft body squirming slowly across the room in the direction of the hapless Major, who seemed to have lost consciousness. Leaning forward to rouse him again, I was startled to hear a low growl. In the glow from the fallen joss sticks I distinctly saw the shadowy form of a small shapeless slimy white animal, about to spring.

I don't mind saying I was at my wits' end. What should I do? The Major settled the question by leaping to his feet with a scream of pain. I could hear him staggering around the room like a drunken man. Then he lurched heavily against me—and we fell together on the floor.

Freeing my right arm, I ran my hand over his body until I felt the slimy pelt of a small hairy animal with its face buried in his neck. There was no question now about the ghost's having materialized in the loathsome form of a deadly vampire.

It was out of the question for me to rise and find the electric switch. The heavy body of the Major had fallen on my left arm and pinned my whole left side to the floor. But I was prepared for just such an emergency.

From my pocket I pulled a small electric torch. Pressing the button, I turned its light full strength on the head of the incubus. The creature let go its hold on the Major's neck and swung around on me. But the bright light proved too much for it. With one growl, it fell to the floor, where it disintegrated and left no sign of its visible existence.

At this point there came a loud and peremptory knocking on the bedroom door. The effect on the Major was immediate. Once more he won my admiration by getting up manfully and walking resolutely to the door.

Outside, backed by a half dozen badly frightened guests, stood an angry—and also frightened—proprietor. To his demands for an explanation of the uproar, my good Major replied with dignity and poise, and not a little ingenuity, that we had been 'rehearsing a play.'

It took me six weeks to lay the ghost. During all of that time I spent part of every night in the room where first he and then he and I together had had the encounters with his strange and terrifying guests. The reason for the long delay was a simple one. I couldn't persuade the spirit of the vindictive old man to go away until I could show him that his victim no longer feared him, and that vengeance was no longer his.

The Cloth of Madness

SEABURY QUINN

Jamison Alvarde, the noted interior decorator, was dying. His family physician knew it; the neat, white-starched nurse—almost waspish in her impersonal devotion to her professional duties—knew it; the eminent graduate of Hopkins and Vienna, called into consultation, whose fee would be more than the annual maintenance of a poor ward in the City Hospital, knew it; Alvarde's next of kin, a niece and nephew, hastily summoned from halfway across the continent, knew it; and—which was most important of all—Jamison Alvarde knew it.

The last rays of the December sun slanted through the casement of the sick man's room, falling directly upon the bed and illuminating his face as though with a rosy spotlight. This was fitting and proper, since he was the principal character in the short tragedy about to be acted.

It was not an ill-looking face the afternoon sun bent its brief valedictory on. Jamison Alvarde's plentiful hair was iron-grey in colour, and swept up from his high, placid forehead in an even-crested pompadour. His eyebrows were heavy and intensely black, and the deep-set eyes beneath them were as grey as frosted glass. While his long illness had etched fine lines about the corners of his eyes and at the ends of his narrow lips, it had not robbed his cheeks of their rich, olive colouring, and even in the ante-chamber of death his mouth retained its firm, almost cruel, set.

In a far corner of the room, the family physician whispered fussily to the next of kin. Waiting for a patient to die is a tiresome business, especially when one is hungry and when one expects to have roast lamb with caper sauce for dinner.

'Yes, yes!' he was saying. 'Mr Alvarde has had a great deal of trouble the last year, a very great deal of trouble. He has never been the same since that terrible affliction fell upon his wife and his friend at his country place in the Highlands. A tragedy, my dear young friends, a very great tragedy; quite enough to break anyone's health. I've no doubt that Mr Alvarde's present illness is directly traceable to that—er—unfortunate occurrence; no doubt whatever.'

Alvarde's wasted, nervous hands paused a minute in their restless fumbling at the bedclothes. His thin, straight lips twisted a moment in an inscrutable smile, and his pale lids slowly lowered till they nearly hid his roving grey eyes. With that unwonted sharpening of the senses which often comes to those weakened in body, he had heard the doctor's whispered conversation.

The mention of that June morning when his wife and friend had been discovered in their rooms, hopelessly imbecile, brought no grimace of horror to the sick man's face. Rather, he smiled whimsically to himself, as if there were something not altogether unpleasing to him in the memory.

The afternoon sun sank behind the line of hills across the river. The great specialist got into his fur-lined overcoat and his imported motor car and drove home. The family physician left instructions to be called immediately there was any change in Mr Alvarde's condition and went home to his lamb and capers. The next of kin tiptoed downstairs to dinner, and Jamison Alvarde was left alone with his thoughts and the white-clad nurse.

'Nurse,' Alvarde raised himself slightly on one elbow,

'open the lower left-hand drawer of the desk and bring me the little black book you'll find there. . . .

'Now give me my fountain pen, please,' he directed, when the sharp-featured girl had brought the book and adjusted the pillows behind his back.

The nurse withdrew to the window, watching the last spots of sunlight on the river, and Alvarde commenced to scribble on the flyleaf of the book before him. As he wrote—difficult, for he was very weak—the same faintly reminiscent smile he had worn in the afternoon settled again on his tight-pressed lips.

Half, three-quarters, of an hour his pen travelled laboriously over the book's blank leaf; then, with a faint sigh of satisfaction, as at a task well done, Jamison Alvarde lay back upon his pillows.

The nurse crossed the room to remove the book and pen, paused a second, looking into her patient's face, then hurried to the telephone to call the family physician.

She might have saved herself the trouble and allowed the good doctor to finish his dinner in peace. Jamison Alvarde had no need of his services, or of any other physician's. Jamison Alvarde was dead.

The customary three days elapsed, and in the morning of the fourth they took Jamison Alvarde from his residence on the Drive to a new home in Shadow Lawns. It was a very stylish and dignified funeral, for Alvarde had left a respectable estate, and the high-priced funeral director who conducted the obsequies understood his business thoroughly.

On the fifth evening Alvarde's attorney—a dapper little man, much addicted to wing collars and neat, double-breasted jackets—called and read his deceased client's last will and testament to the next of kin, who, as was expected, proved also to be his residuary legatees, one-third of the estate having been left the dead man's wife. Then the lawyer took up the business of straightening out Alvarde's affairs.

'It will be necessary,' he informed them, stuffing the will

back into his saddle-leather brief-bag, 'to let me have all your uncle's papers which are in the house.'

'The only papers of Uncle Jamison's we found in the house are bound in a little black book,' the niece remarked. 'He'd been writing in it just before he died.'

When the little book was forthcoming and he had tucked it in his overcoat pocket, the lawyer seated himself in his automobile and started on his homeward trip. Before the motor had traversed two blocks he took out the slender volume and opened it. He was no waster of time; his capacity for making every minute count had won him his enviable standing at the bar.

The first words which struck his eye were written in a weak, straggling hand—the words Jamison Alvarde had penned on the night of his death.

'What the devil!' the lawyer exclaimed as he slowly spelt out the sprawling characters of the inscription. 'Did the old fool try to make another will on his death-bed?'

> I, Jamison Alvarde, being of sound mind and memory (which is more than some I know are), but being weakened in body, and about to die, do declare the following statement to be the true explanation of the mental derangement which occurred to my wife, Edith, and my friend, Hector Fuller, at my country place last summer.
>
> My one regret in publishing this memoir is that I shall not be present to hear the comments of the fools who have sympathized with me in my 'affliction.'
>
> JAMISON ALVARDE.

'Humph,' the lawyer turned the scribbled fly-leaf over. Following the leaf upon which the scrawling introduction was scratched, the book was written in a firm, clear hand, the hand Alvarde had penned in health. The pages were filled with detached paragraphs, like diary entries, but undated. The first sheet was torn diagonally across, so that the first sentence was incomplete.

*

. . . somewhat cool for this time of year. Excepting the tower, the house is fully completed, and we shall live here while the carpenters are finishing up.

I have asked Hector Fuller up for the weekend. Edith protested against his coming; for, with every woman's loathing of the unattainable, she has taken his impregnable bachelorhood as a deliberate affront. But Fuller is my friend, and whether Edith is pleased with his visit or not is of no moment to me. This is my house and Edith is my wife; and I mean to be master of both.

Fuller came this afternoon. I watched Edith narrowly when she greeted him, for I had determined to cut her allowance in two if she were discourteous to him. She blushed to the roots of her hair when she gave him her hand, and his face coloured, too. Fuller looked uncomfortably at me out of the corner of his eye, and I caught a sidelong glance from Edith which reminded me of the look Regina, my Irish setter, gives me when she knows I am about to beat her for worrying the poultry. I was sorry for Fuller; having to be polite to a hostess who dislikes you must be uncomfortable business.

Fuller is a sly old dog! Pretending misogynist that he is, always preaching the joys of an Eveless Eden, I've caught him red-handed in a flirtation with some silly woman—and, I believe, a married one, at that.

This afternoon I came in late from inspecting the decorations of the Grayson mansion drawing-room, and as I was about to mount the stairs I noticed a bit of folded paper lying on the floor. The sight of this trash on my hall carpet angered me; I hate such clutter and disorder.

I was about to pitch the scrap of paper in the fireplace when I noticed that it was house stationery and was written on. I opened it and recognized Fuller's writing.

My darling:

The ordeal was terrible. How I hate to have to pretend; how you hate it; how I hate to see you obliged to do it!

If only you-know-who would go away, so that we could cast aside this hideous mask, how happy we could be!

My dear, there are not words enough in all the languages combined to tell you how I love you. I'd rather kiss the print of your little foot in the dust than the lips of any other woman on earth. Oh, if only that brute could be got rid of!

Only a few more days, dear one, and the ghastly comedy we're playing will be finished. Then I will be at liberty to meet you once more at the old accustomed place.

My darling, my darling, I love you!

HECTOR

'H'm!' I muttered, as I shoved the slushy thing into my jacket pocket. 'That "brute" they're so anxious to be rid of is undoubtedly the lady's husband. Abuse the husband to flatter the wife, every time!'

We husbands are always brutes once we're pledged, with bell, book and candle, to provide a living for some worthless female. We're precious enough before they've put their halter on us, though, I've noticed! I dare say Edith thinks me a brute, though the devil knows it keeps my nose to the grindstone, paying for her fripperies.

I found Fuller in his room, dressing for dinner, and gave him his note.

'Next time, don't be so careless with your *billets d'amour*,' I cautioned. 'Someone might find it and pass it along to her husband, you know.'

The shot went home. Fuller turned as pale as if a ghost had entered the room with me, and faced about with a spring, as though expecting me to attack him.

'I suppose you'll demand that I leave the house immediately?' he asked, when he saw that I had no immediate intention of assaulting him.

I laughed. 'My dear boy,' I told him, 'it's a matter of perfect indifference to me how much you protest your hatred of the sex in public and flirt with them in private.

Only you're so ungodly absent-minded with your mash notes! I found that gummy thing of yours lying in plain sight on the hall floor. Is your brain so addled with love of the fair one that you forget to post your letters to her?'

He regarded me a moment as a condemned criminal might the messenger who brings his reprieve, and jammed the note into his waistcoat pocket.

'Thanks, old man,' he gulped. 'Awfully good of you to bring it to me!'

'Oh, that's all right!' I assured him as I started to my own room to dress. 'Don't bother about thanking me.'

Funny, what a doddering fool love can make of a sensible man like Fuller.

I wish Fuller would use more discretion in his choice of a light o' love. She uses lily of the valley.

Lily of the valley is the one thing about which Edith has defied me. Time and again I've ordered her never to bring the pestilent stuff into my house, and every time I've found a phial of it on her dressing-table I've flung it out the window; yet her hair, her fingertips and her lingerie fairly reek with it, despite my commands.

I came out late from town this evening, and Grigsby, the butler, informed me that Fuller had dropped out during the afternoon and had put up in his usual room. I stopped in his quarters for a little chat before going to bed. He had already turned in, but was still awake. His clothes were sprawled all over the room in the careless way he always throws them when he crawls into bed, and I had no choice but to share the same chair with his dinner jacket.

I'd scarcely gotten seated and lighted a cigar when I began to notice the unpleasant proximity of lily of the valley scent. At first I couldn't make out where the annoying odour came from, but a few sniffs localized its source. Fuller's dinner jacket was redolent with the perfume.

'No doubt you find it very comforting to have your lady love rest her head on your shoulder,' I grumbled, 'but, for heaven's sake, why don't you get her to use some other scent? I loathe this stuff as the devil does holy water.'

He gaped at me like a goldfish viewing the sunlight through the walls of an aquarium.

'What d'ye mean, "some other scent?" ' he asked. 'I don't follow you.'

'Why, this infernal lily of the valley.' I tapped the scented shoulder of his jacket in explanation. 'I hate it more than any other smell this side of H. S, Edith uses it until I think, sometimes, I'll have to commit suicide—or murder—to get rid of it.'

Fuller's eyes widened like a cat's in the twilight.

'D-does Edith—Mrs Alvarde—use that perfume?' he stammered.

'You're devilish well right, she does, *ad nauseam*!' I growled as I got up. 'And for the Lord's sake, get your woman to use something else. It's bad enough to have Edith scenting up the place, without your lugging a lot of the stuff in on your clothes.'

I have thought the whole matter over very carefully. I shall kill them both.

The scales fell from my eyes tonight (perhaps I would better say they were snatched from my eyes) and I see what a blind, fatuous, doting cuckold I have been for the fiend only knows how long. The shame of it is maddening.

Spring has broken early this year and summer is upon us; the roses in the lower garden are budding out, and the double row of dogwood trees which flanks the drive is festival-clad in a white surplice of blossoms.

The decorations of the Grayson house were all completed today, but I had to stay late catching up a few loose ends, so that it was well after dark when I reached home.

Fuller was out on one of the visits which have become rather frequent of late, and he and Edith had dined when I arrived. She was in the music room, strumming idly on the piano and singing softly to herself when I passed through the hall. Fuller had gone to his room for some reason or other. I could hear the sickly sentimental refrain of the popular ballad she was thrumming as I went up the stairs:

There's a kiss that you get from baby,
 There's a kiss that you get from Dad,
There's a kiss that you get from Mother,
 That's the first real kiss you've had.
There's a kiss with a tender meaning,
 Other kisses you recall;
But the kisses I get from you, sweetheart,
 Are the sweetest kisses of all.

Something in the spring air, the shower of pearl moonbeams I'd just driven through, or the appealing lilt of the song downstairs—perhaps all three—set my pulses throbbing at an unwonted tempo; I climbed the last ten steps humming the silly words under my breath:

There's a kiss with a tender meaning,
 Other kisses you recall. . . .

In his room across the hall from mine Fuller was moving about, alternately whistling and humming the same banal refrain. The words came softly through the closed door of his room:

Other kisses you recall,
But the kisses I get from you, sweetheart,
 Are the sweetest kisses of all.

Strange how a snatch of song on a spring evening will carry a man's mind back to scenes he has never thought to see reflected on his memory's screen again. As I knotted my tie I remembered my first sweetheart, pretty and blue-eyed and blonde. I used to have a trick of pulling off her glove when I brought her home from some party, and kissing all five of her pink little fingers.

Poor Elsie; when her husband died he left no insurance and God knows how many children. She came to me for help, but she had no business qualifications, couldn't even type; so there was nothing I could do for her.

Then there was another girl—a slender thing with a painted face, a robemaker's mannequin. Her masculine acquaintances had been the sort who wear coloured derby hats and converse in terms of the race-track and poolroom. I was the first man of breeding she had known, and she was as grateful for the common or garden variety of courtesy as a stray dog for a scrap of meat.

She knew only one medium of exchange, and her timid little offers of passion were pitiful to see.

I gave her three hundred dollars: rather a handsome settlement, considering our respective positions. A child more or less doesn't matter to her kind . . . I've often wondered what became of her. . .

Fuller was still singing to himself when I finished dressing and went down to the dining-room. Edith had left the house and was sitting on a stone bench at the lower end of the terrace, watching the boats go by on the river below. In her white dinner frock, with the moonlight on her arms and shoulders, she was almost as pale as the marble Psyche at the other end of the walk.

A chilly breath of wind swept up from the river, rustling the dogwood blossoms and shaking the scrim curtains at the dining-room windows. Edith felt it as it passed and shivered a little.

'She'll be cold without her wrap,' I speculated as I poured myself a stiff appetizer of Irish whiskey and rang for Grigsby to serve dinner.

A bar from the song recurred to me:

> There's a kiss with a tender meaning . . .
> But the kisses I get from you, sweetheart. . .

I went into the music-room, picked up Edith's China-silk scarf, and stepped through the French window to the lawn.

Walking quietly across the short-cut grass, I approached her from the rear, softly humming the refrain.

'But the kisses I get from you, sweetheart, are the sweetest kisses of all,' I finished aloud, dropping the shawl over her narrow shoulders, putting my hands over her eyes, and bending forward to kiss her full upon the lips.

Her white, thin hands flew up from her lap and clasped about my neck, drawing my cheek close to hers.

'Oh!' she cried, and the exclamation was about a sob, 'my dear, my dear, I've been thinking you'd never come! I've been so lonesome.'

Then she struck me playfully on the cheek and gave a sniff of disapproval.

'Hector,' she scolded, 'you've been drinking that horrid Irish whiskey, and you know how I hate it. *He* uses it!'

I released her eyes and sprang back, livid with fury. But my mind worked with the agility of a leaping cat. Before Edith had time to recover from the horror the discovery of her error had given her. I had landed fairly on my mental feet.

I threw back my head and laughed; laughed naturally, laughed uproariously.

'By the Lord Harry, old girl,' I cried, pounding my thigh in a perfect paroxysm of counterfeit mirth, 'that's the best joke I've heard you spring in years! Everyone knows you hate Hector Fuller worse than a hen hates a rainstorm, and now you call me by his name and pretend you thought you were kissing him!' Again I rocked forward in a spasm of laughter. 'And I can just about imagine how you'd have written the ten commandments on his face with your nails if it really had been Fuller!'

All the while I was watching her as a snake does a bird, noting the look of blank amazement which slowly replaced the terrified gaze she had first turned to me when she discovered her mistake.

'Let's go in the house and have some music; it's too cold for you out here, dear,' I concluded, as soon as I had calmed down my mock amusement.

She rose as obediently as a well-trained dog and accompanied me across the lawn in silence. But she shuddered slightly as I put my arm about her. Women have no control of their emotions.

While I smoked three or four cigarettes, she played and sang for me, and then, pleading a headache—the old, threadbare excuse of all her sex since Eve first left the garden—begged leave to go up to bed.

I let her go and went out to the stable. I harnessed the cob to the village cart and drove furiously along the country lanes for three hours, lashing the horse fiercely whenever he dropped out of a gallop. The poor brute was nearly foundered when I turned him home; but I was as raging wild as ever.

I have thought the whole matter over very carefully. I shall kill them both.

Last night I said I should kill them both. Today I know I *must* kill them. A sentence from Fuller's treacherous note to Edith has been pounding in my head all day with the monody of a funeral dirge:

'. . . if that brute could only be got rid of!'

When faithless wives and false friends conspire to be rid of an inconvenient husband the number of his days is appointed. The dockets of our criminal courts bear eloquent testimony of that.

A weakling would seek divorce as the easy solution of my difficulty; but I am no maudlin fool, ready to efface myself, leaving the way clear for them to flaunt their triumph and my dishonour before the world.

I must be very careful in my execution of these two. Except for them, no one must suspect my vengeance; for it is no part of my plan to die like a felon for having exacted the justice which the law denies me.

I must kill them, but I must be careful—very careful.

If I were a superstitious man I should say that the Fates have decided to aid me in the furtherance of my plans. While I was lunching at the Republique today, Howard Enright dropped into the chair opposite me. I greeted him sourly enough, for I was in no mood for conversation, but he refused to be rebuffed.

He is just back from an extended tour of the East, where he has picked up enough expensive junk for his house to fill three museums and impoverish half a dozen millionaires. Despite my curt answers, he rambled on about the thousand and one *objets de vertu* he'd lugged halfway around the world, until I was ready to believe that he'd brought the whole *Arabian Nights* home with him. Othello's tales of

> . . . anthropophagi,
> And men whose heads do grow below their shoulders,

were hackneyed beside the wonders Enright would display at his galleries.

He had a jade Buddha that caught and held the sunlight until the beholder was ready to swear that the image was filled with living fire. He had lachrymatories from Persia—tall, spindle-necked bottles, coming in pairs, into which the Persian widows wept, that the fulness of the bottles might be an outward and visible sign of the fulness of their grief at their husbands' taking-off. He had a great fan from Korea, where there was an ancient custom that no widow might remarry till her husband's grave was dry. The fan, he explained, was to be used by the lady in hastening the aridness of her lord's burial mound. He had bits of porcelain from the dynasties of Han and Ming—things so fragile that the Chinese called them 'frozen air,' and so precious that they were worth their weight in rubies.

I was thoroughly bored by his graphic cataloguing of the stock of his junkshop, and had given up the attempt to stifle a yawn, when he wound up with:

'And I've something else, Alvarde, that will appeal to you as an interior decorator.'

'Indeed?' I masked the yawn with my hand.

'Yes, sir. Weirdest thing you ever saw; regular old marrow-freezer! They call it "the cloth of madness," and there's a legend to the effect that whoever looks at it loses his reason. Some vengeful old rajah had it woven for the special benefit of some friends he suspected of forgetting that the harem is sacred, inviolate.'

'Well, did it work?' I queried, more for the sake of politeness than anything else.

'They say it did. According to tradition he had an asylumful of crazy friends and acquaintances in less than no time. Anyhow, I couldn't get one of the natives to look at the thing. Rummy lot, these Indians.'

I smiled my appreciation of the wily old maharajah's finesse. 'What does it look like, this "cloth of madness" of yours?'

'Oh,' Enright spread his hands wide in preparation for an eloquent description. 'It's—it's—it's—Oh, hang it all, man, I can't describe the beastly thing to you! All red and full of funny, twisty black lines like snakes and lizards and why, Alvarde, it's like an X-ray of a guilty conscience! Come around to the shop and see for yourself; I'd never be able to make you imagine the thing's damnable fascination.'

'There might be an idea for some bizarre pattern in wall-hanging,' I reflected. 'New designs are hard to find nowadays.' So I went with him to the shop.

He undid several yards of cocomatting wrappings and unfurled a small oblong of crimson cloth for my inspection.

At first sight of the thing I was ready to laugh in his face; for, save for a rather unusual combination of involuted and convoluted black lines and stripes on the cloth's red ground, it seemed to differ in no particular from hundreds of other Oriental tapestries.

Enright must have seen the unspoken scepticism in my face, for the corners of his small hazel eyes wrinkled in amusement.

'Go ahead and laugh,' he invited, 'but I'll bet you ten dollars that you'll be ready to cry "'nough" by the time you've looked at it steadily for five minutes.'

For answer I drew a bill from my pocket and placed it on a tabouret, without taking my eyes from the bit of weaving.

Enright matched my note with one of his, and drew back, smiling whimsically at me through the smoke of his cigar.

'Hand me your ten when the five minutes are up,' I ordered, keeping my gaze fixed on the cloth.

'Easy now,' he counselled, glancing at his watch; 'you've only been looking forty seconds, so far.'

One who has never tried it has no conception of how time drags while the eyes are focused on an immovable object. In the quiet of the storeroom I could hear the ticking of Enright's watch distinctly, and the ticks seemed a minute apart. An almost uncontrollable desire to rub my eyes, to shut them, to direct them anywhere but at the cloth, came over me. The writhing broad and narrow black bands on the ruby surface seemed to be slowly coming to life. They wound and twisted, one upon another, like the shadows of scores of snakes suspended in the sunlight. They seemed alternately to advance and retreat upon their glaring resting-place, and my eyes ached with the effort to follow their serpentine movements.

I began to be obsessed with the thought that there really were reptiles—dozens of them, scores of them, hundreds of them—behind me; that they would drop upon me any moment, smearing my body with their loathsome slime, tearing my flesh with their fangs, filling my blood with their deadly venom.

'Time up?' I called, my voice sounding hoarse and croaking in my own ears.

'Only two minutes more to go,' Enright answered pleasantly.

'I'll—stick—it—out—if—it—kills—me!' I muttered between my teeth, and, covering my eyes with my hands, fell choking and gasping to my knees.

The infernal cloth had won. Scornful and determined as I had been, it had worn my nerves to shreds and made a whimpering, fear-crazed thing of me in three minutes.

'How much will you take for that thing, Enright?' I asked, when I had recovered my composure to some extent.

'More than you're able to give, son,' he replied. 'I'll get a half-grown fortune from some museum for that bit of fancy work or my name isn't Howard Enright.'

'Well,' I temporized, 'will you rent it to me, then? I'd like to have a modified copy of it made by my paper manufacturer. Some client with a diseased mind might want a chamber of horrors done, and a denatured copy of this cloth would be just the thing.'

'Promise me on your honour as a gentleman not to have a duplicate made, and I'll lend it to you for forty-eight hours for nothing,' Enright offered.

'Done!' I agreed.

I took the tapestry to my papermaker this afternoon. I have ordered two rolls of paper made in exact imitation of it. I shall paper the unfinished tower room with it.

The trap is set. Working at night, and without help, I have hung the walls and ceiling of the tower attic room with the paper. This room is small, hardly more than a large closet, and, being originally intended for a lumber room, is without windows or other communication with the outside except a small fresh-air vent in the roof.

With an idea of obtaining the maximum amount of room for storage purposes, I had dispensed with all wood trim and had the door made flush with the wall. This renders the place ideal for my purpose, for I am able to cover every fractional inch of wall space with the paper; so that, when the door is closed, the maddening design is presented to the gaze from every direction except the floor. This I have painted white, the better to reflect the glare from the cluster of high-power nitrogen-filled electric lights I have placed in the ceiling.

Early this morning, when I had finally completed my work, I switched on the full force of light and looked about me.

From above, the glare of the electric bulbs beat down like the fires that destroyed Sodom and Gomorrah; from the white floor the reflection smote my eyes like splinters of incandescent metal, and from the walls and ceiling the writhing, tortuous design of the demoniacal paper glared like (to use Enright's description) 'an X-ray of a guilty conscience.'

I had been careful to leave the door open when I tried my experiment. Lucky for me I did; for I had scarcely glanced once round the hideous apartment when I began to feel the same panic fear I had experienced when I first looked at the cloth in Enright's store. My eyes seemed bulging from their sockets; my breath came hot and quick, like the breath of a sleeper bound fast in a nightmare, and I all but lost my sense of direction. It was with great effort that I found the open door and staggered through it, with the sweat of mortal terror standing on my forehead.

I have been very good to Edith these last few days. I have endeavoured to anticipate her every wish; have come back from the city loaded with bonbons and flowers like a country bumpkin wooing his sweetheart; I have doubled her allowance of spending money.

Last evening, after dinner, she kissed me, of her own volition. I felt my plan for vengeance weaken a little as her arms went around my neck. . . . Fool! Her lips are soiled with another man's kisses; her arms are tainted with the embraces of her paramour.

I looked into her eyes, warm and brown and bright, and wondered how often they had shone with love of Fuller. How long, I wondered, had it been since the same arm which rested on my shoulder had clasped the neck of the man who called himself my friend—and stole my honour like a common thief?

I shall invite Fuller to the house to spend the weekend. My trap is set; now to snare the quarry.

It is done.

Last week I mentioned casually to Edith that I had asked Fuller up for the weekend. I saw her eyes brighten at the suggestion, but chose to misinterpret the sign.

'It's no use making a fuss about it,' I told her. 'I know you don't like him; but I want him here, so you might just as well make the best of it.'

She made no reply, simply rose and left the room. As a play-actor Edith is a sad failure. I suppose she feared her joy would be too apparent, even to a doting fool husband if she remained.

When Fuller came I made a great show of urging her to be courteous to him, and greeted him cordially myself.

Fuller's was a charming personality. Quick-witted, loquacious, well read and much travelled, he was an ideal guest, providing his own and his host's entertainment. We passed a pleasant afternoon together.

I never saw Edith more charming than at dinner that night. There was a faint flush in her face, her eyes were very bright. She was wearing a gown of silver over sapphire, and had a jasmine blossom pinned in the smooth coils of her chocolate-coloured hair.

The corners of my mouth flexed grimly at sight of the flower. Once, when I was in South America, I had seen a vicious knife duel between two men, and when I asked the cause of the brawl, I was told that one had offered the other's sister a jasmine bloom. Jasmine, they explained, was the symbol of inconstancy. Strange, that of all the flowers in my grounds and conservatory Edith should have chosen the badge of infidelity to wear that night!

From my seat at the head of the table I could see Fuller worshipping Edith with his eyes. There was that in his adoring gaze which gave one to think of a medieval knight kneeling humbly at his fair lady's feet, while her husband was off to the crusades.

We had coffee in the music room. Edith seemed ill at ease, fumbling with her cup, twirling the stem of her liqueur glass between her fingers, toying nervously with her cigarette. Before Fuller and I had finished, she rose abruptly and went to the piano.

There was no light burning in the room, and the moon laid a path of mother-of-pearl across the polished floor. With the silver radiance of the moonlight on the silver meshes of her gown, Edith was white as a wraith of the night. A snatch from Oscar Wilde's *Salome* flashed through my mind:

> She is like a dead woman; a dead woman, who covers herself with a veil and goes seeking for lovers.

I smiled to myself in the darkness. 'She will seek no more after tonight,' I reflected.

'Ah, moon of my delight, that knowst no wane,
The moon of heav'n is rising once again;
How oft hereafter rising shall she look
Through this same garden after one—in vain?'

she sang. I rose and began to pace the room.

Gradually, taking great pains to be impersonal about it, I swung the conversation to stories of the vengeance wreaked by outraged husbands on faithless wives and their paramours. Incidentally, I recounted the legend of the cloth of madness; how the Indian prince had demanded his treacherous friends' sanity as the price of their perfidy.

Edith's hands fluttered among the sheets of music on the piano; a leaf of it fell to the floor. Fuller leaped gallantly to his feet to retrieve it for her, and their hands came together in the moonlight. I saw his fingers close round hers and give them a reassuring pressure.

'What would you do, Alvarde, if you caught another man trespassing on your wife's affections?' Fuller suddenly shot at me. 'Kill him?'

Edith gave a short little choking gasp and put her hand to her throat very suddenly. She had always been afraid of me.

'My dear man,' I drawled, 'do I look like such a fool?'

'Fool?'

'Precisely; "fool" is what I said. Why should I hang for another man's sin? I rather think the old rajah's method of revenge would appeal to me.'

'But, you know,' he objected, 'the cloth of madness is only a myth.'

'So is my wife's incontinence,' I answered shortly. 'One is quite as possible as the other.'

And so we let the talk of betrayed friendship and its price drop, and passed to a discussion of interior decorations.

I told them of my more unusual bits of work for a while, then suggested:

'Let's go to the tower rooms. I've evolved a new scheme in wall-hangings for them. One of the rooms especially will interest you two.'

We went through the larger rooms, I pointing out the novelties in colour scheme, pattern and wood trim, they taking only a perfunctory interest in my designs.

At the door of the storeroom I stood aside to let them pass. Edith paused at the threshold, looking questioningly, fearfully, into the velvety darkness of the little chamber. Fuller stepped before her.

'Let me go first,' he said; 'it's dark in there.'

'Yes,' I echoed, all the smouldering resentment I had felt for months flaming up in my voice, 'it is dark in there—we'll lighten it.'

I put out my hand, pushing Edith roughly through the doorway after Fuller, slammed the door, locked it, and pressed the switch which controlled the electric lights. Then I bent listening at the keyhole.

For the space of a long breath all was silent in the little room; then there was a deep-drawn sigh, whether from Edith or Fuller I could not say.

'Well, what's next?' I heard him ask. 'If this is Jamison's idea of a joke, I think he's showing mighty poor taste.'

'Hector,' it was Edith speaking in a still, frightened whisper, 'he *knew*!'

Fuller's steps sounded harshly on the bare, polished floor of the empty room as he strode about it, seeking an exit; his fists pounded the walls in search of the hidden door. I had to stifle the laughter in my throat; for I knew how the rounded walls, the unbroken monotony of the crimson and black paper, and the glaring reflection from the white floor would confound his sense of direction. He was pacing the room like a blind, caged beast, striking the walls again and again in the same place, and meeting with no more success than an imprisoned bumble-bee flying at the transparent walls of a poison-jar.

For several minutes he continued his futile efforts; then I heard him withdraw to the centre of the room.

There was a faint rustle of skirts. She was shrinking up against him.

'She's in his arms, now,' I muttered. 'Let her cling to him; let him hold her. I wish them joy of each other.'

Several minutes more. Then:

'Hector, I'm afraid; I'm terrified. Hold me close, dear.'

I bit my lips. Would that devil's design on the walls never begin to work?

'Hector,' this time the words came quaveringly, as though she were fighting back a chill, 'that paper on the wall—does it seem to you as if the figures on it were moving?'

'Yes, dear.'

'They are like snakes—like horrible twisting snakes. I feel as though they were going to spring at me from the walls.'

'A-a-h!' I murmured to myself. 'They're beginning to notice now.'

Fuller took several quick, decided steps from the room's centre, walking directly toward the door. I drew back and seized a chair, ready to strike him down if he succeeded in breaking through the light wooden frame. I had not counted on his retaining his faculties so long, and had taken no precautions to reinforce the lock, trusting the paper with which it was covered to mask the door effectively.

Within a foot or so of the door he paused irresolutely, waited a moment, and retreated.

'I can't do it!' he almost wailed. 'I can't bear to put my hands against that wall!'

'Hector!' This time there was no mistaking the panic in Edith's voice; every word came with a gasp. 'The paper—the paper on the wall; it—it's—the—cloth—of— madness! It's that awful tapestry he told us about tonight.'

'My God, girl,' his reply came thickly, as though his tongue were swollen in his mouth, 'you're right.'

I could hear them breathing heavily, like spent runners after a race, or those in the presence of mortal danger.

Softly, there came the sound of Edith's sobbing. Very low it was, and very pitiful, like the disconsolate heartbroken sobbing of a little child who has lost its mother, and is afraid.

'Oh!' she whimpered, 'let me hide my face against you, dear. Don't let me look at those ghastly things on the walls. You must shut your eyes, too, dear; you must not look either.'

I waited patiently outside the door. Even closed eyes, I knew, could not withstand the intense glare of those lights and the fascination of those flame-coloured walls.

Her resolution broke even sooner than I had expected.

'I can't bear the darkness,' she wailed. 'I must look, I must see them—the horrible snakes, the hideous snakes that are beckoning to me from the walls. Hold me, Hector, darling; don't let me move—don't let me go to them! Hold me fast in your arms.'

Another pause. Dimly I caught another noise—one that I had not heard before. Sharp and syncopated it was, like the clicking of castanets heard from a distance. It puzzled me at first; then recognition burst upon me, and I had to thrust my tongue against my teeth to keep from laughing aloud. It was a sound I'd heard on very cold nights when I'd passed shivering newsboys filching a little heat from above some engine-room grating. It was the sound of chattering teeth.

It was warm that night; the temperature in that little, poorly ventilated room, with those great lights burning in it, must have been like the entrance to Avernus; yet their teeth were chattering like a monk's clapdish.

I was striding softly across the floor, digging my nails into my palms in an effort to keep from giving audible vent to my feeling of triumph, when my steps were arrested by a titter from the room beyond. Edith was laughing, not mirthfully, but with the shrill cachinnation of hysteria. In a moment her quavering treble was seconded by a deep, masculine baritone. The pair of them were laughing in concert, and from the cracking strain in their voices I knew that, they were trying with all their strength to keep silence, yet laughed the harder as they strove.

I turned on my heel and descended to the dining-room.

No need to listen further, I knew. A few hours more, at most, and my revenge would be complete. I was shivering a little, myself.

Downstairs, I poured out a stiff peg of Scotch. Raising my glass I looked out into the moonlight, apostrophizing the old rajah who invented the cloth of madness.

'Here's to you, brother!' I said as I turned my glass bottom up.

Shortly after midnight I climbed the stairs to the tower and stopped before the door of the little room where I left them. I listened intently for a minute. There was no more sound from beyond the door than if it had barred the entrance to a tomb.

I pressed the electric switch, reducing the force of the lights within by half, then unlocked the door and opened it a crack, peering through the narrow opening.

Inside, everything was still, still as a nursery at midnight.

Fuller was sitting upright in the middle of the floor, an insane smirk overspreading his face. His collar and tie were undone, his waistcoat was unbuttoned, his shirt-front was partly loosened from its studs, and much wrinkled. His tongue protruded from his mouth, hanging flaccidly over his lower lip, as though he had lost control of it. Altogether, he was a figure of comic tragedy, like that character of Victor Hugo's whose face had been so horribly deformed in childhood, that no matter what his emotion was, he could do nothing but grin.

Nearer the door, just as she had fallen, lay Edith. One arm was extended, the hand resting palm up on the floor, the fingers slightly curled, like a sleeping child's. Her cheek lay pillowed on her arms. Her hair was a little disarranged and the jasmine flower had fallen from it. One of her satin pumps had dropped off and lay gaping emptily beside her, exposing her narrow, silk-cased foot. I could see the veins of her instep showing against the white flesh under her silver-tissue stocking. Her lips were parted very slightly.

The air of the place was heavy with the perfume of lily of the valley.

I gathered her in my arms, and she whimpered a little, like a child that is disturbed in its sleep, as I carried her down to her room.

It was a difficult business disrobing her and getting her into bed, for she seemed to have lost all control of her muscles, even being unable to take the pins from her hair.

Fuller was a heavy man, but somehow I managed to drag him downstairs and tumble him into bed, being careful to scatter his clothes about the room as was his custom when turning in late.

Last of all I returned to the tower and worked like a fiend, obliterating every trace of the wallpaper's design with grey paint I had hidden away for that purpose. Two hours' work, and the little room was as demure in its fresh coating of Quaker drab as a nun's cell. A neat, well-lighted store-room it was, nothing more. Every lingering sign of the cloth of madness was hidden away forever.

I slept well in the morning next day, rousing only when Grigsby came rushing into my room and shook me roughly by the shoulder.

'Mr Alvarde, sir,' he panted, his eyes bulging from his face like a terrified frog's, 'something terrible has happened, sir!'

'What's the matter?' I growled at him sleepily. 'Cook gone on a strike?'

'Oh, no, sir, no!' He wrung his hands together in anguish 'It's really terrible sir! Mr Fuller's a-sittin' on the edge of his bed, a-tryin' to put both feet into one leg of his trousers, sir, and he's smilin' something awful.' And Grigsby attempted to twist his heavy features into an imitation of Fuller's demented grin.

I got into my slippers and robe and started across the hall for Fuller's room, running full tilt into Agnes, the waitress. When Edith had failed to come down long after her usual breakfast hour, Agnes had gone upstairs to see what was detaining her, and had come running to me, fear written in every line of her face.

'Oh, sir, something's wrong with Mrs Alvarde! I went in to call her, and she wouldn't answer me, nor look at me, nor nothing; just lies there and laughs and mumbles at herself like she was a baby!'

'You're a pair of fools,' I told her and Grigsby. 'You stay here; I'll go and see for myself.

It was true. Fuller was as perfect an imbecile as was ever confined in an asylum, and Edith's mental timepiece had been turned back thirty-five years. No babe in arms was ever more helpless in body and mind than she.

The papers and the doctors and the neighbours made a great fuss about it. Everyone sympathized with my unfortunate wife and friend and wondered how I could stand my terrible misfortune with such fortitude. I closed the house and sold it at a loss several months later.

Edith is still at a sanitorium, and the physicians look sorrowfully at me when I go out to visit her, and tell me that she will never be anything but a grown-up infant, though she will probably live to a ripe old age.

Fuller's malady has taken a turn for the worse. Last month they had to restrain him with a strait-jacket. He was raving about some strange kind of cloth—what it was they couldn't make out—and threatening to kill me; me, his best and oldest friend!

'Let me go first, it's dark in there!' Fuller said when he and Edith stood at the entrance of the storeroom. I've often wondered which one of them went into the darkness of insanity first. Edith, I imagine; women have no control of their emotions.

I am a sick man. The physician tells me that there's nothing to worry about, but I read my death sentence in his eyes. If there's such a place as the hell the preachers tell of, I suppose I'll go there. At least, I'll have to die to do it; Edith and Fuller got theirs here, and it will last through all the long years they live like brute beasts in their madhouse cells.

Jamison Alvarde's attorney closed the little black book with a snap and pursed his lips. Anyone looking at him would have said that he was about to whistle.

'Yes,' he said meditatively, tapping his knee with the little book, 'if there's a hell he's undoubtedly there now! It's a pity if he isn't. This scheme of things certainly seems to require a hell—a good hot one, too!'

CONTENTS

The Haunted and the Haunters
or, The House and the Brain

Lord Lytton

A friend of mine, who is a man of letters and a philosopher, said to me one day, as if between jest and earnest: 'Fancy! since we last met, I have discovered a haunted house in the midst of London.'

'Really haunted? – and by what? – ghosts?'

'Well, I can't answer that question; all I know is this: six weeks ago my wife and I were in search of a furnished apartment. Passing a quiet street, we saw on the window of one of the houses a bill, "Apartments, Furnished". The situation suited us: we entered the house – liked the rooms – engaged them by the week – and left them the third day. No power on earth could have reconciled my wife to stay longer; and I don't wonder at it.'

'What did you see?'

'Excuse me – I have no desire to be ridiculed as a superstitious dreamer – nor, on the other hand, could I ask you to accept on my affirmation what you would hold to be incredible without the evidence of your own senses. Let me say only this, it was not so much what we saw or heard (in which you might fairly suppose that we were the dupes of our own excited fancy, or the victims of the imposture in others) that drove us away, as it was an undefinable terror which seized both of us whenever we passed by the door of a certain unfurnished room, in which we neither saw nor heard anything. And the strangest marvel of all was, that for once in my life I agreed with my wife, silly woman though she be – and allowed, after the third night, that it was impossible to stay a fourth in that house. Accordingly, on the fourth morning I summoned the woman who kept the house and attended on us, and told her that the rooms did not quite suit us, and we would not stay out our week. She said dryly: "I know why; you have stayed longer than any other lodger. Few ever stayed a second night; none before you a third. But I take it they have been very kind to you."

'"They – who?" I asked, affecting to smile.

'"Why, they who haunt the house, whoever they are. I don't mind them; I remember them many years ago, when I lived in this house, not as a servant; but I know they will be the death of me some day. I don't care – I'm old, and must die soon anyhow; and then I shall be with them, and in this house still." The woman spoke with so dreamy a calmness, that really it was a sort of awe that prevented my conversing with her further. I paid for my week, and too happy were my wife and I to get off so cheaply.'

'You excite my curiosity,' said I; 'nothing I should like better than to a sleep in a haunted house. Pray give me the address of the one which you left so ignominiously.'

My friend gave me the address; and when we parted, I walked straight towards the house thus indicated.

It is situated on the north side of Oxford Street, in a dull but respectable thoroughfare. I found the house shut up – no bill at the window, and no response to my knock. As I was turning away, a beer-boy, collecting pewter pots at the neighbouring areas, said to me: 'Do you want anyone at that house, sir?'

'Yes, I heard it was to be let.'

'Let! – why, the woman who kept it is dead – has been dead these three weeks, and no one can be found to stay there, though Mr J – offered ever so much. He offered mother, who chars for him, a pound a week just to open and shut the windows, and she would not.'

'Would not! – and why?'

'The house is haunted; and the old woman who kept it was found dead in her bed, with her eyes wide open. They say the devil strangled her.'

'Pooh! – you speak of Mr J – . Is he the owner of the house?'

'Yes.'

'Where does he live?'

'In G – Street, number – .'

'What is he? – in any business?'

'No, sir – nothing particular; a single gentleman.'

I gave the pot-boy the gratuity earned by his liberal information, and proceeded to Mr J – , in G – Street, which was close by the street that boasted the haunted house. I was lucky enough to find Mr J – at home – an elderly man, with intelligent countenance and prepossessing manners.

I communicated my name and my business frankly. I said I heard the house was considered to be haunted – that I had a strong desire to examine the house with so equivocal a reputation – that I should be greatly obliged if he would allow me to hire it, though only for a night. I was willing to pay for that privilege whatever he might be inclined to ask. 'Sir,' said Mr J – , with great courtesy, 'the house is at your service, for as short or as long a time as you please. Rent is out of the question – the obligation will be on my side should you be able to discover the cause of the strange phenomena which at present deprive it of all value. I cannot let it, for I cannot even get a servant to keep it in order or answer the door. Unluckily the house is haunted, if I may use that expression, not only by night, but by day; though at night the disturbances are of a more unpleasant and sometimes of a more alarming character. The poor old woman who died in it three weeks ago was a pauper whom I took out of the workhouse, for in her childhood she had been known to some of my family, and had once been in such good circumstances that she had rented that house of my uncle. She was a woman of superior education and strong mind, and was the only person I could ever induce to remain in the house. Indeed, since her death, which was sudden, and the coroner's inquest, which gave it a notoriety in the neighbourhood, I have so despaired of finding any person to take charge of the house, much more a tenant, that I would willingly let it rent free for a year to anyone who would pay its rates and taxes.'

'How long is it since the house acquired this sinister character?'

'That I can scarcely tell you, but very many years since. The old woman I spoke of said it was haunted when she rented it between thirty and forty years ago. The fact is, that my life has been spent in the East Indies, and in the civil service of the Company. I returned to England last year, on inheriting the fortune of an uncle, among whose possessions was the house in question. I found it shut up and uninhabited. I was told that it was haunted, that no one would inhabit it. I smiled at what seemed to me so idle a story. I spent more money in repairing it – added to its old-fashioned furniture a few modern articles – advertised it, and obtained a lodger for a year. He was a colonel on half-pay. He came in with his family, a son and a daughter, and four or five servants: they all left the house the next day; and, although each of them declared that he had seen something different from that which had scared the others, a something still was equally terrible to all. I really could not in conscience sue, nor even blame, the colonel for breach of agreement. Then I put in the old woman I have spoken of, and she was empowered to let the house in apartments. I never had one lodger who stayed more than three days. I do not tell you their stories – to no two lodgers have there been exactly the same phenomena repeated. It is better that you should judge for yourself, than enter the house with an imagination influenced by previous narratives; only be prepared to see and hear something or other, and take whatever precautions you yourself please.'

'Have you never had a curiosity yourself to pass a night in that house?'

'Yes, I passed not a night, but three hours in broad daylight in that house. My curiosity is not satisfied, but is quenched. I have no desire to renew the experiment. You cannot complain, you see, sir, that I am not sufficiently candid; and unless your interest be exceedingly eager and your nerves unusually strong, I honestly add, that I advise you *not* to pass a night in that house.'

'My interest *is* exceedingly keen,' said I, 'and though only a coward will boast of his nerves in situations wholly unfamiliar to him, yet my nerves have been seasoned in such variety of danger that I have the right to rely on them – even in a haunted house.'

Mr J – said very little more; he took the keys of the house out of his bureau, gave them to me – and, thanking him cordially for his frankness, and his urbane concession to my wish, I carried off my prize.

Impatient for the experiment, as soon as I reached home, I summoned my confidential servant – a young man of gay spirits, fearless temper, and as free from superstitious prejudice as anyone I could think of.

'F – ,' said I, 'you remember in Germany how disappointed we were at not finding a ghost in that old castle, which was said to be haunted by a headless apparition? Well, I have heard of a house in London which, I have reason to hope, is decidedly haunted. I mean to sleep there tonight. From what I hear, there is no doubt that something will allow itself to be seen or to be heard – something, perhaps, excessively horrible. Do you think, if I take you with me, I may rely on your presence of mind, whatever may happen?'

'Oh, sir! pray trust me,' answered F – , grinning with delight.

'Very well; then here are the keys of the house – this is the address. Go now – select for me any bedroom you please; and since the house has not been inhabited for weeks, make up a good fire – air the bed well – see, of course, that there are candles as well as fuel. Take with you my revolver and my dagger – so much for my weapons – arm yourself equally well; and if we are not a match for a dozen ghosts, we shall be but a sorry couple of Englishmen.'

I was engaged for the rest of the day on business so urgent that I had no leisure to think much on the nocturnal adventure to which I had plighted my honour. I dined alone, and very late, and while dining, read, as is my habit. I selected one of the volumes of Macaulay's essays. I thought to myself that I would take the book with me; there was so much of healthfulness in the style, and practical life in the subjects, that it would serve as an antidote against the influences of superstitious fancy.

Accordingly, about half-past nine, I put the book into my pocket, and strolled leisurely towards the haunted house. I took with me a favourite dog – an exceedingly sharp, bold, and vigilant bull-terrier – a dog fond of prowling about strange ghostly corners and passages at night in search of rats – a dog of dogs for a ghost.

It was a summer night, but chilly, the sky somewhat gloomy and overcast. Still there was a moon – faint and sickly, but still a moon – and if the clouds permitted, after midnight it would be brighter.

I reached the house, knocked, and my servant opened with a cheerful smile.

'All right, sir, and very comfortable.'

'Oh!' said I, rather disappointed; 'have you not seen or heard anything remarkable?'

'Well, sir, I must own I have heard something queer.'

'What? – what?'

'The sound of feet pattering behind me; and once or twice small noises like whispers close at my ear – nothing more.'

'You are not at all frightened?'

'I! not a bit of it, sir,' and the man's bold look reassured me on one point – viz., that happen what might, he would not desert me.

We were in the hall, the street-door closed, and my attention was now drawn to my dog. He had at first run in eagerly enough, but had sneaked back to the door, and was scratching and whining to get out. After patting him on the head, and encouraging him gently, the dog seemed to reconcile himself to the situation, and followed me and F – through the house, but keeping close at my heels instead of hurrying inquisitively in advance, which was his usual and normal habit in all strange places. We first visited the subterranean apartments, the kitchen and other offices, and especially the cellars, in which last there were two or three bottles of wine still left in the bin, covered with cobwebs, and evidently, by their appearance, undisturbed for many years. It was clear that the ghosts were not wine-bibbers. For the rest we discovered nothing of interest. There was a gloomy little backyard, with very high walls. The stones of this yard were very damp; and what with the damp, and what with the dust and smoke-grime on the pavement, our feet left a slight impression where we passed. And now appeared the first strange phenomenon witnessed by myself in this strange abode. I saw, just before me, the print of a foot suddenly form itself, as it were. I stopped, caught hold of my servant, and pointed to it. In advance of that footprint as suddenly dropped another. We both saw it. I advanced quickly to the place; the footprints kept advancing before me, a small footprint – the foot of a child: the impression was too faint thoroughly to distinguish the shape, but it seemed to us both that it was the print of a naked foot. This phenomenon ceased when we arrived at the opposite wall, nor did it repeat itself on returning. We remounted the stairs, and entered the rooms on the ground floor, a dining parlour, a small back-parlour, and a still smaller third room that had been probably appropriated to a footman – all still as death. We then visited the drawing-rooms, which seemed fresh and new. In the front room I seated myself in an arm- chair. F – placed on the table the candle-stick with which he had lighted us. I told him to shut the door. As he turned to do so, a chair opposite to me moved from the wall quickly and noiselessly, and dropped itself about a yard from my own chair, immediately fronting it.

'Why, this is better than the turning tables,' said I, with a half-laugh; and as I laughed, my dog put back his head and howled.

F – , coming back, had not observed the movement of the chair. He employed himself now in stilling the dog. I continued to gaze on the chair, and fancied I saw on it a pale blue misty outline of a human figure, but an outline so indistinct that I could only distrust my own vision. The dog was now quiet.

'Put back that chair opposite to me,' said I to F – ; 'put it back to the wall.'

F – obeyed. 'Was that you, sir,' said he, turning abruptly.

'I! – what?'

'Why, something struck me. I felt it sharply on the shoulder – just here.'

'No,' said I. 'But we have jugglers present, and though we may not discover their tricks, we shall catch *them* before they frighten *us*.'

We did not stay long in the drawing-rooms – in fact, they felt so damp and so chilly that I was glad to get to the fire upstairs. We locked the doors of the drawing-rooms – a precaution which, I should observe, we had taken with all the rooms we had searched below. The bedroom my servant had selected for me was the best on the floor – a large one, with two windows fronting the street. The four-posted bed, which took up no inconsiderable space, was opposite to the fire, which burnt clear and bright; a door in the wall to the left, between the bed and the window, communicated with the room which my servant appropriated to himself. This last was a small room with a sofa-bed, and had no communication with the landing-place – no other door but that which conducted to the bedroom I was to occupy. On either side of my fireplace was a cupboard, without locks, flush with the wall, and covered with the same dull-brown paper. We examined these cupboards – only hooks to suspend female dresses – nothing else; we sounded the walls – evidently solid – the outer walls of the building. Having finished the survey of these apartments, warmed myself a few moments, and lighted my cigar, I then, still accompanied by F – , went forth to complete my reconnoitre. In the landing-place there was another door; it was closed firmly. 'Sir,' said my servant, in surprise, 'I unlocked this door with all the others when I first came; it cannot have got locked from the inside, for – '

Before he had finished his sentence, the door, which neither of us then was touching, opened quietly of itself. We looked at each other a single instant. The same thought seized both – some human agency might be detected here. I rushed in first, my servant followed. A small, blank, dreary room without furniture – a few empty boxes and hampers in a corner – a small window – the shutters closed – not even a fireplace – no other door but that by which we had entered – no carpet on the floor, and the floor seemed very old, uneven, worm-eaten, mended here and there, as was shown by the whiter patches on the woods; but no living being, and no visible place in which a living being could have hidden. As we stood gazing round, the door by which we had entered closed as quietly as it had before opened: we were imprisoned.

For the first time I felt a creep of undefinable horror. Not so my servant. 'Why, they don't think to trap us, sir; I could break that trumpery door with a kick of my foot.'

'Try first if it will open to your hand,' said I, shaking off the vague apprehension that had seized me, 'while I unclose the shutters and see what is without.'

I unbarred the shutters – the window looked on the little backyard I have before described; there was no ledge without – nothing to break the sheer descent of the wall. No man getting out of that window would have found any footing till he had fallen on the stones below.

F – , meanwhile, was vainly attempting to open the door. He now turned round to me and asked my permission to use force. And I should here state, in justice to the servant, that, far from evincing any superstitious terrors, his nerve, composure, and even gaiety amidst circumstances so extraordinary, compelled my admiration, and made me congratulate myself on having secured a companion in every way fitted to the occasion. I willingly gave him the permission he required. But though he was a remarkably strong man, his force was as idle as his milder efforts; the door did not even shake to his stoutest kick. Breathless and panting, he desisted. I then tried the door myself, equally in vain. As I ceased from the effort, again that creep of horror came over me; but this time it was more cold and stubborn. I felt as if some strange and ghastly exhalation were rising up from the chinks of that rugged floor, and filling the atmosphere with a venomous influence hostile to human life. The door now very slowly and quietly opened as of its own accord. We precipitated ourselves into the landing-place. We both saw a large pale light – as large as the human figure, but shapeless and unsubstantial – move before us, and ascend the stairs that led from the landing into the attics. I followed the light, and my servant followed me. It entered to the right of the landing a small garret, of which the door stood open. I entered in the same instant. The light then collapsed into a small globule, exceedingly brilliant and vivid: rested a moment on a bed in the corner, quivered, and vanished. We approached the bed and examined it – a half-tester, such as is commonly found in attics devoted to servants. On the drawers that stood near it we perceived an old faded silk kerchief, with the needle still left in a rent half repaired. The kerchief was covered with dust; probably it had belonged to the old woman who had last died in that house, and this might have been her sleeping-room. I had sufficient curiosity to open the drawers: there were a few odds and ends of female dress, and two letters tied round with a narrow ribbon of faded yellow. I took the liberty to possess myself of the letters. We found nothing else in the room worth noticing – nor did the light reappear; but we distinctly heard, as we turned to go, a pattering footfall on the floor – just before us. We went through the other attics (in all four), the footfall still preceding us. Nothing to be seen – nothing but the footfall heard. I had the letters in my hand: just as I was descending the stairs I distinctly felt my wrist seized, and a faint soft effort made to draw the letters from my clasp. I only held them the more tightly, and the effort ceased.

We regained the bed-chamber appropriated to myself, and I then remarked that my dog had not followed us when we had left it. He was thrusting himself close to the fire, and trembling. I was impatient to examine the letters; and while I read them, my servant opened a little box in which he had deposited the weapons I had ordered him to bring; took them out, placed them on a table close at my bed-head, and then occupied himself in soothing the dog, who, however, seemed to heed him very little.

The letters were short – they were dated; the dates exactly thirty-five years ago. They were evidently from a lover to his mistress, or a husband to some young wife.

Not only the terms of expression, but a distinct reference to a former voyage, indicated the writer to have been a seafarer. The spelling and hand-writing were those of a man imperfectly educated, but still the language itself was forcible. In the expressions of endearment there was a kind of rough, wild love; but here and there were dark, unintelligible hints at some secret not of love – some secret that seemed of crime. 'We ought to love each other,' was one of the sentences I remember, 'for how everyone else would execrate us if all was known.' Again: 'Don't let anyone be in the same room with you at night – you talk in your sleep.' And again: 'What's done can't be undone; and I tell you there's nothing against us unless the dead could come to life.' Here there was underlined in a better handwriting (a female's), 'They do!' At the end of the letter latest in date the same female hand had written these words: 'Lost at sea the 4th of June, the same day as – .'

I put down the letters, and began to muse over their contents. Fearing, however that the train of thought into which I fell might unsteady my nerves, I fully determined to keep my mind in a fit state to cope with whatever of the Marvellous the advancing night might bring forth. I roused myself – laid the letters on the table – stirred up the fire, which was still bright and cheering, and opened my volume of Macaulay. I read quietly enough till about half past eleven. I then threw myself dressed upon the bed, and told my servant he might retire to his own room, but must keep himself awake. I bade him leave open the door between the two rooms. Thus alone, I kept two candles burning on the table by my bed-head. I placed my watch beside the weapons, and calmly resumed my Macaulay. Opposite to me the fire burned clear; and on the hearth-rug, seemingly asleep, lay the dog. In about twenty minutes I felt an exceedingly cold air pass my cheek, like a sudden draught. I fancied the door to my right, communicating with the landing-place, must have got open; but no – it was closed. I then turned my glance to my left, and saw the flame of the candles violently swayed as by a wind. At the same moment the watch beside the revolver softly slid from the table – softly, softly – no visible hand – it was gone. I sprang up, seizing the revolver with the one hand, the dagger with the other: I was not willing that my weapons should share the fate of the watch. Thus armed, I looked round the floor – no sign of the watch. Three slow, loud, distinct knocks were now heard at the bed-head; my servant called out, 'Is that you, sir?'

'No; be on your guard.'

The dog now roused himself and sat on his haunches, his ears moving quickly backwards and forwards. He kept his eyes fixed on me with a look so strange that he concentrated all my attention on himself. Slowly, he rose up, all his hair bristling, and stood perfectly rigid, and with the same wild stare. I had no time, however, to examine the dog. Presently my servant emerged from his room; and if ever I saw horror in the human face, it was then.

I should not have recognized him had we met in the street, so altered was every lineament. He passed by me quickly, saying in a whisper that seemed scarcely to come from his lips, 'Run-run! it is after me!' He gained the door to the landing, pulled it open, and rushed forth. I followed him into the landing involuntarily, calling him to stop; but, without heeding me, he bounded down the stairs, clinging to the balusters, and taking several steps at a time. I heard, where I stood, the street door open – heard it again clap to. I was left alone in the haunted house.

It was but for a moment that I remained undecided whether or not to follow my servant; pride and curiosity alike forbade so dastardly a flight. I re-entered my room, closing the door after me, and proceeded cautiously into the interior chamber. I encountered nothing to justify my servant's terror. I again carefully examined the walls, to see if there were any concealed door. I could find no trace of one – not even a seam in the dull-brown paper with which the room was hung. How, then, had the THING, whatever it was, which had so scared him, obtained ingress except through my own chamber? I returned to my room, shut and locked the door that opened upon the interior one, and stood on the hearth, expectant and prepared. I now perceived that the dog had slunk into an angle of the wall, and was pressing himself close against it, as if literally striving to force his way into it. I approached the animal and spoke to it; the poor brute was evidently beside itself with terror. It showed all its teeth, the slaver dropped from its jaws, and would certainly have bitten me if I had touched it. It did not seem to recognize me. Whoever has seen at the Zoological Gardens a rabbit, fascinated by a serpent, cowering in a corner, may form some idea of the anguish which the dog exhibited. Finding all efforts to soothe the animal in vain, and fearing that his bite might be as venomous in that state as in the madness of a hydrophobia, I left him alone, placed my weapons on the table beside the fire, seated myself, and recommenced my Macaulay.

Perhaps, in order not to appear seeking credit for a courage, or rather a coolness which the reader may conceive I exaggerate, I may be pardoned if I pause to indulge in one or two egotistical remarks.

As I hold presence of mind, or what is called courage, to be precisely proportioned to familiarity with the circumstances that lead to it, so I should say that I had been long sufficiently familiar with all experiments that appertain to the Marvellous. I had witnessed many very extraordinary phenomena in various parts of the world – phenomena that would be either totally disbelieved if I stated them, or ascribed to supernatural agencies. Now, my theory is that the Supernatural is the Impossible, and that what is called supernatural is only a something in the laws of nature of which we have been hitherto ignorant. Therefore, if a ghost rises before me, I have not the right to say, 'So, then, the supernatural is possible', but rather, 'So, then, the apparition of a ghost is, contrary to received opinion, within the laws of nature – i.e., not supernatural'.

Now, in all that I hitherto witnessed, and indeed in all the wonders which the amateurs of mystery in our age record as facts, a material living agency is always required. On the Continent you will find still magicians who assert that they can raise spirits. Assume for the moment that they assert truly, still the living material form of the magician is present; and he is the material agency by which, from some constitutional peculiarities, certain strange phenomena are represented to your natural senses.

Accept, again, as truthful, the tales of Spirit Manifestation in America – musical or other sounds – writings on paper, produced by no discernible hand – articles of furniture moved without apparent human agency – or the actual sight and touch of hands, to which no bodies seem to belong – still there must be found the MEDIUM of living being, with constitutional peculiarities capable of obtaining these signs. In fine, in all such marvels, supposing even that there is no imposture, there must be a human being like ourselves by whom, or through whom, the effects presented to human beings are produced. It is so with the now familiar phenomena of mesmerism or electro-biology; the mind of the person operated on is affected through a material living agent. Nor, supposing it true that a mesmerized patient can respond to the will or passes of a mesmerizer a hundred miles distant, is the response less occasioned by a material being; it may be through a material fluid – call it Electric, call it Odic, call it what you will – which has the power of traversing space and passing obstacles, that the material effect is communicated from one to the other. Hence all that I had hitherto witnessed, or expected to witness, in this strange house, I believed to be occasioned through some agency or medium as mortal as myself; and this idea necessarily prevented the awe with which those who regard as supernatural things that are not within the ordinary operations of nature, might have been impressed by the adventures of that memorable night.

As, then, it was my conjecture that all that was presented, or would be presented to my senses, must originate in some human being gifted by constitution with the power so to present them, and having some motive so to do, I felt an interest in my theory which, in its way, was rather philosophical than superstitious. And I can sincerely say that I was in as tranquil a temper for observation as any practical experimentalist could be in awaiting the effects of some rare, though perhaps perilous, chemical combination. Of course, the more I kept my mind detached from fancy, the more the temper fitted for observation would be obtained; and I therefore riveted eye and thought on the strong daylight sense in the page of my Macaulay.

I now became aware that something interposed between the page and the light – the page was overshadowed: I looked up, and I saw what I shall find it very difficult, perhaps impossible, to describe.

It was Darkness shaping itself forth from the air in very undefined outline. I cannot say it was of a human form, and yet it had more resemblance to a human form, or rather shadow, than to anything else. As it stood, wholly apart and distinct from the air and the light around it, its dimensions seemed gigantic, the summit nearly touching the ceiling. While I gazed, a feeling of intense cold seized me. An iceberg before me could not more have chilled me; nor could the cold of an iceberg have been more purely physical. I feel convinced that it was not the cold caused by fear. As I continued to gaze, I thought – but this I cannot say with precision – that I distinguished two eyes looking down on me from the height. One moment I fancied that I distinguished them clearly, the next they seemed gone; but still two rays of a pale-blue light frequently shot through the darkness, as from the height on which I half believed half doubted, that I had encountered the eyes.

I strove to speak – my voice utterly failed me; I could only think to myself, 'Is this fear? it is *not* fear!' I strove to rise – in vain; I felt as if weighed down by an irresistible force. Indeed, my impression was that of an immense and overwhelming Power opposed to my volition; that sense of utter inadequacy to cope with a force beyond men's, which one may feel *physically* in a storm at sea, in a conflagration, or when confronting some terrible wild beast, or rather, perhaps, the shark of the ocean, I felt *morally*. Opposed to my will was another will, as far superior to its strength as storm, fire, and shark are superior in material force to the force of man.

And now, as this impression grew on me – now came, at last, horror – horror to a degree that no words can convey. Still I retained pride, if not courage; and in my own mind I said: 'This is horror, but it is not fear; unless I fear I cannot be harmed; my reason rejects this thing; it is an illusion – I do not fear.' With a violent effort I succeeded at last in stretching out my hand towards the weapon on the table: as I did so, on the arm and shoulder I received a strange shock, and my arm fell to my side powerless. And now, to add to my horror, the light began slowly to wane from the candles – they were not, as it were, extinguished, but their flame seemed very gradually withdrawn: it was the same with the fire – the light extracted from the fuel; in a few minutes the room was in utter darkness. The dread that came over me, to be thus in the dark with that dark Thing, whose power was so intensely felt, brought a reaction of nerve. In fact, terror had reached that climax, that either my senses must have deserted me, or I must have burst through the spell. I did burst through it. I found voice, though the voice was a shriek. I remember that I broke forth with words like these: 'I do not fear, my soul does not fear'; and at the same time I found strength to rise. Still in that profound gloom I rushed to one of the windows – tore aside the curtain – flung open the shutters; my first thought was – LIGHT. And when I saw the moon high, clear, and calm, I felt a joy that almost compensated for the previous terror. There was the moon, there was also the light from the gas-lamps in the deserted slumberous street. I turned to look back into the room; the moon penetrated its shadow very palely and partially – but still there was light. The dark Thing, whatever it might be, was gone – except that I could yet see a dim shadow, which seemed the shadow of that shade, against the opposite wall.

My eye now rested on the table, and from under the table (which was without cloth or cover – an old mahogany round table) there rose a Hand, visible as far as the wrist. It was a hand, seemingly, as much of flesh and blood as my own, but the hand of an aged person – lean, wrinkled, small too – a woman's hand. That hand very softly closed on the two letters that lay on the table: hand and letters both vanished. There then came the same three loud measured knocks I had heard at the bed-head before this extraordinary drama had commenced.

As those sounds slowly ceased, I felt the whole room vibrate sensibly; and at the far end there rose, as from the floor, sparks or globules like bubbles of light, many-coloured – green, yellow, fire-red, azure. Up and down, to and fro, hither, as tiny will-o'-the-wisps, the sparks moved, slow or swift, each at its own caprice. A chair (as in the drawing-room below) was now advanced from the wall without apparent agency, and placed at the opposite side of the table. Suddenly, as forth from the chair, there grew a shape – a woman's shape. It was distinct as a shape of life – ghastly as a shape of death. The face was that of youth, with a strange mournful beauty; the throat and shoulders were bare, the rest of the form in a loose robe of cloudy white. It began sleeking its long yellow hair, which fell over its shoulders; its eyes were not turned towards me, but to the door; it seemed listening, watching, waiting. The shadow of the shade in the background grew darker; and again I thought I beheld the eyes gleaming out from the summit of the shadow – eyes fixed upon that shape.

As if from the door, as though it did not open, there grew out another shape, equally distinct, equally ghastly – a man's shape – a young man's. It was in the dress of the last century, or rather in a likeness of such dress (for both the male shape and the female, though defined, were evidently unsubstantial, impalpable – simulacra – phantasms); and there was something incongruous, grotesque, yet fearful, in the contrast between the elaborate finery, the courtly precision of that old-fashioned garb, with its ruffles and lace and buckles, and the corpse-like aspect and ghost-like stillness of the flitting wearer. Just as the male shape approached the female, the dark Shadow started from the wall, all three for a moment wrapped in darkness. When the pale light returned, the two phantoms were as if in the grasp of the Shadow that towered between them; and there was a blood-stain on the breast of the female; and the phantom male was leaning on its phantom sword, and blood seemed trickling fast from the ruffles, from the lace; and the darkness of the intermediate Shadow swallowed them up – they were gone. And again the bubbles of light shot, and sailed, and undulated, growing thicker and thicker and more wildly confused in their movements.

The closet door to the right of the fireplace now opened, and from the aperture there came the form of an aged woman. In her hand she held letters – the very letters over which I had seen *the* Hand close; and behind her I heard a footstep. She turned round as if to listen, and then she opened the letters and seemed to read; and over her shoulder I saw a livid face, the face as of a man long drowned – bloated, bleached – seaweed tangled in its dripping hair; and at her feet lay a form as of a corpse, and beside the corpse there cowered a child, a miserable squalid child, with famine in its cheeks and fear in its eyes. And as I looked in the old woman's face, the wrinkles and lines vanished, and it became a face of youth – hard-eyed, stony, but still youth; and the Shadow darted forth, and darkened over those phantoms as it had darkened over the last.

Nothing now was left but the Shadow, and on that my eyes were intently fixed, till again eyes grew out of the Shadow – malignant, serpent eyes. And the bubbles of light again rose and fell, and in their disordered, irregular, turbulent maze, mingled with the wan moonlight. And now from these globules themselves, as from the shell of an egg, monstrous things burst out; the air grew filled with them; larvae so bloodless and so hideous that I can in no way describe them except to remind the reader of the swarming life which a solar microscope brings before his eyes in a drop of water – things transparent, supple, agile, chasing each other, devouring each other – forms like nought ever beheld by the naked eye. As the shapes were without symmetry, so their movements were without order. In their very vagrancies there was no sport; they came round me and round, thicker and faster and swifter, swarming over my head, crawling over my right arm, which was outstretched in involuntary command against all evil beings. Sometimes I felt myself touched, but not by them; invisible hands touched me. Once I felt the clutch as of cold, soft fingers at my throat. I was still equally conscious that if I gave way to fear I should be in bodily peril; and I concentrated all my faculties in the single focus of resisting, stubborn will. And I turned my sight from the Shadow – above all, from those strange serpent eyes – eyes that had now become distinctly visible. For there, though in nought else around me, I was aware that there was a Will, and a will of intense, creative, working evil, which might crush down my own.

The pale atmosphere in the room began now to redden as if in the air of some near conflagration. The larvae grew lurid as things that live in fire. Again the room vibrated; again were heard the three measured knocks; and again all things were swallowed up in the darkness of the dark Shadow, as if out of that darkness all had come, into that darkness all returned.

As the gloom receded, the Shadow was wholly gone. Slowly, as it had been withdrawn, the flame grew again into the candles on the table, again into the fuel in the grate. The whole room came once more calmly, healthfully into sight.

The two doors were still closed, the door communicating with the servant's room still locked. In the corner of the wall, into which he had so convulsively niched himself, lay the dog. I called to him – no movement; I approached – the animal was dead; his eyes protruded; his tongue out of his mouth; the froth gathered round his jaws. I took him in my arms; I brought him to the fire; I felt acute grief for the loss of my poor favourite – acute self-reproach; I accused myself of his death; I imagined he had died of fright. But what was my surprise on finding that his neck was actually broken. Had this been done in the dark? – must it not have been by a hand human as mine? – must there not have been a human agency all the while in that room? Good cause to suspect it. I cannot tell. I cannot do more than state the fact fairly; the reader may draw his own inference.

Another surprising circumstance – my watch was restored to the table from which it had been so mysteriously withdrawn; but it had stopped at the very moment it was so withdrawn; nor, despite all the skill of the watchmaker, has it ever gone since – that is, it will go in a strange erratic way for a few hours, and then come to a dead stop – it is worthless.

Nothing more chanced for the rest of the night. Nor, indeed, had I long to wait before the dawn broke. Nor till it was broad daylight did I quit the haunted house. Before I did so, I revisited the little blind room in which my servant and myself had been for a time imprisoned. I had a strong impression – for which I could not account – that from that room had originated the mechanism of the phenomena – if I may use the term – which had been experienced in my chamber. And though I entered it now in the clear day, with the sun peering through the filmy window, I still felt, as I stood on its floors, the creep of the horror which I had first there experienced the night before, and which had been so aggravated by what had passed in my own chamber. I could not, indeed, bear to stay more than half a minute within those walls. I descended the stairs, and again I heard the footfall before me; and when I opened the street door, I thought I could distinguish a very low laugh. I gained my own home, expecting to find my runaway servant there. But he had not presented himself, nor did I hear more of him for three days, when I received a letter from him, dated from Liverpool, to this effect:

Honoured Sir:

I humbly entreat your pardon, though I can scarcely hope that you will think that I deserve it, unless – which Heaven forbid! – you saw what I did. I feel it will be years before I can recover myself; and as to being fit for service, it is out of the question. I am therefore going to my brother-in-law at Melbourne. The ship sails tomorrow. Perhaps the long voyage may set me up. I do nothing now but start and tremble, and fancy IT is behind me. I humbly beg you, honoured sir, to order my clothes, and whatever wages are due to me, to be sent to my mother's, at Walworth – John knows her address.

The letter ended with additional apologies, somewhat incoherent, and explanatory details as to effect that had been under the writer's charge.

This flight may perhaps warrant a suspicion that the man wished to go to Australia, and had been somehow or other fraudulently mixed up with the events of the night. I say nothing in refutation of that conjecture; rather, I suggest it as one that would seem to many persons the most probable solution of improbable occurrences. My belief in my own theory remained unshaken. I returned in the evening to the house, to bring away in a hack cab the things I had left there, with my poor dog's body. In this task I was not disturbed, nor did any incident worth note befall me, except that still, on ascending and descending the stairs, I heard the same footfall in advance. On leaving the house, I went to Mr J – 's. He was at home. I returned him the keys, told him that my curiosity was sufficiently gratified, and was about to relate quickly what had passed, when he stopped me, and said, though with much politeness, that he had no longer any interest in a mystery which none had ever solved.

I determined at least to tell him of the two letters I had read, as well as of the extraordinary manner in which they had disappeared, and I then inquired if he thought they had been addressed to the woman who had died in the house, and if there were anything in her early history which could possibly confirm the dark suspicions to which the letters gave rise. Mr J – seemed startled, and, after musing a few moments, answered: 'I am but little acquainted with the woman's earlier history, except, as I before told you, that her family were known to mine. But you revive some vague reminiscences to her prejudice. I will make inquiries, and inform you of their result. Still, even if we could admit the popular superstition that a person who had been either the perpetrator or the victim of dark crimes in life could revisit, as a restless spirit, the scene in which those crimes had been committed, I should observe that the house was infested by strange sights and sounds before the old woman died – you smile – what would you say?'

'I would say this, that I am convinced, if we could get to the bottom of these mysteries, we should find a living human agency.'

'What! you believe it is all an imposture? for what object?'

'Not an imposture in the ordinary sense of the word. If suddenly I were to sink into a deep sleep, from which you could not awake me, but in that sleep could answer questions with an accuracy which I could not pretend to when awake – tell you what money you had in your pocket – nay, describe your very thoughts – it is not necessarily an imposture, any more than it is necessarily supernatural. I should be, unconsciously to myself, under a mesmeric influence, conveyed to me from a distance by a human being who had acquired power over me by previous *rapport*.'

'But if a mesmerizer could so affect another living being, can you suppose that a mesmerizer could also affect inanimate objects: move chairs – open and shut doors?'

'Or impress our senses with the belief in such effects – we never having been *en rapport* with the person acting on us? No. What is commonly called mesmerism could not do this; but there may be a power akin to mesmerism and superior to it – the power that in the old days was called Magic. That such a power may extend to all inanimate objects of matter, I do not say; but if so, it would not be against nature – it would only be a rare power in nature which might be given to constitutions with certain peculiarities, and cultivated by practise to an extraordinary degree. That such a power might extend over the dead – that is, over certain thoughts and memories that the dead may still retain – and compel, not that which ought properly to be called the SOUL, and which is far beyond human reach, but rather a phantom of what has been most earth-stained on earth to make itself apparent to our senses – is a very ancient though obsolete theory, upon which I will hazard no opinion. But I do not conceive the power would be supernatural. Let me illustrate what I mean from an experiment which Paracelsus describes as not difficult, and which the author of the *Curiosities of Literature* cites as credible: A flower perishes; you burn it. Whatever were the elements of that flower while it lived are gone, dispersed, you know not whither; you can never discover nor re-collect them. But you can, by chemistry, out of the burnt dust of that flower, raise a spectrum of the flower, just as it seemed in life. It may be the same with the human being. The soul has as much escaped you as the essence or elements of the flower. Still you may make a spectrum of it. And this phantom, through the popular superstition it is held to be the soul of the departed, must not be confounded with the true soul; it is but the eidolon of the dead form. Hence, like the best attested stories of ghosts or spirits, the thing that most strikes us is the absence of what we hold to be the soul; that is, of superior emancipation intelligence. These apparitions come for little or no object – they seldom speak when they do come; if they speak, they utter no ideas above those of an ordinary person on earth, they utter no ideas above those of an ordinary person on earth. American spirit-seers have published volumes of communications, in prose and verse, which they assert to be given in the names of the most illustrious dead – Shakespeare, Bacon – Heaven knows whom. Those communications, taking the best, are certainly not a whit of higher order than would be communications from living persons of fair talent and education; they are wondrously inferior to what Bacon, Shakespeare, and Plato said and wrote when on earth. Nor, what is more noticeable, do they ever contain an idea that was not on earth before. Wonderful, therefore, as such phenomena may be (granting them to be truthful), I see much that philosophy may question, nothing that it is incumbent on philosophy to deny – viz., nothing supernatural. They are but ideas conveyed somehow or other (we have not yet discovered the means) from one mortal brain to another. Whether, in so doing, tables walk of their own accord, or fiend-like shapes appear in a magic circle, or bodyless hands rise and remove material objects, or a Thing of Darkness, such as presented itself to me, freeze our blood – still am I persuaded that these are but agencies conveyed, as by electric wires, to my own brain from the brain of another. In some constitutions there is a natural chemistry, and those constitutions may produce chemic wonders – in others a natural fluid, call it electricity, and these may produce electric wonders. But the wonders differ from Normal Science in this – they are alike objectless, purposeless, puerile, frivolous. They lead on to no grand results, and therefore the world does not heed, and true sages have not cultivated them. But sure I am, that of all I saw or heard, a man, human as myself, was the remote originator; and I believe unconsciously to himself as to the exact effects produced, for this reason: no two persons, you say, have ever told you that they experienced exactly the same thing. Well, observe, no two persons ever experienced exactly the same dream. If this were an ordinary imposture, the machinery would be arranged for results that would but little vary; if it were a super-natural agency permitted by the Almighty, it would surely be for some definite end. These phenomena belong to neither class; my persuasion is that they originate in some brain now far distant; that that brain had no distinct volition in anything that occurred; that what does occur reflects but its devious, motley, ever-shifting, half-formed thoughts; in short, that it has been but the dreams of such a brain put into action and invested with a semi-substance. That this brain is of immense power, that it can set matter into movement, that it is malignant and destructive, I believe; some material force must have killed my dog; the same force might, for aught I know, have sufficed to kill myself, had I been as subjugated by terror as the dog – had my intellect or my spirit given me no countervailing resistance in my will.'

'It killed your dog! that is fearful! indeed it is strange that no animal can be induced to stay in that house; not even a cat. Rats and mice are never found in it.'

'The instincts of the brute creation detect influences deadly to their existence. Man's reason has a sense less subtle, because it has a resisting power more supreme. But enough; do you comprehend my theory?'

'Yes, though imperfectly – and I accept any crotchet (pardon the word), however odd, rather than embrace at once the notion of ghosts and hobgoblins we imbibed in our nurseries. Still, to my unfortunate house the evil is the same. What on earth can I do with the house?'

'I will tell you what I would do. I am convinced from my own internal feelings that the small unfurnished room at right angles to the door of the bedroom which I occupied forms a starting-point or receptacle for the influences which haunt the house; and I strongly advise you to have the walls opened, the floor removed – nay, the whole room pulled down. I observe that it is detached from the body of the house, built over the small back-yard, and could be removed without injury to the rest of the building.'

'And you think, if I did that – '

'You would cut off the telegraph wires. Try it. I am so persuaded that I am right, that I will pay half the expense if you will allow me to direct the operations.'

'Nay, I am well able to afford the cost; for the rest, allow me to write to you.'

About ten days after, I received a letter from Mr J – , telling me that he had visited the house since I had seen him; that he had found the two letters I had described, replaced in the drawer from which I had taken them; that he had read them with misgivings like my own; that he had instituted a cautious inquiry about the woman to whom I rigidly conjectured they had been written. It seemed that thirty-six years ago (a year before the date of the letters) she had married, against the wish of her relations, an American of very suspicious character; in fact, he was generally believed to have been a pirate. She herself was the daughter of very respectable tradespeople, and had served in the capacity of a nursery governess before her marriage. She had a brother, a widower, who was considered wealthy, and who had one child of about six years old. A month after the marriage, the body of this brother was found in the Thames, near London Bridge; there seemed some marks of violence about his throat, but they were not deemed sufficient to warrant the inquest in any other verdict than that of 'found drowned'.

The American and his wife took charge of the little boy, the deceased brother having by his will left his sister the guardian of his only child – and in the event of the child's death, the sister inherited. The child died about six months afterwards – it was supposed to have been neglected and ill-treated. The neighbours deposed to have heard it shriek at night. The surgeon who had examined it after death said that it was emaciated as if from want of nourishment, and the body was covered with livid bruises. It seemed that one winter night the child had sought to escape – crept out into the backyard – tried to scale the wall – fallen back exhausted, and been found at morning on the stones in a dying state. But though there was some evidence of cruelty, there was none of murder; and the aunt and her husband had sought to palliate cruelty by alleging the exceeding stubbornness and perversity of the child, who was declared to be half-witted. Be that as it may, at the orphan's death the aunt inherited her brother's fortune. Before the first wedded year was out, the American quitted England abruptly, and never returned to it. He obtained a cruising vessel, which was lost in the Atlantic two years afterwards. The widow was left in affluence: but reverses of various kinds had befallen her: a bank broke – an investment failed – she went into a small business and became insolvent – then she entered into service, sinking lower and lower, from housekeeper down to maid-of-all-work – never long retaining a place, though nothing decided against her character was ever alleged. She was considered sober, honest, and peculiarly quiet in her ways; still nothing prospered with her. And so she had dropped into the workhouse, from which Mr J – had taken her, to be placed in charge of the very house which she had rented as mistress in the first year of her wedded life.

Mr J – added that he had passed an hour alone in the unfurnished room which I had urged him to destroy, and that his impressions of dread while there were so great, though he had neither heard nor seen anything, that he was eager to have the walls bared and the floors removed as I had suggested. He had engaged persons for the work, and would commence any day I would name.

The day was accordingly fixed. I repaired to the haunted house – we went into the blind, dreary room, took up the skirting, and then the floors. Under the rafters, covered with rubbish, was found a trap-door, quite large enough to admit a man. It was closely nailed down, with clamps and rivets of iron. On removing these we descended into a room below, the existence of which has never been suspected. In this room there had been a window and a flue, but they had been bricked over, evidently for many years. By the help of candles we examined this place; it still retained some mouldering furniture – three chairs, an oak settle, a table – all of the fashion of about eighty years ago. There was a chest of drawers against the wall, in which we found, half-rotted away, old-fashioned articles of a man's dress, such as might have been worn eighty or a hundred years ago by a gentleman of some rank – costly steel buckles and buttons, like those yet worn in court dresses, a handsome court sword. In a waistcoat which had once been rich with gold lace, but which was now blackened and foul with damp, we found five guineas, a few silver coins, and an ivory ticket, probably for some place of entertainment long since passed away. But our main discovery was in a kind of iron safe fixed to the wall, the lock of which it cost us much trouble to get picked.

In this safe were three shelves, and two small drawers. Ranged on the shelves were several small bottles of crystal, hermetically stopped. They contained colourless volatile essences, of the nature of which I shall only say that they were not poisons – phosphor and ammonia entered into some of them. There were also some very curious glass tubes, and a small pointed rod of iron, with a large lump of rock-crystal, and another of amber – also a loadstone of great power.

In one of the drawers we found a miniature portrait set in gold, and retaining the freshness of its colours most remarkably, considering the length of time it had probably been there. The portrait was that of a man who might be somewhat advanced in middle life, perhaps forty-seven or forty-eight.

It was a remarkable face – a most impressive face. If you could fancy some mighty serpent transformed into man, preserving in the human lineaments the old servant type, you would have a better idea of that countenance than long descriptions can convey: the width and flatness of frontal – the tapering elegance of contour disguising the strength of the deadly jaw – the long, large, terrible eye, glittering and green as the emerald – and withal a certain ruthless calm, as if from the consciousness of an immense power.

Mechanically I turned round the miniature to examine the back of it, and on the back was engraved a pentacle; in the middle of the pentacle a ladder, and the third step of the ladder was formed by the date 1765. Examining still more minutely, I detected a spring; this, on being pressed, opened the back of the miniature as a lid. Withinside the lid was engraved 'Marianna to thee – Be faithful in life and in death to – .' Here follows a name that I will not mention, but it was not unfamiliar to me. I had heard it spoken of by old men in my childhood as the name borne by a dazzling charlatan who had made a great sensation in London for a year or so, and had fled the country on the charge of a double murder within his own house – that of his mistress and his rival. I said nothing of this to Mr J – , to whom reluctantly I resigned the miniature.

We had found no difficulty in opening the first drawer within the iron safe; we found great difficulty in opening the second: it was not locked, but it resisted all efforts, till we inserted in the chinks the edge of a chisel. When we had thus drawn it forth, we found a very singular apparatus in the nicest order. Upon a small thin book, or rather tablet, was placed a saucer of crystal; this saucer was filled with a clear liquid – on that liquid floated a kind of compass, with a needle shifting rapidly round; but instead of the usual points of a compass were seven strange characters, not very unlike those used by astrologers to denote the planets. A peculiar, but not strong nor displeasing odour, came from this drawer, which was lined with a wood that we afterwards discovered to be hazel. Whatever the cause of this odour, it produced a material effect on the nerves. We all felt it, even the two workmen who were in the room – a creeping tingling sensation from the tips of the fingers to the roots of the hair. Impatient to examine the tablet, I removed the saucer. As I did so the needle of the compass went round and round with exceeding swiftness, and I felt a shock that ran through my whole frame, so that I dropped the saucer on the floor. The liquid was spilt – the saucer was broken – the compass rolled to the end of the room – and at that instant the walls shook to and fro, as if a giant had swayed and rocked them.

The two workmen were so frightened that they ran up the ladder by which we had descended from the trap-door; but seeing that nothing more happened, they were easily induced to return.

Meanwhile I had opened the tablet: it was bound in plain red leather, with a silver clasp; it contained but one sheet of thick vellum, and on that sheet were inscribed, within a double pentacle, words in old monkish Latin, which are literally to be translated thus: 'On all that it can reach within these walls – sentient or inanimate, living or dead – as moves the needle, so work my will! Accursed be the house, and restless be the dwellers therein.'

We found no more. Mr J – burnt the tablet and its anathema. He razed to the foundations the part of the building containing the secret room with the chamber over it. He had then the courage to inhabit the house himself for a month, and a quieter, better-conditioned house could not be found in all London. Subsequently he let it to advantage, and his tenant has made no complaints.

The 'Ouanga' Charm

W. B. Seabrook

'Go bring me a humming bird,' said Maman Célie, 'and we'll see what can be done.'

She was talking to her tall grandson, Paul, Emanuel's boy, who had been moping about the habitation for days because a young, high-breasted black damsel down by the spring, who seemed to him more desirable than all the other young black damsels on the mountain, had tossed her crinkly head and sent him about his business.

It was through this idyllic episode of the humming bird that I discovered Maman Célie to be a sorceress, as well as a priestess of Voodoo. The two functions do not necessarily concur.

It seemed to me, however, that she had set her grandson a somewhat difficult task. I had seen humming birds occasionally down yonder among the tropical flowers and fig-banana groves, tiny, fragile, iridescent, darting sprites, as incorporeal as soap-bubbles, as swift to disappear at a threatened touch. To catch one of them seemed almost as difficult as trapping a sunbeam. I knew vaguely that naturalists made use of delicate and cunningly constructed nets, and I had heard with equal vagueness of tiny shotguns spraying microscopic pellets, but Paul was equipped only with his natural wits.

Next day he returned with the humming bird. He had trapped it with a sort of birdlime made of a sticky, gummy sap. It was already dead and Maman Célie hung it up to dry in the sunshine. Meanwhile she persuaded Paul to show me, reluctantly, a former love-charm she had fabricated for him, but which apparently had failed of its purpose, though he still wore it next to his skin in a little sack strung around his neck. She explained its construction and use. Two needles of equal length are stood upright, side by side, baptized with suitable incantations, and are given the names of the youth and his unwilling girl. The two in this particular case were called Paul and Ti-Marie. The needles are then left side by side, parallel but reversed, so that the point of each presses against the eye of the other. The point is symbolic of the phallus and the eye symbolic of the vulva. The reverse doubling simply increases the potency of the charm; it has no perverse significance. The needles are placed between twigs from the roots of the *bois chica* tree, whittled smooth and straight, and then wound round with thread. Like all charms of every sort in Haiti, it was called a *ouanga*. There are love-*ouangas*, hate-*ouangas*, birth-*ouangas*, protective-*ouangas*, and murder-*ouangas*. Sometimes they work, and sometimes they don't. Apparently this one hadn't worked, and Paul now centred all his hopes in the humming bird.

Aware of my curiosity about these matters, Maman Célie permitted me to see her make the new *ouanga*. It was a less weird, less cabalistic business than one might guess, though midnight and moonlight were in it, as she crouched, crooning her incantations, but there was nothing mysteriously dreadful. In a little wooden mortar, which they call *pilon*, she ground the dried body of the humming bird into a dustlike powder, droning, 'Wood of the woods, bird of the woods, woman you were created by God. Bird of the woods, fly into her heart. I command you in the name of the three Marys and in Ayida's name. *Dolor, Dolori, passa.*' There was much more of it, untranslatable and cryptic. And with the dried powder of the humming bird she mixed a few dried drops of her grandson's blood, also of his semen, likewise the pollen of jungle flowers.

When all this had been duly ground together into dustlike fineness, she transferred it to a leather pouch made (as Spanish shepherds often do to hold their love-charms) from the scrotum of a he-goat, and gave it to Paul next day.

I was told, for I did not see it, that on the following Saturday evening, at the *danse Congo*, as Ti-Marie swayed past him laughing, he threw the dust full in her face, and that half blinded, with the dust in her eyes and nostrils and mouth, she spat like a young wildcat, and cried out that she would kill him – but she lay with him that night in the forest, and on Monday morning he fetched her home. Doubtless a deeper magic than Maman Célie's was also at work, but I think it would be a mistake to assume *a priori* that without Maman Célie's incantations and the humming bird, Ti-Marie would have yielded.

There were two other occasions when I saw her magic work effectively. I saw her, by processes which she considered magical, cure a dying girl and catch a thief. She said and believed that it was magic. Words are merely labels, and we do not always explain the inner essence of things by rejecting the old labels and inventing new ones. The Lady of Shalott gazed in her crystal mirror to behold scenes far away, and that was sorcery; now we experiment with television, and that is science. The Witch of Endor was a witch, but Svengali is a hypnotist. Old Nostradamus working over his crucibles called it alchemy when he sought to transform lead to gold, but now the Germans are engaged in the same experiment and call it advanced chemistry. I realize that there is a flaw in these parallels. But the scientific-minded Carrel, after his long stay at Lourdes, came away convinced that there were invisible powers unknown to any science at work there, and that the probable power of immaterial emanations to produce constructive or destructive changes in material substances, for instance the human body, was a thing which saints still knew more about than savants. When such things occur at holy shrines, they are called miracles; when they occur in a psychological laboratory, they are called science; when they occur in the Haitian jungle, they are called Voodoo magic. These words are all tags, labels, nothing more. Life and the forces of life remain shrouded in eternal mystery.

Maman Célie's sorcery was principally benevolent, as when she presently began gathering materials for the construction of a *ouanga* packet for me – it seemed that I was to have one of my very own, like that of Louis, which was the first I had ever seen, down in my back yard at Port-au-Prince – and that it was to preserve me safe from all harm amid these mountains. It was to be used also, she told me, in the special ceremonial that would occur when I was finally led into the *houmfort* to face certain of the ultimate Voodoo mysteries. I would need it then, she assured me earnestly.

How much I believed in that *ouanga* packet, and in what manner I believed what I did believe, are questions difficult to answer. I suspect that generally in such matters it is easier to believe in things which are sinister, perhaps dangerous, than it is to believe in things which are benevolent. It is always easier to fear ghosts, hobgoblins, and demons than it is to feel the hovering presence of guardian spirits. How many millions of people have been terrorized by ghosts and sworn trembling afterwards to their reality, compared with the few score in the history of the world who, like Saint Augustine and Joan of Arc, have conversed with angels. I knew that certain other *ouanga* packets in this Voodoo sorcery, horridly devised, were sometimes as definitely deadly as the murderer's knife or poison. There is no question about that. Every white man who has lived long enough with primitive peoples, no matter what his hard scientific background, no matter how rational the texture of his mind, has come finally to an often reluctant admission of the fact. One may find the semi-scientific explanation of how so-called black magic can kill, in the fifteen volumes, more or less, of Frazer's *Golden Bough*; the condensed edition in two volumes has been emasculated. But if one has ever lived, I mean geographically, outside the limits of our well-ordered rule-of-thumb world where every effect is politely assumed to trace back to respectably explicable causes, it will scarcely be necessary to read Frazer to understand that I am not treating here of superstition. Superstition would have had naught to do with my fleeing from that mountain if word had come to my ears that these people were secretly contriving for me the black death-*ouanga*, and even fleeing I might not have been safe. White men have died in London – and the records are in Scotland Yard – because some monk in the mountains of Tibet marked them to die, and sat droning in his far-off cell among the Himalayas. A subtle poison leaving no trace? Who knows? How can one be ever sure?

But the *ouanga* packet they were now preparing to make for me was to be bright-coloured, friendly and protective, and for those very reasons I found it more difficult to view it seriously, to separate it from obvious elements which were merely superstition. Yet had I not accepted it seriously I should have been wrong, for into its making went something more than aromatic leaves and powders; into it went also the imponderable will-to-protect of a community, so that whatever it was or was not magically, it not only deserved respect but had an actual potency-value as the sacred symbol and earnest of their protection.

It was the realization of this, I think, that enabled me to see, somewhat with their eyes, as more than mummery, the ceremony of this *ouanga* packet's making.

In a small, bare room inside Maman Célie's dwelling-house, from which a sleeping-pallet and other common household gear had been removed, a large cowhide was spread, hairy side upward, on the earthern floor, and around it in a circle sat solemnly a dozen negroes whom I knew, mostly of our immediate household. There were eight men and four women. It was night time. The only light flickered upward on their faces from small candles arranged as a geometric pentagram on the cowhide. Barring the doorsill were two crossed machetes, their broad, naked blades inscribed with white chalk symbols, the swirling serpent, the phallic staff, the enmeshed triangles.

Spread in the centre of the candle pentagram, on the cowhide, was a square red cloth, like a napkin, which was to be the covering of my *ouanga* packet. Bright ribbons, red and yellow, lay beside it, and also feathers brilliantly dyed. In little, separated piles upon the cowhide were balsam leaves, leaves of the castor-bean plant, roots of the lime tree; a saucer of flour, a saucer of ashes, a bottle of *clairin*, a bottle of perfume, a tiny iron crucifix.

Maman Célie and I sat on one side in the circle, Papa Théodore facing us. While they chanted almost in undertones, '*Papa Legba, ouvri barrière pour lie; tout Mystère 'gider lie*' (Legba, open the gate for him and every Mystery protect him), old Théodore took some of the roots and leaves, mixed them in a brazier, charred them together in a mortar. The two machetes were taken from the doorsill and planted upright in the ground, flanking him on each side. A *bocor* (magician) filled his mouth with *clairin* and sprayed it, sputtering, over all the paraphernalia on the cowhide, to drive away evil spirits. While Papa Théodore continued rhythmically pounding his materials in the mortar, the *bocor* began picking up balsam leaves and castor-bean leaves, one by one, marking each with a chalked cross and depositing it on the napkin, until a new pile was made there. Atop these leaves he now laid the crucifix, also a tuft of hair (tied together with thread) which had been cut previously from the central crown of my head; a paring from my right thumb-nail, and a small square cut from a shirt which had been worn next to my skin. Something of this sort runs through all primitive magic, whether the purpose be benevolent or evil. Articles intimately connected with the individual to be affected, a part of his own body such as hair or nail-paring if it can be procured, or a piece of clothing saturated with his perspiration or grease, are used variously as a substitution for himself. One of the most dreaded forms of Haitian-African magic includes the dressing of a corpse in a garment of the person marked for vengeance and then exposing it to rot away in some secret place in the jungle. Men have gone stark mad seeking that jungle-hidden horror, and others have died hopelessly, searching. Fear, hunger, thirst, jungle-terror, one may say. Names again, tags, labels. But marked for death by the Voodoo curse, they died. In the case of the death-*ouanga* packet, poisonous leaves are used with other corroding and defiling substances. Frazer contends that for magic of this sort to operate fatally without supplementary human agency the victim must *know* and *believe*. Probably this is true. But in the case of unbelievers they sometimes make use of appallingly pragmatic methods to instil faith. I am told that when some years ago 'Bank' Williams, the saturnine, cynical, fearless Yankee manager of the bank which is Haiti's treasury, was thus marked for death, on one occasion a dog died in agony lapping pure water from the seemingly innocent clean bowl in which his morning coffee might have been poured had not the bowl been suspected, and on another occasion, deadly poison was found inside an egg whose shell had apparently never been broken. He survived, I am told, because he fought the devil with fire; for weeks, until definite events made his death no longer desired, every particle of food that passed his lips, every garment that touched his skin, first went through the hands of an old wrinkled woman from Martinique who knew every trick of black magic and served him with single-hearted fidelity.

So there was an additional element beyond anything that could be connected with credulity, superstition, or a belief in supernormal agencies that caused in me this knowledge that Voodoo magic was pragmatically effective, whether for good or evil; that caused me to believe in a definite sense that this bright, protective charm which they were engaged in preparing for me now constituted a real and actual protection. There is a queer point involved here which I find difficulty in putting into words. It will doubtless seem to many readers superstitious when I aver that I actually believe the protective virtue would have been destroyed in this charm unless I myself had faith in it. But, suppose I had sat there deeming their whole performance, well, say – silly, or funny? Suppose I had viewed it as futile, childish charlatanism? I do not mean, 'Suppose I had laughed or sneered in their faces.' I do not mean anything as clearly defined as that. These people were intuitively sensitized to shades of unexpressed feeling, almost like animals. Is it sure that if I had felt a humorous or contemptuous scorn, even secret and unexpressed, I should have been as well protected by this *ouanga*, as safe thereafter among these people in the mountain? I tell you that my believing gave it power. And connected with this truth are many deep collateral truths concerning the power of all magic, miracles, and prayer.

When Papa Théodore had finished pounding the charred aromatic herbs, the *bocor* took a pinch of the substance between his fingers and sprinkled it, muttering incantations, on the pile of green leaves surmounted by the crucifix and the objects which had been a part of myself, of my living body. All arose, and slowly circling, took similarly a pinch of the charred mixture and sprinkled it. I, last of all, was instructed to do likewise. When we were reseated, the *bocor*, with a small glowing brand from the fire, touched off successively three little piles of gunpowder on the cowhide to drive away evil spirits. Then he and Papa Théodore drew the two cabalistically marked machetes from the earth and clashed them violently together above all our heads.

Maman Célie handed me a copper coin and instructed me to place it on the packet. And now, before it was tied up, she told me to make a prayer (wish). I hesitated, then stood with both arms stretched straight out before me, palms downward, as I had seen them do and said in English:

'May Papa Legba, Maîtresse Ezilée and the Serpent protect me from misrepresenting these people, and give me power to write honestly of their mysterious religion, for all living faiths are sacred.'

On the afternoon of the Friday set for my blood baptism, more than fifty friends and relatives gathered at the habitation of Maman Célie. There was no reason to suppose that we might be disturbed, but as an extra precaution a gay *danse Congo* was immediately organized to cover the real purpose of our congregation. Maman Célie had told me that I would get no sleep that night; so despite the noise I napped until after sunset, when she awakened me and led me across the compound to the *houmfort*.

Through its outer door, which Emanuel stood guarding like a sentinel and unlocked for us, we entered a dim, windowless, cell-like anteroom in which were tethered the sacrificial beasts, a he-goat, two red cocks and two black, an enormous white turkey, and a pair of doves. Huddled there in a corner also was the girl Catherine, Maman Célie's youngest unmarried daughter; why she was there I did not know, and it is needless to say that I wondered.

From this dim, somewhat sinister antechamber we passed through an open doorway into the long, rectangular mystery room, the temple proper, which was lighted with candles and primitive oil lamps that flickered like torches. Its clay walls were elaborately painted with crude serpent symbols and anthropomorphic figures. Papa Legba, guardian of the gates, god of the crossroads, was represented as a venerable old black farmer with a pipe between his teeth; Ogoun Badagris, the bloody warrior, appeared as an old-time Haitian revolutionary general in uniform with a sword; Wangol, master of the land, drove a yoke of oxen; Agoué, master of the seas, puffed out his cheeks to blow a wind and held in the hollow of his hand a tiny boat; the serpent symbols stood for the great Damballa Oueddo, almighty Jove of the Voodoo pantheon, and his consort Ayida Oueddo.

At the near end of the room, close to the doorway through which we had entered, was the wide, low altar, spread over with a white lace tablecloth. In its centre was a small wooden serpent, elevated horizontally on a little pole as Moses lifted up the serpent in the wilderness; around this symbol, which was ancient before the Exodus, were grouped thunderstones, Christian crucifixes made in France or Germany, necklaces on which were strung snake vertebrae, others from which hung little medallions of the Virgin Mary. On the corner of the altar nearest me, my *ouanga* had been placed. Grouped also on the altar were earthern jugs containing wine, water, oil; platters of vegetables and fruits, plates containing common bread, and plates containing elaborate sweet fancy cakes, bought days before down in the plain. There were bottles of expensive French-labelled grenadine and orgeat, a bottle of rum, kola-champagne, etc. There were also three cigars, not of the rough sort the peasants smoke, but fat and smooth in their red-gilt bands. With a naïve but justifiable rationality, these worshippers, whose gods were vitally, utterly real, saw no anachronism in offering to their deities the best of everything that could be procured. Maman Célie herself, accompanied by Papa Théodore, had gone by narrow trails across mountains and valleys, leading a donkey down to the modern city, shopping there for their celestial guests and returning with the donkey's panniers heavy laden.

On the altar also was a cone-like mound of cornmeal surmounted by an egg, and before the altar candles were burning, and wicks floating in cocoanut shells of oil. At the left were the three *Rada* drums, at the right was a low wooden stool placed for me.

At the other end of the mystery room, so that a ten-foot open space was left before the altar, were seated on the ground the eighteen or twenty people, all close relatives or trusted friends, who were to witness the ceremony. When I entered, they were swaying and singing:

Papa Legba, ouvrí barrière pour moins!
Papa Legba, coté petits ou?
Papa Legba, ou oué yo!
Papa Legba, ouvrí barrière pour li passer!

(Father Legba, open wide the gate!
Father Legba, where are thy children?
Father Legba, we are here.
Father Legba, open wide the gate that he may pass!)

The *papaloi*, a powerful clean-shaven black man of middle age with red turban and a bright-coloured embroidered stole over his shoulders, traced with cornmeal a cabalistic design on the bare earth before the altar. It measured perhaps twelve feet from end to end. Its circles, it was afterwards explained to me, represented, from left to right, earth, sky, and sea. (Adepts of the esoteric will read here earth, air, and water, or if of a certain school will read earth, air, fire, and water, accepting a central sky-circle as a symbol also of the sun.) All these matters indeed entered into it, but the simpler interpretation was dominant. Forked marks, all connecting, with lines interjoining them with three circles, thence radiating towards the altar and reversely towards the worshippers, were symbols of the invisible paths through which the gods and mysteries would move.

Into the earth circle the *papaloi* poured oil, flour, and wine, while the people chanted, '*Wangol maît' la terre*' (Wangol is master of the earth). Into the sky circle he poured rum and ashes, while they chanted, '*Damballa Oueddo, ou maît' la ciel*' (Damballa Oueddo, thou art master of the sky). Into the sea circle he poured water, while they sang, '*Papa Agoué, li maît' la mer*' (Father Agoué, he is master of the sea).

A number of solos interspersed this general chanting. It was impossible to retain them all in memory. I could not make pencil notes there; not even Maman Célie was able afterwards to repeat them all for me, and the next day some of the singers were gone. There was one song to Papa Agoué, however, which I partly remembered because it had seemed to me beautiful, and later I rode to find the singer and transcribe it. It was:

Agoué, woyó! woyó!
Maîtr' Agoué reter lans la mer;
Li tirer canot.

Bassin blé
Reter toi zilet;

Nèg coqui' lans mer zorage;
Li tirer canot là.

Agoué, woyó! woyó!

(Hail to Father Agoué
Who dwells in the sea!
He is the Lord of ships.

In the blue gulf
There are three little islands.
The negro's boat is storm-tossed,
Father Agoué brings it safely in.
Hail to Father Agoué!)

When this singing and pouring of libations were ended, the *papaloi* sealed the open doorway by tracing across its earthen sill. Evil or unwelcome forces which sought to enter would become entangled in the lines and go wandering from circle to circle like lost souls among the stars.

This done, he began the real service, for which all thus far had been but a preparation. He stood with arms raised before the altar and said solemnly, '*Lans nom tout Loi et tout Mystère*' (In the name of all the Gods and all the Mysteries).

Maman Célie advanced at a sign from the *papaloi* and was invested by him, with the scarlet robe and headdress of ostrich feathers black and red, as *mamaloi* or priestess. This was accompanied by a shrill chant:

Ayida Oueddo, ou couleuvre moins!
Qui lé ou filer ou cou z'éclai!

(Ayida Oueddo, my serpent goddess,
When you come it is like the lightning flash!)

At the same time now I heard through the chanting a sharp long-drawn continuous hissing. It was Maman

Célie, hissing like a snake, drawing and expelling the breath through her teeth.

I looked for Maman Célie's familiar sweet, gentle face, but beneath the black and scarlet plumes I saw now only what seemed a rigid mask. I felt that I was looking into the face of a strange, dreadful woman, or into the face of something which I had never seen before. As I watched, the cheeks of this black mask were deeply indrawn so that the face became skull-like, and then alternately puffed out as if the skull had been covered with flesh and come alive.

As the chanting died away, she whirled three times and flung herself prostrate before the altar with her lips pressed against the earth.

Emanuel, without donning sacerdotal garb, but now acting as a sort of altar servant, brought in the two red cocks. Each was handled gently, almost reverently, by the *papaloi*, as he knelt holding it and with white flour traced on its back a cross. One of the small sweet cakes was crumbled, and each cock must peck at it from the *mamaloi's* hand. This was awaited patiently. At the moment when each bird consented to receive the consecrated food, the priestess seized it and rose wildly dancing, whirling with the cock held by its head and feet in her upstretched hands, its wings violently fluttering. Round and round she whirled while the drums throbbed in a quick, tangled, yet steady rhythm. With a sudden twist the cock's head was torn off and as she whirled the blood flew out as if from a sprinkling-pot. The other birds, the black cocks and the doves, were dealt with similarly. As she danced with the white living doves, it was beautiful, and it seemed to me natural also that they should presently die. Blood of the doves was saved in a china cup.

A thing which had a different, a horror-beauty like a mad Goya etching, occurred when the black priestess did her death dance with the huge white turkey. Though far from feeble, possessed of great vitality, she was a slender woman, slightly formed, whose nervous strength lay not in muscular weight. When the turkey's wings spread wide and began to flap frantically above her head as she whirled, the great bird seemed larger and more powerful than she; it seemed that she would be dragged from her feet, hurled to the ground, or flown away with fabulously into the sky. And as she sought finally to tear off its head, sought to clutch its body between her knees, it attacked her savagely, beating her face and breasts, beating at her so that she was at moments enfolded by the great white wings, so that bird and woman seemed to mingle struggling in a monstrous, mythical embrace. But her fatal hands were still upon its throat, and in that swanlike simulacre of the deed which for the male is always like a little death, it died.

So savage had this scene been that it was almost like an anti-climax when the sacrificial goat was now led through the doorway to the altar, but new and stranger things, contrasting, were yet to happen before other blood was shed. He was a sturdy brown young goat, with big, blue, terrified, almost human eyes, eyes which seemed not only terrified but aware and wondering. At first he bleated and struggled, for the odour of death was in the air, but finally he stood quiet, though still wide-eyed, while red silken ribbons were twined in his little horns, his little hoofs anointed with wine and sweet-scented oils, and an old woman who had come from far over the mountain for this her one brief part in the long ceremony sat down before him and crooned to him alone a song which might have been a baby's lullaby.

When it was finished, the *papaloi* sat down before the little goat and addressed to it a discourse in earnest tones. He told the little goat that it would soon pass through the final gates before us all, instructed it in the mysteries, and pleaded with it concerning its conduct on the other side. But before it passed through the gate, he explained, certain magical changes, making its path easier, would occur on this side. Therefore it need have no fear. Upon its forehead he traced a cross and circle, first with flour and afterwards with blood of the doves. Then he presented to it a green, leafy branch to eat.

This goat had by now become inevitably personal to me. I had conceived an affectionate interest in him while the old woman was singing. I recalled what had happened to the other creatures at the moment they touched food, and I had an impulse to cry out to him, 'Don't do that, little goat! Don't touch it!' But it was a fleeting, purely sentimental impulse. Not for anything, no matter what would happen, could I have seriously wished to stop that ceremony. I believe in such ceremonies. I hope that they will never die out or be abolished. I believe that in some form or another they answer a deep need of the universal human soul. I, who in a sense believe in no religion, believe yet in them all, asking only that they be alive – as religions. Codes of rational ethics and human brotherly love are useful, but they do not touch this thing underneath. Let religion have its bloody sacrifices, yes, even human sacrifices, if thus our souls may be kept alive. Better a black *papaloi* in Haiti with blood-stained hands who believes in his living gods than a frock-coated minister on Fifth Avenue reducing Christ to a solar myth and rationalizing the Immaculate Conception.

And so I did not cry out.

And the goat nibbled the green leaves.

But no knife flashed.

In the dim, bare anteroom with its windowless grey walls, the girl Catherine had remained all this time huddled in a corner, as if drugged or half asleep.

Emanuel had to clutch her tightly by the arm to

prevent her from stumbling when they brought her to the altar. Maman Célie hugged her and moaned and shed tears as if they were saying good-bye forever. The *papaloi* pulled them apart, and someone gave the girl a drink of rum from a bottle. She began to protest in a dull sort of angry, whining way when they forced her down on her knees before the lighted candles. The *papaloi* wound round her forehead red ribbons like those which had been fastened around the horns of the goat, and Maman Célie, no longer as a mourning mother but as an officiating priestess, with rigid face aided in pouring the oil and wine on the girl's head, feet, hands, and breast.

All this time the girl had been like a fretful, sleepy, annoyed child, but gradually she became docile, sombre, staring with quiet eyes, and presently began a weird song of lamentation. I think she was extemporizing both the words and the melody. She sang:

Cochon marron saché chemin caille;
Moins mandé ça li gagnin.
'Nans Léogane tout moon malade O!'

Béf marron saché chemin caille.
Moins mandé ça li gagnin.
'Nans gros morne tout moon malade O!'

Cabrit marron saché chemin caille.
Moins mandé ça li gagnin.
'Nans Guinea tout moon malade O!'

M'pas malade, m'a p'mourri!
(The wild pig came seeking me;
I said why have you come?
'Every one is sick in Léogane!'

The wild bull came seeking me;
I said why have you come?
'Every one is sick in the mountains!'

The wild goat came seeking me;
I said why have you come?
'Every one is sick in Africa!'

So I who am not sick must die!)

And so that black girl sang, and as the inner meaning of her song came to me, I seemed to hear the voice of Jephtha's daughter doomed to die by her own father as a sacrifice to Javeh, going up to bewail her virginity on Israel's lonely mountain. Her plight in actuality was rather that of Isaac bound by Abraham on Mount Moriah; a horned beast would presently be substituted in her stead; but the moment for that mystical substitution had not yet come, and as she sang she was a daugher doomed to die.

The ceremony of substitution, when it came, was pure effective magic of a potency which I have never seen equalled in Dervish monastery or anywhere. The goat and the girl, side by side before the altar, had been startled, restive, nervous. The smell of blood was in the air, but there was more than that hovering; it was the eternal, mysterious odour of death itself which both animals and human beings always sense, but not through the nostrils. Yet now the two who were about to die mysteriously merged, the girl symbolically and the beast with a knife in its throat, were docile and entranced, were like automatons. The *papaloi* monotonously chanting, endlessly repeating, 'Damballa calls you, Damballa calls you,' stood facing the altar with arms outstretched above their two heads. The girl was now on her hands and knees in the attitude of a quadruped, directly facing the goat, so that their heads and eyes were on a level, less than ten inches apart, and thus they stared fixedly into each other's eyes, while the *papaloi's* hands weaved slowly, ceaselessly above their foreheads, the forehead of the girl and the forehead of the horned beast, each wound with red ribbons, each already marked with the blood of a white dove. By shifting slightly I could see the big, wide, pale-blue, staring eyes of the goat, and the big, black, staring eyes of the girl, and I could have almost sworn that the black eyes were gradually, mysteriously becoming those of a dumb beast, while a human soul was beginning to peer out through the blue. But dismiss that, and still I tell you that pure magic was here at work, that something very real and fearful was occurring. For as the priest wove his ceaseless incantations, the girl began a low, piteous bleating in which there was nothing, absolutely nothing, human; and soon a thing infinitely more unnatural occurred; the goat was moaning and crying like a human child. I believe that through my Druse and Yezidee accounts I have earned a deserved reputation for being not too credulous in the face of marvels. But I was in the presence now of a thing that could not be denied. Old magic was here at work, and it worked appallingly. What difference does it make whether we call it supernatural or merely supernormal? What difference does it make if we say that the girl was drugged – as I suspect she was – or that both were hypnotized? Of course they were, if you like. And what then? We live surrounded by mysteries and imagine that by inventing names we explain them.

Other signs and wonders became manifest. Into this little temple lost among the mountains came in answer to goat-cry girl-cry the Shaggy Immortal One of a thousand names whom the Greeks called Pan. The goat's lingam became erect and rigid, the points of the girl's breasts visibly hardened and were outlined sharply pressing against the coarse, thin, tight-drawn shift that was her only garment. Thus they faced each other motionless as two marble figures on the frieze of some ancient phallic temple. They were like inanimate twin lamps in which a sacred flame burned, steadily yet unconsuming.

While the *papaloi* still wove his spells, his hands

moving ceaselessly like an old woman carding wool in a dream, the priestess held a twig green with tender leaves between the young girl and the animal. She held it on a level with their mouths, and neither saw it, for they were staring fixedly into each other's eyes as entranced mediums stare into crystal globes, and with their necks thrust forward so that their foreheads almost touched. Neither could therefore see the leafy branch, but as the old *mamaloi's* hand trembled, the leaves flicked lightly as if stirred by a little breeze against the hairy muzzle of the goat, against the chin and soft lips of the girl. And after moments of breathless watching, it was the girl's lips which pursed out and began to nibble at the leaves. Human beings, normally, when eating, open their mouths and take the food directly in between their teeth. Except for sipping liquids they do not use their lips. But the girl's lips now nibbling at the leaves were like those of a ruminating animal. Her hands, of course, were flat on the ground so that in a sense she perforce must have eaten without using them, somewhat in the manner of a quadruped; but in a castle near the edge of the Nefud desert I once watched closely a woman eating whose hands were tied behind her back, and that woman, opening her mouth and baring her teeth, took the fragments of food directly between her teeth, as any normal human being would. But this girl now pursed her lips and used them nibbling as horned cattle do. It sounds a slight thing, perhaps, in the describing, but it was weird, unnatural, unhuman.

As she nibbled thus, the *papaloi* said in a hushed but wholly matter-of-fact whisper like a man who had finished a hard, solemn task and was glad to rest, '*Ca y est*' (There it is).

The *papaloi* was now holding a machete, ground sharp and shining. Maman Célie, priestess, kneeling, held a *gamelle*, a wooden bowl. It was oblong. There was just space enough to thrust it narrowly between the mystically identified pair. Its rim touched the goat's hairy chest and the girl's body, both their heads thrust forward above it. Neither seemed conscious of anything that was occurring, nor did the goat flinch when the *papaloi* laid his hand upon its horns. Nor did the goat utter any sound as the knife was drawn quickly, deeply across its throat. But at this instant, as the blood gushed like a fountain into the wooden bowl, the girl, with a shrill, piercing, then strangled bleat of agony, leaped, shuddered, and fell senseless before the altar.

At the moment the knife flashed across the goat's throat, the company had begun to chant, not high or loud but with a sort of deep, hushed fervour, across which the girl's inhuman bleating had shrilled sharp as another invisible blade. Now they continued chanting while the celebrants performed their various offices. They chanted:

Damballa Oueddo odan q'icit
Mandé ça la! Oué!
Ayida Oueddo odan q'icit
Mandé ça la! Oué!

(Damballa and Ayida, behold the deed we have done as you commanded).

The body of the goat was thrown as a ritually useless and no longer sacred thing through the door into the anteroom. The body of the unconscious girl, spattered with blood, was lifted carefully into Emanuel's arms and carried away, followed by two old women versed in magic who would attend her recovery. If Maman Célie, her face still like a terrible, inspired mask, bestowed one fleeting glance on either body, I did not see it. She was revolving slowly before the altar with the bowl in her outstretched arms and now held it to the *papaloi*, who received it, drank, then placed it on the altar, and with a little china cup poured libations within each of the three cabalistic circles on the earth. They also sang an invocation to Ybo, another of the ancient gods.

There was a pause, a lull, in which I who had been for hours too utterly absorbed to give myself a thought, recalled that all this ceremonial was leading up to an event which concerned me more deeply than any other present. The time had now come. A very old black man, deeply wrinkled, with a beard that was like Spanish moss turned snowy white, who had been sitting silent all the while, took from a bag at his feet a white cloth which he wound around his head, and a white embroidered garment like a cassock which he put over his shoulders. He invested himself without the aid of other hands as a black pope or emperor might have done. He was not of our mountain. He had come riding upon a donkey from beyond the great Morne. Maman Célie had summoned him and had paid the expenses from her own purse. It was a thing for which she would never permit me to repay her. As he arose and beckoned me to kneel at last before the altar, there was absolute silence. He was Voodoo of the Voodoo, but as he laid his hand upon my head it was neither in Creole that he spoke, nor French, nor even the almost forgotten language of old Guinea. I heard as in a dream, low, clear, and deep as the voices of old men rarely are, '*In nomine Patris, et Filii, et Spiritus Sancti. Amen.*'

And when still kneeling there with my eyes closed, I heard as from a great distance and as an echo from years long past his sure voice intoning that most marvellous and mysterious of all Latin invocations, 'Rosa Mystica . . . Tower of David . . . Tower of Ivory . . . House of Gold . . . Gate of Heaven,' it seemed to me that I heard too the rolling of mighty organs beneath vaulted domes . . .

Oil, wine, and water were poured upon my head, marks were traced upon my brow with white flour, and then I was given to eat ritually from the cakes upon the altar, to drink from the wine, rum, and syrups there. Parts of many cakes were crumbled together in a little cup and were put into my mouth with a spoon; likewise were mingled a few drops from each of the many bottles.

This, it seemed, had been a preliminary consecration rite in sincere inclusion of the Christian divinities, saints, and powers. Now the Voodoo chanting recommenced, and for the first time my own name was mingled with the Creole and African words. They were beseeching Legba to open wide the gates for me, Damballa and Ayida to receive me. A sort of mad fervour was again taking possession of them all. The old *hougan*, shouting now so that his voice could be heard above the singing, demanded once more silence, and placing both hands heavily upon my head, pronounced a long mixed African and Creole invocation, calling down to witness all the gods and goddesses of ancient Africa. Still commanding silence, he dipped his hand into the wooden bowl and traced on my forehead the bloody Voodoo cross.

Then he lifted the bowl, hesitated for a queer instant as if in courteous doubt – it was a strange, trivial thing to occur at such a moment – and then picked up a clean spoon. Maman Célie interfered angrily. So the bowl itself was held to my lips and three times I drank. The blood had a clean, warm, salty taste. In physical fact, I was drinking the blood of a recently slain goat, but by some mysterious transubstantiation not without its parallels in more than one religion other than Voodoo, I was drinking the blood of the girl Catherine who in the body of the goat had mystically died for me and for all miserable humanity from Léogane to Guinea.

One small thing yet remained to be done. I had been told that it would be done, and its meaning explained to me. I had been told also that for no white man alive or dead had it ever been done before. The *papaloi* took from the altar an egg which had surmounted a little pyramid of cornmeal, and holding it aloft in his cupped hands, pronounced incantation. As the blood had represented the mystery of death, sacrifice, and purification, likewise fertilization as it was poured upon the earth, the egg now represented rebirth, productivity, fertility, re-creation. Maman Célie, the priestess, took it from the hands of the *papaloi*, traced with it a new cross on my forehead, and dashed it to the earth. My knees were spattered. Then the priestess tore off her feathered headdress, and Maman Célie, the old woman, sank down beside me, put her arms around me, and cried, 'Legba, Papa Legba, open wide the gates for this my little one.'

Green Jewel of Death

Princess Catherine Radziwill

To say that one emerald – no matter how huge – affected the history of a great nation for more than three hundred years is to create at once what lawyers call a reasonable doubt. And to suggest further that its influence was due to an ancient curse put upon the stone is not only a sure way to win ridicule, but also to be accused of an imagination lacking originality.

So let me say at the outset that I do not believe the legend about the Great Emerald being bewitched.

After one has come to America and has become a citizen of a nation with a rational history, and when one rides in subways and works in tall steel buildings, one forgets such things. Yet I must admit that when I first saw the green light of that big stone glittering from the bosom of the Empress Alexandra, and heard the indiscreet whisper of the story from a lady of the court as she counted off on her fingers the Great Emerald's victims, I was inclined to be credulous. For all of the story, except the part about the witch, is plain history that anyone may read.

There *was* such a man as Nikita Romanoff, and there *was* such a man as Boulouk Khan with a beautiful daughter. Nikita Romanoff *did* die a horrible death, and many Romanoffs thereafter, with the jewel always at hand to reflect tragedies in its cold green facets.

Remember, the last Czar and the Empress Alexandra were murdered in that cellar at Ekaterinburg *after* I had heard the story! So, you see, it is not an easy story to forget. Let me tell it as simply as possible.

First, a necessary bit of political history. When Ivan the Terrible died in 1584, he left the throne to his son, the feeble-minded Feodor. Then followed the 'troubled years' of Russian history, when Tartars, Poles, and Swedes fought for possession of Russia's dreary and lonesome plains and for the conquest of the three hundred churches and shrines of stately Moscow, with the great treasures they contained.

Fortunately, perhaps, for Russia, Feodor was married to a beautiful woman, Irene Godounoff, who contrived that her famous brother, Boris, should rule the land in Feodor's name. This Boris Godounoff was a determined, relentless man, full of ambition, who made up his mind to become the next Czar. So when Feodor died, and Irene was hailed as Czarina by the assembled nobles, or boyars, as they were called, she refused the throne, and with her own hands placed on her brother's head the crown her husband had worn.

Boris triumphed, yet he knew himself to be a usurper. He knew that, even after Feodor's younger brother, Dmitry, had been assassinated at his command, there still existed lawful successors to the Russian throne in the persons of the Romanoffs, direct descendants of the great Rurik.

There were three of these Romanoffs – Feodor, Ivan, and Nikita – and to their destruction Boris set his hand.

The first was forced to enter holy orders after having been separated from his wife, Marfa, who was shut up in the solitude of the Ipatieff Convent in Kostroma. (What Boris never knew was that, thanks to the connivance of the Abbess of Ipatieff, Marfa continued to see her husband, and gave birth to a son who was one day to become the first of the Romanoff czars.)

The second brother, Ivan, died of a mysterious illness with which was mixed up a suspicion of poison. But the third, Nikita, was not so easy to dispose of. He had too many friends.

He was handsome and brave, beloved by women and popular with men. He was truly a hero of romance, and romantic adventures followed him throughout his career.

Nikita was the only one of the Romanoffs who did not care for politics, and who had no ambition to see the diadem of the Monomaques put upon his head. He cared only for a good time, to look into the dark eyes of a lovely maiden, or to enjoy a sumptuous banquet. He, the pious orthodox descendant of that Grand Duchess Olga who had brought Christianity to Russia, had become infatuated with an infidel, with a Moslem girl, the only daughter of a Tartar Prince, Boulouk Khan.

Boulouk – one of the few Tartars whose family had remained in Moscow after the khans had been driven back to Kazan – lived very quietly in a small house under the very ramparts of the Kremlin, and received few people. One of them, however, was Nikita Romanoff.

Nikita had met the beautiful Isma by chance, at a banquet given by the Czarina; and although Moslem women were not allowed to show their faces to men, he contrived to have an affair with her, and out of it a son was born.

Boulouk Khan asked Nikita to marry the girl. The younger boyar refused, saying that his religion forbade him to unite himself in wedlock with an infidel. The tartar was furious, but kept silent.

So far, we have nothing but historical facts. Now

comes the legend, which I will relate in the form that has come down to this day. It seems that Boulouk Khan, on the night following his interview with Nikita, went to seek the help of an old and famous witch.

The old woman received him in her den, a dark, underground cavern in a lonesome spot shunned by everybody. She listened to Boulouk's story and then asked him:

'You wish to be revenged on this man for the wrong he has done your daughter?'

'Yes, I do,' replied the Tartar, 'and not only on him but on all his race in the centuries to come.'

The hag laughed, a harsh and cruel laugh.

'Your wish will be granted,' she said, 'and your revenge will perhaps be more terrible than you suspect. Wait a moment!'

She retired behind a curtain that divided her gruesome abode, and after a few minutes returned, holding in her hand an uncut emerald set in gold, fashioned as a clasp for a man's cloak.

The Tartar extended his hand towards it.

'Don't touch it!' exclaimed the old woman. 'Don't touch it until I allow you to. The devil himself is in that stone.'

She walked towards a cauldron and dipped the jewel in it, murmuring as she did so strange words in a strange language. Then she came back to where the terrified Boulouk Khan was standing.

'Here,' she said, 'take the jewel. Its beauty is unsurpassed, and its worth will go on increasing as the years pass by. But it is an accursed stone, and it will bring misfortune, sorrow, suffering, and death to all those who will possess it. Give it to Nikita Romanoff and you will see what havoc it will work. Now leave me the purse I see hanging from your waist, and go away from here, for this is no place for any but the Master of Evil to loiter in!'

That is the legend of the origin of the Great Emerald. Now we turn back to history, and find Boulouk Khan writing the following letter to Nikita Romanoff, the text of which has been preserved in the Russian archives:

Boulouk Khan, the humble servant of the great and mighty Boyar Nikita Nikitich Romanoff, humbly craves his presence at a banquet at his house, and hopes he will honour his slave with his presence at it.

'The old dog evidently has forgotten all about his anger of the other day, and wants to make amends for it,' the young man must have thought.

He went to the feast and enjoyed himself immensely.

Boulouk Khan had spared neither money nor trouble to make it sumptuous, and the day was already dawning before anyone thought of retiring. As Nikita was preparing to depart, his host stopped him.

'Great and mighty Boyar,' he said, 'grant me one last favour before you leave my house. Here is a stone that came to me from my ancestors, and which is supposed to have belonged to our great Genghis Khan himself. I have had it set as a clasp for your cloak. Honour me by accepting it, just to prove to me that you bear me no ill will for any differences we may have had in the past.'

With these words he handed over to the astonished young man the Great Emerald.

Three nights later Nikita Romanoff was sound asleep in the arms of a woman to whom, it is said, he had been secretly married, when a great noise at the door of his room awakened him. The house was surrounded and invaded by a troop of armed men, the soldiers of Boris Godounoff.

Whether the usurper, who had spies everywhere, had heard the tale of the Great Emerald and fancied that the powers of darkness were now on his side, or whether he had simply become weary of waiting and decided to risk the anger of Nikita's friends, we shall never know. The fact remains that the young Boyar was seized and bound with heavy chains and thrown into a sledge waiting at his door.

He protested and cried out for help; but all his servants had been put out of the way, and, in spite of the entreaties of his wife, he was hurried away. For long weeks the prisoner and his guards travelled towards the Siberian wastes, Nikita lying on his back at the bottom of the sledge, so tightly chained he could move neither hand nor foot. All his money had been taken away; but, by design or coincidence, the emerald of Boulouk Khan had been left in his possession.

At last the sledge stopped in the midst of an apparently endless plain. Night was beginning to fall.

The officer in command of the escort gave a brisk order, and two men began digging a hole in the frozen ground. When the men climbed out of the deep pit they had made, the officer measured the depth of it and nodded his head.

He gave a signal, and the soldiers seized Nikita and flung him into the deep hole. The top was covered over with a rude roof and without further ado the escort rode away.

Nikita Romanoff lived on for three long years, sunk in the pit, without even the possibility of looking up at the sky. From time to time a piece of bread was thrown down and a pitcher of water lowered to him. At last, one day, the guard, hearing no sound from the living tomb, peered down and saw that Nikita Romanoff was dead at last.

They did not remove his body. Godounoff had given his orders, and all that was done was to fill up the pit with earth.

Time went on, and after Godounoff's death Nikita's nephew, Michael Romanoff, was hailed as Czar by the Muscovite boyars in the Ipatieff Convent at Kostroma. The new dynasty began its reign, which was to last exactly three hundred and four years.

Nikita Romanoff lay in his unconsecrated grave, forgotten by the world, until the day when, for a short period, Russia was ruled by a woman – the handsome, imperious Czarina Sophia, sister of the man who was to be known as Peter the Great.

She remembered the dark story of the victim of Godounoff's ambition and cruelty and sent men to Siberia with instructions to look for the mortal remains of her murdered kinsman. When they were found, she had them properly buried, and a chapel erected on the spot of his awful martyrdom.

Among the remnants of clothes dug from Nikita Romanoff's grave was found the Great Emerald of Boulouk Khan. Its gold setting had not tarnished, and the jewel itself had lost none of its weird beauty. The Czarina's messengers brought it back to her, and Sophia found it so fascinating that she immediately began to wear it on a chain around her neck. Her attendants and even her confessor warned her against it, for by this time the legend of the curse was being whispered around Moscow.

Sophia laughed at these warnings. She believed herself absolutely secure.

But the boy under whose name she was reigning was the great Peter. He also wanted to reign, and to reign alone.

One day Sophia was rudely dragged out of her Kremlin Palace and thrust into a convent. Only once did she ever emerge from her cell. This was on a fateful afternoon when, by order of her brother, she was taken to a window under which a scaffold had been erected and was forced to see each one of her faithful Stryeltsi officers led up in succession and beheaded. The miserable woman fainted at last, and, when she recovered her senses, found herself back in her religious prison, where she remained until her death.

But, before she had been led away from the Terem she was never to see again, the Czarina had contrived to squeeze into the hand of Eudoxia Lopoukhina, the wife of her brother Peter, the emerald of Nikita Romanoff. Not long afterwards, Eudoxia also fell into disgrace, and was banished by her merciless husband to make way for the Livonian peasant girl who was to become Empress of All the Russias.

When Eudoxia was bidding goodbye to her only son, Alexis, she gave him the emerald.

This unbalanced youth, who imagined himself strong enough to resist the will of his father, the Great White Czar, was tortured to death in the dark dungeons of the fortress of Saints Peter and Paul. Peter himself lashed him with the knout, and dealt the blow that killed him.

Alexis turned his eyes upon the Czar, and murmured, 'Father, I forgive you!' then feebly put his hands to a little silk bag he wore around his neck, and clung to it until death mercifully released him. In the bag was Nikita Romanoff's emerald. It was brought to Peter after his son's body had been laid in his coffin. But the Emperor refused to touch it; instead he had it taken to the Treasury and put under lock and key.

There it remained until his niece, the Empress Anna Ivanovna, ascended the throne of Russia. The first time she looked through the imperial jewels, she took a fancy to the stone and presented it to her favourite, the famous Biren, who became Duke of Courland. The latter was disgraced and sent into exile by Anna's successor, the Empress Elizabeth Petrovna.

Remembering the evil reputation the stone possessed, Biren sent it back to his sovereign, in the hope, it was said, that it would work her evil. Elizabeth, however, did not care for it. She had it set in a ring, which she gave to her nephew – the man who later became Peter III.

Peter was celebrating his marriage to a young girl who later became known as Catherine the Great. Those who doubt the Great Emerald's evil influence point out that the sole gift of Catherine's hand would have been enough to bring tragedy into any man's life – even a nobler one than the coarse and brutal Peter.

The fact remains, though that not long after Peter succeeded his aunt to the throne, he was deposed by the Palace Guards and later strangled in the castle of Ropscha by Gregory Orloff, Catherine's favourite.

The emerald of Nikita Romanoff was removed from his finger with great difficulty after his death and brought back to the Imperial Treasury. The Empress Catherine refused at first to have anything to do with it.

The great sovereign was not a superstitious woman, yet somehow this stone inspired terror in her.

One day, after many years had passed and the murder that had taken place at Ropscha was beginning to be forgotten, curiosity overcame her. She had the Great Emerald brought to her, and was so captivated with its beauty that she decided to have it reset as an ornament for Marie Feodorovna, the wife of her son Paul. Two hours after she had sent for the court jeweller to discuss the matter with him, Catherine was struck down by an apoplectic fit and died that same evening.

After this, no one at court would touch without gloves the emerald of Nikita Romanoff, and friends urged Paul I to get rid of it. But the Emperor refused to entertain the idea of parting with this remarkable jewel. Instead, he had it set in the handle of a sword to wear on state occasions.

On the evening of the day when Paul had worn the sword for the first time, conspirators, acting under the direction of his son Alexander, broke into the Czar's bed-chamber, demanding his abdication.

Paul leaped up and seized the sword that bore the Great Emerald and attempted to defend himself. In the scuffle the stone was broken from its setting – and its owner mortally wounded.

Paul's son, Alexander I, would never even look at the jewel, and conceived the idea of presenting it to some church or shrine. But his confessor, the famous Abbot Photius, told him this could not be done, because the stone was supposed to have been cursed by Satan himself. This opinion the next sovereign, Nicholas I, seemed to share, and as long as he occupied the throne Nikita Romanoff's emerald remained hidden away in one of the strong-boxes of the Imperial Treasury.

There it lay until, many years later, the morganatic wife of Alexander II, the Princess Dolgorouky, having heard its sinister story, asked her husband to allow her to examine it. The Czar himself had never seen the fateful emerald, and when it was brought to him one morning at breakfast, he admired it immensely – so much, indeed, that, after having promised his consort to have it set for her in a pendant, he put it in his pocket to show to his favourite cousin, the Grand Duchess Catherine Michaelovna, with whom he was to dine that day.

On his way back to the Winter Palace, Alexander was blown to pieces by bombs thrown at him by nihilist conspirators.

The next day a police officer picked the emerald out of a snow bank on the spot where the Czar had fallen, and took it to the palace.

Once again Nikita Romanoff's jewel went into retirement. Alexander III and his consort, the Empress Marie, believed absolutely in its uncanny influence, and would not even allow it to be kept in any of the strong-boxes where their personal belongings were stored. The Empress, in particular, never wished it to be even mentioned in her presence, and is to this day persuaded that it caused all the calamities of the Romanoff dynasty.

Perhaps it was out of opposition to the Empress Marie that her daughter-in-law, the late Alexandra, refused to admit that a mere jewel could bring misfortune. She persuaded Czar Nicholas II to have the emerald set into a pendant, which she wore continually.

It was on Alexandra's neck that I saw this fatal jewel.

She took it with her into exile when she went with her husband and her children to Siberia. Doubtless she was wearing it on that fatal and mysterious night in Ekaterinburg when the great Romanoff dynasty came to its tragic end.

Where is Nikita Romanoff's emerald now?

No one seems to know.

It has not appeared among the crown jewels that have been sold by the present rulers of Russia.

Superstitious people may be tempted to say that, having worked out its curse, it has been taken back by the devil to whom it belonged. But that, of course, is nonsense.

The Phantom Coach

Elma B. Edwards

The circumstances I am about to relate to you have truth to commend them. They happened to me, and my recollection of them is as vivid as if they had taken place only yesterday. Twenty years, however, have gone by since that night. During those twenty years I have told the story to but one other person. I tell it now with a reluctance which I find it difficult to overcome. All I ask, meanwhile, is that you will abstain from forcing your own conclusions upon me. I want nothing explained away. I desire no arguments. My mind on this subject is quite made up, and, having the testimony of my own senses to rely upon, I prefer to abide by it.

Well! It was just twenty years ago, and within a day or two of the end of the grouse season. I had been out all day with my gun, and had had no sport to speak of. The wind was due east; the month, December; the place, a bleak wide moor in the far north of England. And I had lost all sense of direction. It was not a pleasant place in which to lose one's way, with the first feathery flakes of a coming snowstorm just fluttering down upon the heather, and the leaden evening closing in all around. I shaded my eyes with my hand, and stared anxiously into the gathering darkness, where the purple moorland melted into a range of low hills, some ten or twelve miles distant. Not the faintest smoke-wreath, not the tiniest cultivated patch, or fence, or sheep-track, met my eyes in any direction. There was nothing for it but to walk on, and take my chance of finding what shelter I could, by the way. So I shouldered my gun again and pushed wearily forward, for I had been on foot since an hour after daybreak and had eaten nothing since breakfast.

Meanwhile, the snow began to come down with ominous persistence, and the wind fell. After this, the cold became more intense, and the night came rapidly on. As for me, my prospects worsened with the darkening sky, and my heart grew heavy as I thought how my young wife was already watching for me through the window of our little inn parlour, and thought of all the suffering in store for her throughout this weary night. We had been married four months, and, having spent our autumn in the Highlands, were now lodging in a remote little village situated just on the verge of the great English moorlands. We were very much in love, and, of course, very happy. This morning, when we parted, she had implored me to return before dusk, and I had promised her that I would. What would I not have given to have kept my word!

Even now, weary as I was, I felt that with a supper, an hour's rest, and a guide, I might still get back to her before midnight, if only some help could be found.

And all this time the snow fell and the night became darker. I stopped and shouted every now and then, but my cries seemed only to emphasize the silence that reigned everywhere. Then a vague sense of uneasiness came upon me, and I began to remember stories of travellers who had walked on and on in the falling snow until, exhausted, they sank down to embrace a sleep from which they never awoke. Would it be possible, I asked myself, to keep going all through the long, lonely night? Would there not come a time when my limbs must fail, and my resolution give way? When I, too, must sleep the sleep of death. Death! I shuddered. How hard to die just now, when life a few hours ago had seemed so full of promise! How hard for my darling, whose loving heart – but that thought was not to be borne! To banish it, I shouted again, louder and longer, and then listened eagerly. Was my shout answered, or did I only fancy that I heard a far-off cry? I halloed again, and again the echo followed. Then a wavering speck of light came suddenly out of the dark, shifting, disappearing, growing momentarily nearer and brighter. Running towards it as quickly as I could, I found myself, to my great joy, face to face with an old man and a lantern.

'Thank God!' was the exclamation that burst involuntarily from my lips.

Blinking and frowning, he lifted his lantern and peered into my face.

'What for?' growled he, sulkily.

'Well – for you. I began to fear I should be lost in the snow.'

'Eh, then, folks do get cast away hereabouts fra', time to time, an' what's to hinder you from bein' cast away likewise, if the Lord's so minded?'

'If the Lord is so minded that you and I shall be lost together, friend, we must submit,' I replied; 'but I don't mean to be lost without you. How far am I now from Dwolding?'

'A gude twenty mile, more or less.'

'And the nearest village?'

'The nearest village is Wyke, an' that's twelve mile 'other side.'

'Where do you live, then?'

'Out yonder,' said he, with a vague jerk of the lantern.

'You're going home, I presume?'

'Maybe I am.'

'Then I'm going with you.'

The old man shook his head, and rubbed his nose reflectively with the handle of the lantern.

'It ain't o' no use,' growled he. 'He won't let you in – not he.'

'We'll see about that,' I replied, briskly. 'Who is He?'

'The master.'

'Who is the master?'

'That's nowt to you,' was the unceremonious reply.

'Well, well; you lead the way, and I'll see to it that the master shall give me shelter and a supper tonight.'

'Eh, you can try him!' muttered my reluctant guide; and, still shaking his head, he hobbled, gnome-like, away through the falling snow. A large mass loomed up presently out of the darkness, and a huge dog rushed out, barking furiously.

'Is this the house?' I asked.

'Ay, it's the house. Down, Bey!' And he fumbled in his pocket for the key.

I drew up immediately behind him, determined to go in with him, and saw in the little circle of light shed by the lantern that the door was heavily studded with iron nails, like that of a prison. In another minute he had turned the key and I had pushed past him into the house.

Once inside, I looked round with curiosity, and found myself in a great raftered hall, which served, apparently, a variety of uses. One end was piled to the roof with corn, like a barn. The other was stored with flour-sacks, agricultural implements, casks, and all kinds of miscellaneous lumber; while from the beams overhead hung rows of hams, flitches, and bunches of dried herbs for winter use. In the centre of the floor stood a large object gauntly dressed in a dingy wrapping-cloth, and reaching half way to the rafters. Lifting a corner of this cloth, I saw, to my surprise, a telescope of considerable size, mounted on a rough moveable platform, with four small wheels. The tube was made of painted wood, bound round with bands of metal; the speculum, so far as I could estimate its size in the dim light, measured at least fifteen inches in diameter. While I was yet examining the instrument, and asking myself whether it was not the work of some self-taught star-gazer, a bell rang sharply.

'That's for you,' said my guide, with a malicious grin. 'Yonder's his room.'

He pointed to a low black door at the opposite side of the hall. I crossed over, rapped somewhat loudly, and went in, without waiting for an invitation. A huge, white-haired old man rose from a table covered with books and papers, and confronted me sternly.

'Who are you?' said he. 'How came you here? What do you want?'

'James Murray, barrister-at-law. On foot across the moor. Meat, drink, and sleep.'

He bent his bushy brows into a portentous frown.

'Mine is not a house of entertainment,' he said, haughtily. 'Jacob, how dare you admit this stranger?'

'I didn't admit him,' grumbled the old man. 'He followed me over the muir, and shouldered his way in before me. I'm no match for six foot two.'

'Tell me, sir, by what right have you forced an entrance into my house?'

'The same by which I should have clung to your boat, if I were drowning. The right of self-preservation.'

'Self-preservation?'

'There's an inch of snow on the ground already,' I replied, briefly; 'and it would be deep enough to cover my body before daybreak.'

He strode to the window, pulled aside a heavy black curtain, and looked out.

'It is true,' he said. 'You can stay, if you choose, till morning. Jacob, serve the supper.'

With this he waved me to a seat, resumed his own, and became at once absorbed in the studies from which I had disturbed him.

I placed my gun in a corner, drew a chair to the hearth, and examined my quarters at leisure. Smaller and less incongruous in its arrangements than the hall, this room contained, nevertheless, much to awaken my curiosity. The floor was carpetless. The white-washed walls were in parts scrawled over with strange diagrams, and elsewhere covered with shelves crowded with instruments, the uses of many of which were unknown to me. On one side of the fireplace stood a bookcase filled with shabby folios; on the other, a small organ, fantastically decorated with painted carvings of mediaeval saints and devils. Through the half-opened door of a cupboard at the further end of the room I saw a long array of geological specimens, surgical preparations, crucibles, retorts, and jars of chemicals; while on the mantelshelf beside me, amid a number of small objects, stood a model of the solar system, a small galvanic battery, and a microscope. Every chair had its burden. Every corner was heaped high with books. The very floor was littered over with maps, casts, papers, tracings, and learned lumber of all conceivable kinds.

I stared about me with an amazement increased by every fresh object upon which my eyes chanced to rest. So strange a room I had never seen before; yet stranger still was its presence in a solitary farmhouse amid these wild and lonely moors! If what I saw aroused a keen curiosity, I was no lest intrigued as to the identity of my host and how he came to be living here. His head was singularly fine; but it was more the head of a poet than of a philosopher. Broad in the temple, prominent over the eyes, and clothed in an unruly shock of perfectly white hair, it had the appeal and much of the ruggedness that characterizes the head of Lüdwig van Beethoven. While I was yet observing him, the door opened, and Jacob brought in the supper. His master then closed his book, rose, and with more courtesy than he had yet shown, invited me to the table.

A dish of ham and eggs, a loaf of brown bread, and a bottle of admirable sherry, were placed before me.

'I have but the homeliest farmhouse fare to offer you, sir,' said my host. 'Your appetite, I trust, will make up for the deficiencies of our larder.'

I had already fallen upon the viands, and now protested, with the enthusiasm of a starving sportsman, that I had never eaten anything so delicious.

He bowed stiffly, and sat down to his own supper, which consisted primitively, of a jug of milk and a basin of porridge. We ate in silence, and when we had done, Jacob removed the tray. I then drew my chair back to the fireside. My host, somewhat to my surprise, did the same, and, turning abruptly towards me, said:

'Sir, I have lived here in strict retirement for three-and-twenty years. During that time I have not seen many unknown faces and I have not read a single newspaper. You are the first stranger who has crossed my threshold for more than four years. Will you favour me with a little information respecting that outer world from which I have parted company so long?'

'Pray interrogate me,' I replied. 'I am willingly at your service.'

He bent his head in acknowledgment; leaned forward, with his elbows resting on his knees and his chin supported in the palms of his hands; stared fixedly into the fire; and proceeded to question me.

His inquiries related chiefly to scientific matters, with the later progress of which, as applied to the practical purposes of life, he was almost wholly unacquainted. No student of science myself, I replied as well as my slight knowledge permitted; but the task was far from easy, and I was much relieved when, passing from interrogation to discussion, he began to formulate his own conclusions upon the facts which I had been attempting to place before him. He talked, and I listened spellbound. Later on I believe he almost forgot my presence, and only thought aloud. I had never heard anything like it then nor since. Familiar with most schools of philosophy, subtle in analysis, bold in generalization, his thoughts were expressed in an uninterrupted stream, and, still leaning forward in the same moody attitude with his eyes fixed upon the fire, wandered from topic to topic, from one speculation to another, like an inspired dreamer. From practical science to mental philosophy; from Watts to Mesmer, from Mesmer to Reichenbach, from Reichenbach to Swedenborg, Spinoza, Condillac, Descartes, Berkeley, Aristotle, Plato, and the Magi and mystics of the East, were transitions which, however bewildering in their variety and scope, seemed easy and harmonious upon his lips as sequences in music. By and by – I forget now by what link of conjecture or illustration – he passed on to that field which lies beyond the boundary of even conjectural philosophy, and reaches no man knows where. He spoke of the soul and its aspirations; of the spirit and its powers; of second sight; of prophecy; of those phenomena which, under the names of ghosts, spectres, and supernatural appearances, have been denied by sceptics and attested by the credulous, of all ages.

'The world,' he said, 'grows hourly more and more sceptical of all that lies beyond its own narrow radius; and our men of science foster the fatal tendency. They condemn as fable all that resists experiment. They reject as false all that cannot be brought to the test of the laboratory or the dissecting-room. Against what superstition have they waged so long and obstinate a war, as against the belief in apparitions? And yet what superstition had maintained its hold upon the minds of men so long and so firmly? Show me any fact in physics, in history, in archaeology, which is supported by testimony so wide and so various. Attested by all races of men, in all ages, and in all climes, by the soberest sages of antiquity, by the rudest savage of today, by the Christian, the Pagan, the Pantheist, the Materialist, this phenomenon is treated as a nursery tale by the philosophers of our century. Circumstantial evidence weighs with them as a feather in the balance. The comparison of cause with effect, however valuable in physical science, is put aside as worthless and unreliable. The evidence of competent witnesses, however conclusive in a court of justice, counts for nothing. He who pauses before he pronounces, is condemned as a trifler. He who believes, is a dreamer or a fool.'

He spoke with bitterness, and, having said thus, relapsed for some minutes into silence. Presently he raised his head from his hands, and added, with an altered voice and manner:

'I, sir, paused, investigated, believed, and was not ashamed to state my convictions to the world. I, too, was branded as a visionary, held up to ridicule by my contemporaries, and excluded from that field of science in which I had laboured with honour during all the best years of my life. These things happened just three-and-twenty years ago. Since then I have lived as you see me living now, and the world has forgotten me, as I have forgotten the world. You now know my history.'

'It is a very sad one,' I murmured, scarcely knowing what to answer.

'It is a very common one,' he replied. 'I have only suffered for the truth, as many a better and wiser man has done before me.'

He rose, as if desirous of ending the conversation, and went over to the window.

'It has ceased snowing,' he observed, as he dropped the curtain and came back to the fireside.

'Ceased!' I exclaimed, starting eagerly to my feet,

'Oh, if it were only possible – but no! It is no use. Even if I could find my way across the moor, I could not walk twenty miles tonight.'

'Walk twenty miles tonight!' repeated my host. 'What are you thinking of?'

'Of my wife,' I replied, impatiently. 'Of my young wife, who does not know that I have lost my way, and who is at this moment, I am sure, in despair over my absence.'

'Where is she?'

'At Dwolding, twenty miles away.'

'At Dwolding,' he echoed, thoughtfully. 'Yes, the distance, it is true, is twenty miles; but – are you that anxious to make the journey before dawn?'

'So very, very anxious, that I would give ten guineas at this moment for a guide and a horse.'

'Your wish can be gratified at less cost,' he said, smiling. 'The night mail from the north, which changes horses at Dwolding, passes within five miles of this spot, and will be due at a certain cross-road in about an hour and a quarter. If Jacob were to go with you across the moor and put you along the old coach-road, you could find your way, I suppose, to where it joins the new one?'

'Easily – gladly.'

He smiled again, rang the bell, gave the old servant his directions, and, taking a bottle of whisky and a wineglass from the cupboard in which he kept his chemicals, said:

'The snow lies deep and it will be difficult walking tonight on the moor. A glass of usquebaugh before you start?'

I would have declined the spirit, but he pressed it on me, and I drank it. It went down my throat like liquid flame and almost took my breath away.

'It is strong,' he said; 'but it will help to keep out the cold. And now you have no time to spare. Good night!'

I thanked him for his hospitality and would have shaken hands with him but that he had turned away before I could make the gesture. In another minute I had traversed the hall, Jacob had locked the outer door behind me, and we were out on the wide white moor.

Although the wind had fallen, it was bitterly cold. Not a star glimmered in the black vault overhead. Not a sound, save the crunch of snow beneath our feet, disturbed the heavy stillness of the night. Jacob, not too well pleased with his mission, ambled along in sullen silence, his lantern in his hand and his shadow at his feet. I followed, with my gun over my shoulder, as little inclined for conversation as himself. My thoughts were full of my late host. His voice still rang in my ears, his eloquence yet held my imagination captive. I remember to this day, with surprise, how my mind, greatly stimulated, retained so much of what he had said, troops of brilliant images, and fragments of splendid reasoning, in the very words he himself had used. Musing thus over what I had heard, and striving to recall a lost link here and there, I strode on at the heels of my guide, absorbed and unobservant. Presently – and it seemed only a few minutes since we had set off – Jacob came to a sudden halt, and said:

'Yon's your road. Keep the stone fence to your right hand and you can't fail to find your way.'

'This, then, is the old coach-road?'

'Ay, 'tis the old coach-road.'

'And how far do I go before I reach the cross-roads?'

'Nigh upon three mile.'

I pulled out my purse, and he became more communicative.

'The road's a fair road enough,' said he, 'for foot passengers; but 'twas over-steep and narrow for the northern traffic. You'll mind where the parapet's broken away, close again' the sign-post. It's never been mended since the accident.'

'What accident?'

'Eh, the night mail pitched right over into the valley

below – a gude fifty feet an' more – just at the worst bit o' road in the whole county.'

'Horrible! Were many lives lost?'

'All. Four were found dead, and t'other two died next morning.'

'How long is it since this happened?'

'Just nine year.'

'Near the sign-post, you say? I will bear it in mind. Good night.'

'Gude night, sir, and thankee.' Jacob pocketed his half-crown, made a faint pretence of touching his hat, and trudged back by the way he had come.

I watched the light of his lantern till it disappeared, and then turned to pursue my way alone. I had not now the slightest cause for concern, for, despite the darkness the line of stone fence showed distinctly enough against the pale gleam of the snow. How silent it seemed now, with only my footsteps to listen to; how solitary! A strange disagreeable sense of loneliness however soon stole over me. I walked faster. I hummed a fragment of a tune. I cast up enormous sums in my head, and accumulated them at compound interest. I did my best, in short, to forget the startling speculations to which I had but just been listening, and, to some extent, I succeeded.

Meanwhile, the night air seemed to become colder and colder, and though I walked fast I found it impossible to keep myself warm. My feet were like ice. I lost sensation in my hands, and grasped my gun mechanically. I even breathed with difficulty, as though, instead of traversing a quiet North-country highway, I were scaling the uppermost heights of some gigantic mountain. This last symptom became presently so distressing that I was forced to stop for a few minutes and lean against the stone fence. As I did so I chanced to look back up the road, and there, to my infinite relief, I saw a distant point of light, like the gleam of an approaching lantern. At first I thought that Jacob had retraced his steps and followed me; but even as the conjecture presented itself, a second light flashed into sight – a light evidently parallel with the first, and approaching at the same rate of motion. It needed no second thought to show me that these must be the carriage-lamps of some private vehicle, though it seemed strange that any such conveyance should take a road no longer used and regarded as dangerous.

There could be no doubt, however, of the fact, for the lamps grew larger and brighter every moment, and I even fancied I could already see the dark outline of the carriage between them. It was coming up very fast, and quite noiselessly, the snow being nearly a foot deep under the wheels.

And now the body of the vehicle became distinctly visible behind the lamps. It looked strangely lofty. A sudden suspicion flashed upon me. Was it possible that I had passed the cross-roads in the dark without observing the sign-post and could this be the very coach which I had come to meet?

No need to ask myself that question a second time, for here it came round the bend of the road, guard and driver, one outside passenger, and four steaming greys, all wrapped in a soft haze of light, through which the lamps blazed out, like a pair of glowing meteors.

I jumped forward, waved my hat, and shouted. The vehicle came down at full speed, and passed me. The coachman pulled up; the guard, muffled to the eyes in capes and comforters, and apparently sound asleep in the rumble, neither answered my hail nor made the slightest effort to dismount; the outside passenger did not even turn his head. I opened the door for myself, and looked in. There were but three travellers inside, so I stepped in, shut the door, slipped into the vacant corner, and congratulated myself on my good fortune.

The atmosphere of the coach seemed, if possible, colder than that of the outer air and was pervaded by a singularly damp and disagreeable smell. I looked round at my fellow-passengers. They were three of them, men, and all silent. They did not seem to be asleep, but each leaned back in his corner of the vehicle, as if absorbed in his own reflections. I attempted to open a conversation.

'How intensely cold it is tonight,' I said, addressing my opposite neighbour.

He lifted his head, looked at me, but made no reply.

'The winter,' I added, 'seems to have begun in earnest.'

Although the corner in which he sat was so dim that I could distinguish none of his features very clearly, I saw that his eyes were still turned full upon me. And yet he spoke no word.

At any other time I should have felt, and perhaps expressed, some annoyance, but at the moment I felt too ill to do either. The icy coldness of the night air had struck a chill to my very marrow, and the strange smell inside the coach was so powerful that it gave me a feeling of intense nausea. I shivered from head to foot, and, turning to my neighbour on the left, I asked if he had any objection to an open window?

He neither spoke nor stirred.

I repeated the question rather more emphatically, but with the same result. Then I lost my patience and let the sash down. As I did so, the leather strap broke in my hand, and I noticed that the glass was covered with a thick coat of mildew, the accumulation, apparently, of years of neglect. My attention being thus drawn to the condition of the coach, I examined it more carefully, and saw by the uncertain light of the outer lamps that it was in the last stage of dilapidation. Every part of it was not only decrepit but in a condition of decay. The sashes splintered at a touch and the leather fittings were encrusted with mould, and literally rotting from the woodwork. The floor was I could see, in a dangerous condition. The vehicle, in fact, was foul with damp, and had evidently been dragged from some outhouse in which it had been mouldering away for years, to do another day or two of duty on the road.

I turned to the third passenger, whom I had not yet addressed, and hazarded one more remark.

'This coach,' I said, 'is in a deplorable condition. The regular mail, I suppose, is under repair?'

He moved his head slowly, and looked me in the face, without speaking a word. I shall never forget that look while I live. I turned cold at heart under it. I tremble even now when I recall it. His eyes glowed with a fiery unnatural lustre and his face was as livid as that of a corpse. His bloodless lips were drawn back as if in the agony of death, and showed the gleaming teeth between.

The words that I was about to utter died upon my lips, and a strange horror – an unspeakable dread – came upon me. My sight had by this time become used to the gloom of the coach, and I could see with tolerable distinctness. I turned to my opposite neighbour. He, too, was looking at me with the same startling pallor in his face and the same awful glitter in his eyes. I passed my hand across my brow. I turned to the passenger on the seat beside my own, and saw – oh, Heaven! how shall I describe what I saw? I saw that he was no living man – that none of them were living men, like myself! A pale phosphorescent light – the light of putrefaction – played upon their awful faces; upon their hair, dank with the dews of the grave; upon their clothes, earth stained and falling to pieces; upon their hands, which were as the hands of corpses long buried. Only their eyes, their terrible eyes, were living; and those eyes were all turned menacingly upon me!

A shriek of terror, a wild, unintelligible cry for help and mercy, burst from my lips as I flung myself against the door and strove in vain to open it.

In that single instant, brief and vivid as a landscape held in the flash of summer lightning, I saw the moon shining down through a rift of stormy cloud – the ghastly sign-post rearing its warning finger by the wayside – the broken parapet – the plunging horses – the black gulf below. The coach reeled like a ship in heavy seas. Then came a mighty crash – a sense of crushing pain – and then darkness.

It seemed as if years had passed when I awoke one morning from a deep sleep and found my wife watching at my bedside. I will not describe the scene that ensued and will tell you, in a few words, the tale she told me with tears of thanksgiving. I had fallen over a precipice, quite close to the junction of the old coach-road and the new, and had only been saved from certain death by lighting upon a deep snowdrift that had accumulated at the foot of the rock beneath. In this snowdrift I was discovered at daybreak by a couple of shepherds, who carried me to the nearest shelter, and brought a surgeon to my aid. He found me in a state of delirium, with a broken arm and a compound fracture of the skull. The letters in my pocket-book showed my name and address; my wife was summoned to nurse me; and, thanks to my youth and robust constitution and to the care I received I survived the dangerous phases of my illness. The place of my fall, I need scarcely say, was precisely that at which a frightful accident had happened to the north mail nine years before.

I never told my wife the fearful events which I have just related to you, but confided in the surgeon who attended me; but he treated the whole adventure as a mere dream born of the fever in my brain. We discussed the affair on several occasions until we found that our differing views provoked too sharp an argument and we never referred to it again. Others may form what conclusions they please – I *know* that twenty years ago I was the fourth passenger inside the Phantom Coach.

Ghosts Come to Hell

Pat Scholer

People who don't believe in ghosts are usually content to say so and pass on to other matters but not dapper, forty-year-old Welsh actor John Heel, now living in Sydney.

Early in his life Heel decided against the existence of ghosts. Since then he has devoted much of his time to proving he took the right line.

During his search for certainty, Heel became a member of England's Ghost Club, an association of people dedicated to coming to grips with Things.

He visited reputedly haunted buildings, confronted invisible barriers, pursued disembodied footsteps, fled from a voice urging him to kill himself, and explored the Great Pyramid of Egypt while leaving his body safe at home in his London flat.

Though these experiences might have shaken another man's disbelief in the supernatural, Heel has stuck to his theory that there's nothing about ghosts that science can't explain, given a little more time.

Ghosts, he insists, are not spirits returned from the

grave, but a type of photograph. Everybody, so he reasons, leaves some impression or image in the atmosphere, and a person under stress leaves a very strong image which someone else may later see and call a ghost.

American scientists, he points out, claim they have developed a time camera, an infra-red device which looks back through time and takes pictures of what it sees. This camera, focused on an empty parade ground, is said to have taken a photograph of soldiers who were there some time previously.

Doesn't this, Heel asks, rather point up his theory that people leave an image in the atmosphere?

Heel would have appreciated having some such device as the time camera along with him on his ghost hunts. It might have come in handy, for instance, in that seventeenth century house in North Wales which was the scene of one of his first encounters with the Unexplained. Heel explored the house with a friend when he was only seventeen.

'The place was in excellent condition, yet it had been vacant for years because it was disturbed,' Heel says in that richly dramatic voice which has interpreted so many roles in the English theatre.

'Ah yes, undoubtedly it was disturbed. Doors opened and shut. Across the staircase there was an invisible barrier so strong that when we tried to break through it we couldn't.'

Would that be the work of a photograph? 'Let's say of – a force,' Heel replies, and his voice drops to a sibilant murmur which is quite unsettling. 'Something had happened in that house. Something – rather horrible, I imagine, had left behind this super-charged atmosphere. Perhaps we disturbed it. Perhaps a sort of electricity caused the doors to open and shut.'

One of Heel's lighter encounters with the supernatural (for lack of a more scientific word) occurred on Snowdon, the highest mountain in Wales.

'This is a story I cannot account for,' Heel admits candidly. 'All I can say is it happened.' And the resonant voice takes up the tale of the Tylwydd Teg.

'The Welsh,' he explains, 'are a romantic and imaginative people. Through the centuries they have cherished the tradition of the Tylwydd Teg – the fairy music of Snowdon. I have heard this music.

'I was staying at the foot of Snowdon. One moonlit night it occurred to me that it was bright enough to climb a little way up the mountain and have a look at the view. I must confess that the thought also came into my mind – "I'll find out about the Tylwydd Teg business".'

By two o'clock in the morning, Heel had climbed some way up Snowdon. He was resting, admiring the moonlit view, when he saw, moving slowly down the mountain, a figure – a misty, wild-looking figure.

It was an old shepherd. 'We greeted each other. And then I said to him, "I've been wondering if there's anything to this Tylwydd Teg business".'

According to Heel, the shepherd told him there certainly was, and if he'd just keep quiet he'd probably hear for himself. 'So we sat whispering for about a quarter of an hour,' Heel relates, 'and then suddenly I heard the music. Clearly, like dozens of tiny, tinkling bells – the fairy music of Snowdon.'

He smiles as if he were still listening to that magical sound. 'Well, after about a quarter of an hour the music died away. I said to the old boy, "I'm privileged, I never thought I'd hear that. Astonishing".'

'The old boy,' however, pointed out that there was little call for astonishment, because after all he had been sitting inside one of the enchanted circles of Snowdon – circles of bracken trodden down by the dancing feet of fairies.

'I looked around,' Heel says, 'and right enough, there was the ring of dead bracken, and I was inside it.' In those circumstances, of course, he declares it was not remarkable that he'd heard the Tylwydd Teg.

Heel was in York, with Emlyn Williams' theatrical company, the next time he tangled with a Something which science has yet to explain. On this occasion the puzzle was set by the shade of a nun, known as the Grey Lady of the Theatre Royal.

According to talk around York, this stage-struck ghost often joined the actors during a performance or stood quietly watching them from the auditorium.

'The walls and foundations of this theatre, which was near York Minster, belonged to an ancient nunnery,' Heel explains. 'Below the stage was the nunnery well, where it was the custom of the artists to throw in a penny and make a wish – I did it myself.

'The stalls bar was one of the most perfect examples in all England of a Norman crypt.

'The backstage entrance was through a long, low, dark, stone tunnel. You felt there was something eerie there. The whole atmosphere was one of foreboding.'

It being wartime when he was in York, Heel was often rostered on fire-watching duty after a show closed. It was on one of these occasions, when he was on duty with a member of the stage crew, that he heard the footsteps of the Grey Lady.

'Everything was quiet. We were having a cup of coffee together,' Heel relates, 'when I heard a sound like the pattering of footsteps in the tunnel. So I said to this chap, "What was that sound?" He said, "Don't worry. Happens all the time. Forget it".'

Heel, as a member of the Ghost Club, was simply not the man to accept advice of that sort. 'The pattering sound crossed the wooden stage. I followed. I couldn't see anybody or anything.

'The footsteps led me up the spiral stairs to the dressing rooms. I knew the doors were locked, yet now they were opening as if at a touch. Lights were going on.

'I followed the steps from one dressing room to another. I followed them down the stairs again, I followed them down the stone passage and right out through the stage door. And there they just faded out on the roadway, in the direction of the Great West Door of York Minster.'

In the following year in another theatre, the Royal in Leicester, he had another supernatural experience.

'The place was about one hundred and twenty-seven years old,' he says. 'I was managing it, as well as acting there. I had so much work to do I often stayed on in the theatre after everyone else had gone.

'I'd never had time to explore the place, so one night after the show finished I thought I'd take a look around. I'd heard there was a lot of furniture stored under the stage and I began with that.

'The furniture turned out to be simply covered with dust. Filthy. I was in evening dress, so I decided to leave it for another time.'

And then, he says, some impulse prompted him to make his way up through the gloom into the network of catwalks and galleries forty feet above the stage.

He explored the fly gallery, from which the scenery was manipulated, and the paint gallery, used by the scenic artists. He was halfway over the catwalk across the proscenium arch when he saw, in the wall next to him, a trapdoor.

He hesitated, then wrenched it open. There, stretching back across the roof of the auditorium, was a huge storeroom strewn with the debris of perhaps a century of super-colossal productions; papier mache columns, urns, tattered costumes, plaster statues mantled in the dust of the years.

Shutting the trapdoor, Heel proceeded along the catwalk, feeling his way through shadow pierced weakly by a small pilot light. 'And now – ' Heel's voice sinks, as he relates the story, 'now came the first and only occasion in all this ghost business that I have been absolutely terrified.

'I began to get a feeling. A very curious feeling. Remember, I was forty feet above the stage. And I heard these words: "Jerry wants you to do it – jump over. Jerry wants you to do it – jump over."'

After a long pause – 'Of course,' Heel says in a normal voice, 'I'm willing to admit I might not really have heard those words, that they might perhaps have existed merely in my subconscious –

'Anyway, I ran. I simply turned and ran. I got out of that theatre as fast as I could.'

Next morning Heel called in the stage manager and the electrician who had worked for years at the Royal and asked them if there were any queer stories about the theatre.

Well, they said, there was a stagehand who went berserk. He'd rushed into the fly gallery, put a rope around his neck and thrown himself over. Now, what was his name again? Of course – Jerry.

They mentioned that there was the black shadow which sometimes appeared when they were working late. It had a habit of moving across the spotlight, blotting it out, they said. The shadow carried with it a clammy, chill feeling and a nasty smell.

'But although I stayed back with those men several times, hoping to see the shadow,' Heel says, 'I admit it never appeared when I was there. From which you might gather that I'm not the type to claim to see things when I don't.'

Another case about which Heel gives a fairly detached report was that of St Margaret's vicarage, Leicester. He remembers discussing this case with the Bishop of Leicester as they waited for their respective trains.

'When I first caught sight of the Bishop,' Heel tells, 'I noticed there was something odd about him. Then I realized what it was. He was not wearing his gaiters.

'Well, I greeted him in the usual way – "How d'you do, my lord, long time no see", and so on – and then I got around to the subject of St Margaret's vicarage. I knew he'd arranged to visit the place and I asked him how he'd got on.

'Well, he was a broad-minded man, charming – so many bishops aren't, but he was. He said to me, "Johnny, you'll have noticed I'm not wearing my gaiters". So I said, "Why yes, my lord".

'He said, "Johnny, between you and me, at that vicarage I was scared right out of them".'

One of the disturbing phenomena of St Margaret's was a phosphorescent green light which would fill a closed room. Once the door was opened the light would fade, after which the air would be rent by a sound which might be described as a screaming laugh – or, perhaps, as a laughing scream.

Then of course there was the black-robed figure which walked up and down a flagged stone passageway – doing little harm, actually, by comparison with another figure in white which kept turning up in the staff quarters and frightening away the servants.

The vicar's harassed wife had to manage a household where cloths were pulled off tables by invisible hands (or something), sheets and blankets were whisked off beds and made to disappear in front of her, and cups and saucers took off from their shelves and sailed away into nothingness.

'Finally she'd lose her temper,' Heel recalls, 'and shout out, "Oh, for heaven's sake give me back my things." Then back they'd come, you know. Mysteriously, they'd all be returned to her, and the house would be quiet for a while.'

Heel is certain that most of the phenomena at St Margaret's were due to a poltergeist – defined in the dictionary as 'a noisy ghost, a spirit assumed as the explanation of rappings and other unexplained noises.'

'Poltergeists,' Heel says, 'are two a penny.'

In his opinion, though, they are not spirits, but

manifestations of something in the mind of an adolescent, usually a girl. The adolescent is seldom aware of the poltergeist's behaviour, which often suggests that of a disembodied bogie.

'Poltergeists can be horrible, evil,' Heel insists. 'But also they're silly. I mean, where's the point in picking up a chair, whirling it around and throwing it down again? Ridiculous.

'There was the case of the Battersea poltergeist. I saw the girl myself, just sitting there quietly watching television, unaware of this poltergeist thing operating all around her – hats flying, tapping on walls, a piece of chalk drawing a face on a blind.

'Oh yes. I watched that piece of chalk myself. Moving through the air, drawing, and nothing holding it.'

Heel did not return to the vicarage to investigate the poltergeist of St Margaret's. The Bishop asked him not to because he disliked the publicity which often attended an investigation by Ghost Club members.

Heel's relations with other churchmen in Leicester were not always so happy, especially after he produced James Bridie's 'Mr Bolfry,' a play which brings the devil on to the stage to claim the soul of a parson.

Cast as the parson, Heel evolved what he feels was one of his most spectacular make-ups to turn himself into the crabbed old churchman. 'I had to take the play off after three nights,' Heel told us. 'The church people said it was sacrilegious.'

In 1951 Heel moved to London and because of an acute accommodation shortage, he and his wife and mother had to settle into shabby lodgings. It was then Heel read that the Dover Museum wished to sell an Egyptian mummy which had been in a room damaged in an air raid.

'I wrote,' Heel recalls. 'Purely for a joke, of course. I was invited down to Dover, however, and found that the mummy had lost some of its bandages – it seemed that workmen had searched it for ornaments – but I was impressed by the fine preservation of the body.

'I made an offer for it. An absurd offer, really – £3. And the museum jumped at it.

'When I recovered from the shock it seemed to me extremely peculiar that the museum should be glad to dispose of the mummy for such a small sum. However, I arranged with a road cartage firm to pick up the mummy and deliver it to my digs. Their charge was 25s.

'That made £4 5s. altogether for a mummy – a twenty-one-year-old boy, according to the museum, a priest of Isis of 2,500 years ago.

'Later I received a letter from the museum saying that a chap living in south London had been interested in the mummy, and would like to meet its new owner. So I wrote to this man – Stanley Forsythe – and he invited me to go to see him.'

Forsythe explained to Heel that, as a child, he'd spent many happy hours in the Dover Museum looking at the mummies and so he had a particular interest in the specimen Heel had acquired.

'I'm going to make you an offer,' Forsythe told Heel. 'At the top of this house there's a furnished flat, five rooms, self-contained. I'll let you have it for 35s. a week if you will bring your mummy with you, store it in the basement, and allow me to help with the restoration.'

That was the way Heel acquired a comfortable flat and a famous address – 34 Lancaster Road, South Norwood. It was at No. 34 that such celebrities as Sir Oliver Lodge and Sir Arthur Conan Doyle had attended seances. 'That house,' Heel says, 'was literally saturated with psychic emanations.'

Forsythe, the landlord, turned out to be a writer with a side interest in Egyptology and anatomy. After sessions in the basement cleaning up the coffin and re-winding the outer bandages of the mummy, Forsythe became convinced that the body was not that of a twenty-one-year-old boy but of a girl of about sixteen. In the hope that spirits would confirm his theory, he arranged a seance.

For the occasion, the mummy was carried upstairs to the dining-room. There, under the bright light of an electric chandelier, the seance proceeded in the presence of reporters from the London papers, three spiritualists, Forsythe and Heel, and two friends.

The medium who conducted the seance over the Egyptian mummy was, in Heel's words, 'a young woman who kept a confectionery shop and couldn't even tell you who Tutankhamen was.

'Yet after she'd gone into a trance,' Heel relates, 'she came straight over to me and in a strange voice, the voice of an old, old man, described a temple. It seemed to be a cross between a Greek and Roman building, and I couldn't make much sense out of it.

'The voice said a girl had died and had paid a terrible price for a crime committed. Then the voice changed into that of a young girl. And this is the message I received (I make no comment on it):

'"My name is Katrina. I was accounted fair in the eyes of the Pharaoh and all the land of Egypt. I died and was buried. I sinned against my Pharaoh and I paid the price.

'"I was a priestess in the temple of Orkon. You have saved my body from destruction and so long as you shall keep me safe within these walls I will do harm to all those who would hurt the dwellers within these walls. Protect me, preserve me. In life I suffered acutely from a painful disease."

'A few weeks later a young doctor said he'd like to examine the mummy and I gave him permission.

'Somehow the newspapers got hold of the story. My word, you know, it's a good job I've got a sense of humour, otherwise I might easily have lost my temper. The heading the *Sunday Dispatch* gave the story was, "He is sending his mummy to see a doctor."

'Ah well. Three days later I received the doctor's report. It said that the mummy was the remains of a girl of sixteen, that there were not sufficient internal organs to give a definite cause of death, and that she had suffered from spondylitis.

'In other words, the medium's Katrina voice had been right in claiming the body as a girl's, and right about her suffering from a painful disease.'

Confirmation of statements made in the medium's old-man voice came, Heel adds, from Egyptologist Sir Alan Gardiner. He wrote that the mummy dated from the Graeco-Roman period of Egyptian history and probably from the reign of Osorkon II or III.

Later, despite her promises to be nice to her hosts, Katrina began to misbehave. Heel's mother insisted she had seen queer shadows moving about in the basement.

'I suspected something was disturbing the dust so as a test I spread powdered cement over the floor. I locked the door so that nobody could go in. Later, I inspected the place. The dust had been disturbed. Then, lights began to go on and off in our flat. We began to hear footsteps. One afternoon they crossed the room behind the settee where my wife and I were sitting.'

All this indicated to Heel that Katrina must be dissatisfied with life in a basement, so he brought her upstairs and gave her a room of her own in his flat. Sure enough, the disturbances ceased.

'But then a very curious thing happened,' he says. 'I spent all one night wandering, so it seemed, inside the Great Pyramid of Egypt.

'Everything was clear, as real as anything I'm looking at now. I seemed to be searching for somebody. I felt I wanted to tell them something.

'I said to my wife in the morning, "I've had a wonderful time – I've spent the entire night in the Great Pyramid. I seemed to be looking for somebody." Of course she laughed – "Looking for your mummy, were you?"

'Now, nobody else heard what I said. Yet when I came home that evening I received a note left by my landlord's wife.

'She had written, "I have a strange story to tell you. Last night I dreamed I was in the Great Pyramid of Egypt. I was looking for you and couldn't find you. It seemed I had something to tell you about your mummy."

'Well, that shocked my wife pretty badly.'

It was rather a relief to Mrs Heel to leave the mummy behind when, in February, 1958, she and her husband emigrated to Australia.

In his new country, Heel has maintained his interest in the disturbed images usually referred to as ghosts. His investigations have led him to a suspected poltergeist or two, but there's really been nothing to come up to his experiences in Britain.

'There are simply no very ancient buildings here,' he points out. 'No crumbling arches. None of those marvellous ruins.

'Though, of course,' he adds thoughtfully, 'It isn't strictly necessary for a house to be old to be haunted.

'Why, in Croydon, England, it happened in a new pair of semi-detached red brick council houses. The tenants had been in them only a few weeks when the trouble started. They were haunted by a crying baby.

'This baby just cried and cried. You could hear it from the roadway. You could even pinpoint the spot in the room where the noise came from. But you just couldn't see any baby.

'In the end, the tenants of both the houses moved out.

'Mind you,' Heel adds, 'that's not to say there was a ghost. No doubt there is some perfectly rational explanation. I'm sure there is. And one of these days, science will find it.'

Wages of Envy

Mark Bartholomeusz

Juse Appuhamy, Sinhalese, never liked those who talked too much. Unnecessary speech, he felt, was a sign that the speaker was a man of words, rather than deeds. So as a golden rule, more or less, he minded his own business, kept himself to himself, worked like a galley slave at his job of selling vegetables at the neighbouring fairs, and looked after his family with commendable zeal.

As a result of his labours over the years, he slowly but surely began to thrive. One day he found that he was able to afford the money to buy a new cart and even more important, a fine, sturdy bull, to take his produce to market.

Most of Juse Appuhamy's neighbours in the Ceylon village, where he lived, hated to see him perched on top of his fully laden new cart, driving his bull to market with the arrogance of a king. It irked them to think that Juse Appuhamy who had started life as a labourer, like many of them, working in the rice fields for others, had over the years become successful. There was a time, they recalled, when he could hardly afford a rag to his back.

But now he always wore a well laundered shirt and a new sarong.

They regarded with envy his neat little tiled cottage with its even neater compound, swept regularly every day by Ran Menika, Juse's wife. Every bit as industrious as her husband, she, too, was careful of her appearance even when she was busy in the kitchen. The couple's detractors preferred to ignore the fact that it was their own indolence that had kept them poor. Neither would they admit that Juse Appuhamy and his wife had thrived because of their own efforts. Rarely did their day begin later than cocks-crow and the couple's three healthy children were a credit to their parents.

While the rest of the village slept, Juse would be feeding his bull and preparing for his daily round to the outlying districts.

Meanwhile Ran Menika – so named because of her ran or golden complexion – would start baking the hoppers which Juse relished as though they were the rarest delicacies. She always felt that her toil was well worthwhile, when she saw with what relish her husband ate the meal she had prepared for him. On rare occasions he would even tell her, quietly but with a tenderness she was quick to recognize:

'There is not a woman in this village, Menika, who can bake a better hopper or make a finer coconut sambol.'

Ran Menika would pause in her work for a moment, glance at her husband, as if to remind herself of how handsome he was, and say:

'It's your belly talking again.'

Juse would answer with a smile, 'No, that's not quite true. I am sure you know it isn't.'

So while Juse Appuhamy and his wife prospered, there grew between them and the villagers a veritable wall of resentment. Among the most hostile was Juse's immediate neighbour, Marthelis, a thin, characterless man who lived with his wife and family on three acres of land which had been given to him many years ago by the government. Now, Marthelis had allowed more than half of his acreage to be reclaimed by the jungle and his attempts to grow coconuts and vegetables on the remainder were only half-hearted. He preferred to spend too much of this time earning easy money by selling an illicit brew to the villagers and using most of this income to challenge all-comers to a game of cards called 'Buruwa'.

He was not a very good card player though, and lost more often than he won. His wife, Prema, an unkempt creature with hard eyes and sunken cheeks, had truly little to be happy about. She shared with her husband and children a broken-down hut the roof of which leaked badly whenever it rained.

Every time Marthelis or his wife looked towards the opposite compound and saw the neat reliable red tiles on their neighbours' roof, their envy increased.

Prema especially, by that queer logic peculiar to villagers, began to feel that their poverty was due, in some inexplicable way to their neighbours. Never for a moment did she ascribe it to her husband's feckless ways; for strangely enough, she cared for him despite the scant attention he gave her or the children. One night it rained so heavily that in no time at all the hut was full of little pools of water. Prema's two small daughters had hardly a place that was dry to sleep in and began to cry and whimper. In desperation Prema drugged them to sleep with a herbal concoction well known to the villagers and placed them on a mat in the one dry place in the room. When they finally dozed off to sleep she joined her husband, who sat quietly smoking a beedi (a rolled leaf like tobacco).

For a long time neither spoke. They were both deep in their own thoughts. The rain continued its steady murmur for a while and then slowly dwindled to a drizzle. Prema at length unburdened herself of her thoughts.

'I know who has brought us all this bad luck over the years,' she said dolefully.

'Who?' asked Marthelis innocently, though half suspecting the answer.

'Who else but that filthy woman in the next plot,' said Prema viciously. 'It isn't natural for our family to go on having this bad luck for so long. Yes, for fifteen years I have been your wife and I haven't even a tiled roof to show for it. I live in the same mud hut as you brought me to when I first got married. Only now it leaks a lot more.'

'So how could that woman cause our ill-luck?' asked Marthelis.

'Aiyo,' said Prema. 'As though you don't know.'

'Do you think they have done something?'

'I don't think they have done something. I know it.'

Marthelis' latent hatred towards his neighbours allured his interest in what his wife was saying.

'How do you know for certain?' he asked quietly.

'I went to the Pusari (priest) this morning at the shrine in the forest.'

'You went to see the Pusari?'

'Yes.'

'Alone?'

'Yes.'

'You shouldn't have done it,' said Marthelis. 'Not when you have a husband to go with you.'

'When a woman has a husband who plays cards for most of the day,' said Prema, with a trace of annoyance, 'she must learn to do things for herself.'

Marthelis merely took a long pull at his beedi. For a few moments there was silence. But his curiosity got the better of him.

'What did the Pusari say?' he asked nonchalantly.

'He went into a trance first before the shrine to his God and then the God spoke through him.'

'I know. I know all that,' said Marthelis impatiently, wondering why his wife had to waste his time with all these very familiar details. 'What I want to know is what did the God say?'

Prema came to the point at last.

'In a deep voice which seemed to come from his belly, he said that a tall, fair, well dressed woman with a mole on her right cheek, living almost next to our property, had buried a charm in our garden.'

'Charm!' Marthelis could not conceal the fear he felt when he heard the dreaded word.

'Yes,' said Prema. 'And who else but Ran Menika? Is she not as the God described her, even to the mole on her right cheek?'

Marthelis paused for a moment deep in thought. 'The God cannot be wrong,' he said at length, 'if he described our neighbour so exactly. Where did he say the charm was buried?'

'It is the kind of charm which no one can ever find and was buried many years ago.'

'No one can ever find?' Marthelis really was alarmed.

'Yes. But don't be frightened. The Pusari also said that the power of this charm could be cut.'

'By whom?'

'By him, of course.'

Marthelis sighed with relief. He felt as though a great load had been lifted from his chest. 'I suppose,' he said, finally, 'we will have to take him an offering of some kind when next we go to see him.'

'Yes,' said Prema. 'When I went for water this morning at the wewa (lake) I asked Aunt Marthina what I would have to take, apart from the nine limes and the husked coconut that the Pusari asked me to bring for the cutting ceremony and she said that all we needed was a two rupee note.'

About a week after this conversation Marthelis and Prema both found that they were constantly thinking of what had been done to them by their neighbours, to bring them under the spell of an evil demon, and their consequent misfortunes and poverty. It rankled so much within them that they could not help but speak about it to others in the village. Very soon, the revelation of the Pusari concerning Juse and his wife became known to everybody.

Villagers nodded their heads wisely and said, 'We always knew that those two were not people to be trusted. The Forest God is never wrong. This explains why they have far more money than the rest of us. They are people who dabble in charms and are able to secure the aid of the demons to help them prosper.' Prema and her husband agreed whole-heartedly. Even the handful of acquaintances, who had no grudge against Juse and his wife, began to regard them as something of a threat. They didn't want too many dabblers in black magic in their midst.

The couple had no inkling of the evil rumours that daily were whispered behind their backs. Juse, of course, was aware of the part played by gossip in village life, but he would hardly have believed it even if he had been warned of the dangerous situation that was developing.

Perhaps the last straw was when Juse acquired a handsome transistor set and Prema and her husband heard the sound of music from their neighbour's compound. They were furious as they huddled together in their miserable hovel and, there and then, decided they would no longer delay their visit to the Pusari so that the evil spell which had bound them to poverty for so long should be destroyed for ever.

A visit to the Pusari was not an easy undertaking but Prema and Marthelis were determined to bring about a change in their fortunes or ensure, at least, the ruin of Juse Appuhamy and his wife. So, one morning, they packed a loaf of bread and some bananas into a cloth bag and also took with them a husked coconut, nine limes and a note worth two rupees as offerings.

Shortly after starting their journey they left the road that led out of the village and took to a path through the thick forest. They had five miles to trudge before they came to the shrine. Marthelis thought the journey would never end. He was afraid of the great forest and the silence and gloom. The sun overhead could not penetrate the barrier created by the height of the enormous trees and every shadow filled Marthelis with foreboding. He wondered what he would do if a leopard crossed their path and could hardly repress a shudder on remembering that his wife not long ago had come here alone. The only sign of wild life was that of an occasional jungle fowl which darted into the undergrowth as they approached.

After about two hours they finally came to a clearing at the end of which stood a great tree under which was a crude little structure built of stone and cement and consisting of two rooms. In one of them the Pusari slept, ate and lived, in the other he communicated his revelations from the deity.

As Marthelis and Prema approached the Pusari was intoning a litany before the God he worshipped, symbolized by a massive black image only vaguely suggesting a human outline. On each side of the idol, which stood upon an altar or stone shelf, stood jars containing smouldering joss sticks. Streamers of smoke coiled and uncoiled as they burned, radiating a sickly sweet perfume. At the foot of the image a large flame burned steadily in the clay receptacle filled with oil. Behind the flame was a mirror which appeared to glow eerily as it reflected the rays from the flame.

The Pusari appeared to sense that Prema and Marthelis were watching him from the entrance. Unhurriedly he concluded his devotions and came out to meet his visitors.

'So you've come,' he said quietly addressing Prema rather than her husband.

'Yes,' said Prema, shifting uneasily.

'I'm glad you have brought your husband with you. It will be easier for me to cut the power of the charm.'

Marthelis glanced at the Pusari but was too awed to speak to a man said to have power over spirits and demons. The priest had a strong, bony face and a commanding presence.

'Have you brought the limes?' he asked.

'Yes,' said Prema.

'Give them to me,' he said.

Prema rummaged within the cloth bag which still hung from her husband's neck, brought out the limes and gave them to him.

'Have you brought the husked coconut?' asked the Pusari again.

This time it was Marthelis who answered. 'Yes,' he said, and extracted the coconut from his bag. The Pusari took the coconut without a word and re-entered the shrine room.

Prema and Marthelis followed quietly behind him. The Pusari placed the limes and the coconut on a side of the altar and then he took a red sash which lay there and tied it round his waist. All he wore below the sash was a white cloth which extended up to his knees. His hairy chest was bare of clothing and was streaked horizontally with markings of ash.

'I shall start praying to the God,' he said quietly.

Prema thought the whiteness of his eyes was startling and so was the blackness of his face, which was also streaked with ash. His reddish brown beard like the hair on his head was matted. For a moment she felt frightened in his presence.

The ascetic seemed to sense her fear. 'Now,' he said, 'I want you to calm yourself and to be silent. Your husband too. The great god of the forest will come only if you deserve his aid.' With these words he clasped his palms together, bowed his head and began to mumble something in a slow monotone.

Neither Prema nor Marthelis could understand what he said. Gradually the priest's voice rose from a whisper to a full-throated call while, at the same time, the upper part of his body began to sway from side to side.

Marthelis and Prema watched intently the weird movement of the Pusari's body. Quite suddenly he became convulsed and his body began vibrating at tremendous speed. His words became a meaningless babel and with each vibration there was a report like a pistol shot; so that ultimately Prema and Marthelis both felt as though the room was filled with the staccato rattle of some curious machine. The noise ceased as suddenly as it had begun and with it all movement by the Pusari himself. A deathly silence filled the room. The ascetic turned slowly away from the image to face Prema and Marthelis.

Prema couldn't repress a shudder when she saw the ascetic's eyes. They were gazing at her and yet through her. Then he slowly raised his hand and placed it on her forehead. He spoke now in a deep voice, so deep thought Prema, that it couldn't possibly belong to a human being.

'You and your husband have suffered greatly,' he said in clear intelligible Sinhalese. 'But the God of the Forest will bring your sufferings to an end.'

Prema felt as though a strange force was radiating from his fingers and coursing through her whole body. She was quite convinced that the God himself was talking. The ascetic touched Marthelis' forehead too in a similar manner. He turned slowly towards the altar and took one of the limes and then a knife. Resting the lime on Prema's head he cut it gently. For a moment he gazed at the two halves of the lime and then threw them on the floor.

Once again Prema and Marthelis heard the priest speak strangely as if the words of another were being transmitted through him.

'Not till a seed within the lime is cut exactly in half is the spell that binds you to poverty destroyed,' it said.

With this pronouncement the ascetic took another lime

from his altar and this time cut it over the head of Marthelis. Once again the seeds were whole and intact. He continued the ceremony using the remaining limes over the heads of Prema and her husband in turn. But every time the seeds remained intact. Prema and Marthelis had almost given up hope when he came to the eighth lime. This time he severed the lime in two over Marthelis' head.

'Ah,' intoned the ascetic. 'The seed has been cut exactly in half. The God of the Forest has destroyed the spell. Go back to your hut. You will no more be under its evil influence.'

Both Prema and Marthelis felt at that moment as though a tremendous burden had been lifted from their spirits. They were overjoyed at their reprieve but there was hatred in their hearts for the people who had kept them poor.

The ascetic turned again towards the image and with head bowed low started to pray. Once more his body began to vibrate violently, but this time there were no staccato sounds. Gradually the rapid movement of the body ceased and he seemed to become his usual self again.

His chest was bathed with sweat as he came up to Prema and Marthelis and spoke to them in his normal voice. They could hardly believe that this was the same Pusari who had spoken to them earlier.

'You have a long way to go now, haven't you?' he asked casually.

'Not too far,' said Prema making light of the situation.

'Do not worry about the future,' he said.

But Prema had made up her mind that she would do something much more positive than await the arrival of better times. She would take her revenge for all that had been done to them. Yes, she was going to visit Malhamy the famous sorcerer who lived in the village next to their own. She would seek his aid to bring misfortune upon Ran Menika and her husband. When she whispered her thoughts to her husband he fully agreed. So with a final nod to the ascetic they left the shrine in the forest. But before they did so they dropped a two rupee note into the bowl kept at the entrance for the offerings of those who came for assistance.

For a few days after the visit to the forest shrine, Prema was aware of a great sense of relief; that oppressive burden of continued poverty which weighed down the spirits of both her and her husband seemed to become lighter. Even Marthelis no longer felt as despondent as he once did about his domestic affairs. Both he and Prema decided that it was the power of the Forest God, wielded through the agency of the Pusari, that had brought them this change in spirit; this feeling that all would be well in the future.

But after about a week, doubts began to nag them. As long as Ran Menika was alive and capable of doing something to them again she was a threat to their security. It was not that they doubted the Pusari's assurances but it seemed like folly not to see Malhamy the Kattadiya (sorcerer) at once. They could tell him what the God had revealed to them through the ascetic and ask for a charm with which to take their revenge.

No sooner they had decided on this trip than they made the journey to the village in which Malhamy lived. It wasn't more than ten miles away and it cost very little by bus from their own home.

Malhamy, contrary to what Prema expected of him, was not the thin, diabolic sorcerer with deep set penetrating eyes that she had imagined. He was a fat, hairy chested man with a great round belly and a face as full as a ripe melon. His eyes twinkled good-naturedly as he stood barefoot on the veranda of his home, clad only in a sarong.

What was even more surprising was that his home was quite different from the majority of mud huts in their village. It was built of brick, neatly white-washed, and had a roof of red tiles. A radio set stood ornamentally in the principal room and there was even a carpet on the veranda floor. A large Ford Prefect stood outside the porch and Malhamy had obviously climbed from humble origins to become one of the more prosperous people in the village.

At first, despite the twinkle in his eye, Prema and Marthelis were awed by the signs of opulence they saw. But Malhamy soon put them at their ease.

'Sit down,' he said in hearty manner, rubbing his naked paunch with two fat palms.

The feeling of awe soon thawed and Marthelis even succeeded in smiling as he took a seat on one of the upright chairs placed along the veranda. Prema followed suit.

Malhamy sat down on another easy chair opposite his clients and began to talk.

'Now,' he said, smiling broadly, 'what is your trouble?'

As usual Prema did most of the talking. 'Our neighbours buried a kodivinia (charm) in our garden many years ago,' she said.

'Kodivinia!' Malhamy had ceased to smile.

'Yes,' said Prema.

'How do you know they did this?'

'The God of the Forest told us. We've had bad luck for fifteen years.'

Malhamy nodded his head as she spoke. These were not the first clients to come to him with revelations from the famous Pusari.

'The God of the Forest is rarely wrong,' he said. 'Well, what do you want me to do?'

'We want you to help us to take our revenge,' said Prema.

'Do you want your neighbours to die?'

'No,' said Marthelis promptly. 'We do not desire their death.'

'Do you want them to be harassed by spirits or demons so that they can never prosper again?'

'Yes,' said Prema. 'If you can do that, specially to Ran Menika the woman mainly responsible for our misery, we will be amply revenged. It is time her pride was humbled.'

'It is not a difficult matter,' said Malhamy. 'But you will have to assist me.'

'We will do anything you ask,' said Prema.

'Very well,' said Malhamy. 'Bring me a three by four inch sheet of copper leaf tomorrow and leave it with me. I shall require also the names of your neighbours, both wife and husband, and their birth dates if you happen to know them. If you don't it won't matter. A charm is generally more effective however, when used on significant occasions such as birthdays. I will charm the copper leaf and then return it so that all you've got to do is bury it somewhere near your neighbours' dwelling. If Ran Menika walks over the buried charm at any time it will take effect.

'Within two weeks she will be so completely in the grip of the power invoked by the charm that she will become the victim of terrifying nightmares. Illness will overcome her and, for as long as the demon continues to haunt their home, your neighbours will experience nothing but despair and misfortune.'

Malhamy ceased talking and looked intently at his clients, trying to fathom the impact of his words. Marthelis was plainly a little scared, now that he began to see the implications of his mission. But Prema smiled as she asked, 'Are you sure all this will come to pass?'

Malhamy laughed. 'I haven't been known as the most powerful Kattadiya in these parts for nothing,' he said. 'People come all the way from the big city of Colombo to this remote village to see me.'

Prema remained thoughtful. Malhamy, she reflected, lived in great comfort and he could hardly have succeeded in doing so all these years on a false reputation.

'I will bring you the copper leaf tomorrow,' she said, 'and also the information you require. But how much will we have to pay you?'

'I will accept payment only if my charm is successful,' said Malhamy, smiling broadly again. 'Of course rich people from the big towns sometimes pay me as much as five hundred rupees for a successful kodivinia.'

Prema started. Five hundred rupees was a fortune. But the sorcerer soon allayed her fears.

'Don't be dismayed,' he said, benignly. 'From people who are villagers like myself I very rarely accept more than fifty rupees.'

Marthelis shifted uneasily in his seat while Prema was silent. Even fifty rupees was a large sum to people as poor as themselves.

Malhamy seemed to read their thoughts. 'I can see that even fifty rupees would be too much for you,' he said. 'Very well, I shall do this for you as a special favour for thirty rupees. Only I don't want you to mention this to anyone in your village.'

'Hondhemai,' (we agree) said Prema and Marthelis, together. 'For that price we are willing to bind ourselves to pay you.'

Malhamy's face creased into a happy smile. 'Now you must remember,' he said, 'that this is a special favour. For those who really cannot afford I don't believe in charging sinful prices.'

Prema and Marthelis returned to their village after their audience with the sorcerer. It wasn't easy for them to secure the necessary information about the exact date of birth of their neighbour Menika. But after some delicate enquiries, made so skilfully that nobody suspected her motives, Prema finally managed to learn the details. The next day, armed with this information she bought the necessary copper leaf from the village goldsmith and took the bus to Malhamy's place, accompanied by her husband.

A week later Malhamy returned the copper leaf to his clients. The plain surface of the leaf was now etched on either side with two charts consisting of squares. Within each square were strange symbols, like birds or reptiles' numbers and occasional letters from the Sinhala alphabet. What these meant neither Prema nor Marthelis could fathom.

Prema took the copper leaf from the sorcerer and handled it gently as though it was some precious metal.

'We are very grateful to you,' she said.

'We will let you know if it is successful,' said Marthelis.

'It should succeed,' said Malhamy, in a sinister tone. 'It is now invested with the power of the Yaksa Lokey.'

Prema almost dropped the charm when she heard the words which meant 'Demon World'.

'Don't worry,' said Malhamy reassuringly. 'You can safely hold it in your palm. It only works against those whom it is intended to harm.'

There was nothing more for Prema and Marthelis to do but return to their hut and wait for nightfall. They were both determined to put their plan into action at the earliest moment. Fortunately it was a moonless night and after one o'clock, while the whole village slept, they could bury the charm unobserved.

Marthelis was the first to suggest a suitable place. 'Let's bury it at the entrance to their veranda,' he said, as he and Prema stood in their own doorway, about to set out on their mission.

'No,' said Prema, after a little thought. 'It's too close to their rooms. Somebody might hear us digging. I think it would be better if we buried it right opposite their main gate. Ran Menika goes to market daily and she is bound to walk over the charm.'

Marthelis thought there was sense in what she suggested. So taking a little torch, a garden fork, and of course, the charm, he and his wife walked quietly through their own front garden till they came to the main road. A few yards walk down this road brought them to the gateway of their neighbours' home.

Marthelis soon got down to digging a hole. It wasn't a difficult task as the soil was soft and sandy. When he reached a depth of a foot or so he buried the charm and then filling up the hole with earth, he covered the traces of his deed with the fine grained sand that formed the outer surface of the soil.

'Nobody will suspect that a charm has been buried here,' said Prema, approvingly, as she flashed the torchlight and examined the surface of the earth. Marthelis rose with a grunt. He too, was well pleased. It was time to return to their own hut and await developments.

They were about to do so when they heard a sudden, furtive rustle. It came from the bushes which stood on either side of the main gate. Prema and Marthelis were both startled. Had they been observed? For a few seconds they stood quite still but nothing happened. Prema switched on the torch and played the light around and then sighed with relief. All they saw was the rear of a rabbit darting away into the darkness.

Juse Appuhamy and his wife meanwhile remained entirely unaware of the sinister scheme of their neighbours. Juse drove his vegetable cart to the market, as was his custom, while his wife, Ran Menika, fulfilled her daily chores with her usual thoroughness.

In the evenings at about five o'clock, when she'd finished washing the two younger of her children at the well, she would take her shopping bag and go to the village store to buy her provisions for the next day. Her eldest daughter, now close upon thirteen years in age, looked after the two younger children, until she returned.

Now this was a routine that Prema was well aware of

and, ever since the night the charm was buried, she began to keep watch at her window waiting for something dramatic to happen.

But for about two weeks nothing unusual took place. Prema, whose desire to harm her neighbours had long become a mania with her, felt her hatred of Ran Menika more unbearable than ever with every day that passed without event.

'May lightning strike the bitch,' she'd swear, to herself, as she saw Ran Menika return daily from shopping, her bag laden with provisions and none the worse for the charm. She seemed to walk proudly, like a queen, through the gateway, as if to announce to the whole village that nothing in the world would ever break her spirit or that lovely slender body of hers so neatly encased in its close fitting jacket. When Prema compared her own shabby and dirty dress with that of Ran Menika the contrast was so great that she spat through the window in spite.

One night Ran Menika went to bed as usual after tucking her three children to sleep. As she sank on to her comfortable mattress she snuggled up to her husband, Juse, who was already snoring and let her thoughts drift. It was good to be sleeping on a mattress, she thought. How many villagers could boast of a nice solid bed and a mattress? She remembered the first years of her marriage when she had nothing more than a mat to sleep on. Ah, it was good to have a husband like Juse, a hard-working honest man who had provided her and the children with all their needs. It was worth loving and being loved by him. She didn't regret the many sacrifices she had made in the way of clothes and even food just to see him happy, with more money to improve his business and now they were about the most flourishing couple in the village.

The flame from the kerosene lamp on the table by their bed cast its ray over Juse's face. His hair was beginning to turn grey she noticed. Poor man; he worked very hard and now time was beginning to show its marks. But his body was still bronzed and sinewy and tough. His face, though ever so slightly wrinkled beneath the eyes, exuded confidence. Yes. He was still handsome. He was her man.

As these thoughts passed through her mind, Ran Menika felt a strange sense of warmth, security and above all tenderness. Slowly she sank into sleep.

After about an hour of dreamless sleep she began to enter a strange world. She was in a dark and dismal forest with long overhanging creepers and she was walking alone through an animal track which seemed to stretch endlessly into the distance. She passed a shrine under a huge tree and she espied an aged ascetic mumbling before a little effigy. She kept on walking. Elephants and leopards began to pad behind her, following, following all the time. She tried to run but couldn't. The track ahead of her became gloomier and gloomier. She was filled with panic as the animals kept up their pursuit and she made a final despairing effort to run, when she saw a little hut standing isolated on a side of the track. With a tremendous effort she got to the door of the hut and pulled at its handle with every ounce of strength in her body. The door burst open and she saw . . . the dead, staring eyes of her husband, whose body was sprawled on the floor, with a serpent sliding over him. She screamed as she reached despairingly for the body of her husband . . .

Juse Appuhamy woke up with a start when he heard his wife's cries and he found her writhing on the bed clutching desperately at him. He caught her firmly by the arm and jolted her into awareness. Her body was trembling and hot with perspiration. She took one look at her husband's face. heaved a huge sigh of relief and rested her head upon his chest.

'What was it, Sudha?' (darling) he asked, tenderly as he took her in his arms.

'I had an awful dream that you were dead,' she whispered, as a fresh tremor passed through her whole body. 'It was terrible.'

The next day Ran Menika was much too busy to worry about her dream of the previous night. There were so many things to be done in the house for her husband and children that she hardly noticed the passing of time as one chore followed another.

When the evening was far gone she went to the store once again for provisions. About half an hour later dusk began to settle over the village and Ran Menika finished her marketing as quickly as she could in order to be with her family before it got dark. It didn't take her more than fifteen minutes to get to her little home but in that short space of time the whole atmosphere of the village seemed to change. In the half light which preceded darkness it was hushed. It was the time when villagers believed that spirits and phantoms begin their nocturnal prowling.

Ran Menika felt a little uneasy that she happened to be returning home so late that day. She recalled the dream of the previous night and a little shudder passed through her body. She wondered for a moment whether it meant bad luck. Was it a warning of things to come? It was in this sombre frame of mind that she turned through the entrance to her home when suddenly a rabbit darted out of the undergrowth, crept swiftly between her feet and disappeared. As the animal brushed past her she felt a sudden charge of fear and a rush of blood through her heart, so much so that she nearly dropped her bag of provisions. She was still trembling when she walked through the gate to her home, trembling so much that the blood seemed to drain out of her face and Juse, who had also returned home, couldn't help but notice the paleness of her features under the rays from the veranda lamp. He reached for the lamp which hung suspended from a beam and turned the flame a little higher, to have a closer look at her. She looked ghastly under the flame.

'What happened?' he asked, trying to conceal his alarm.

'A rabbit . . . a rabbit . . . a . . . a . . .' stuttered Menika finding it difficult to explain what she felt.

'Well. What's wrong about a rabbit?' asked Juse slightly mystified.

'It . . . it . . . darted between my feet and . . . and . . . disappeared,' said Menika still feeling her body tremble with a fear that she couldn't explain.

'Where did it happen?' asked Juse quietly.

'At the gate, just when I was walking through it.'

'But surely, you don't have to fear a rabbit that darts between your feet?'

'I know. I know. But, but, I was still very frightened,' said Menika, her words trailing to a whisper. 'I don't know, I don't know why I should have been so frightened.'

'Come Sudha' (darling), said Juse, slowly, as he relieved his wife of the provisions. 'Let's go to the kitchen and have our meal.'

He sensed at that moment that what his wife needed was solace and a chance to forget, not questions.

Before he went to bed that night Juse was a little perturbed and he could read the look of worry on his wife's face, although she didn't say anything. She seemed to carry out her duties of seeing that the children ate their rice and curry early, in a listless, half hearted manner. She hardly said a word as she gave him, too, his meal and stood by him till he finished. Finally, she ate herself, following the custom, by which she had her meal only after the rest of the household had eaten.

The unusual silence on the part of Ran Menika seemed to depress even the spirits of the children who hardly said a word between them as they ate. On any other occasion there'd generally be a babble of sound from the rickety table at which they sat opposite their father, mildly disputing with each other over something or other.

Juse felt the onset of a sudden uneasiness because of the unaccustomed silence. He was used to laughter and chatter from the children and the bright cheerful voice of his wife who had always something to tell him at dinner time about the village gossip or the antics of the children.

He tried to appear nonchalant. So rising from his seat he closed a window and then switched on the little transistor set which lay on another table. As the cheerful Sinhala music of Sarala Gee (light songs) filled the room with its rhythms, the oppressive atmosphere seemed to lift.

But the music of the radio brought only temporary relief. At eleven o'clock the announcer closed the station for the night and the children had long since gone to sleep on their mats. The silence was disturbing. Apart from a 'Yes' or 'No' Ran Menika had hardly spoken a word. When she got to bed with her husband she moved close to him as if she needed all the protection he could give her.

It didn't take her long to fall asleep but for Juse, to whom sleep usually came quickly, it was different for once. He was worried about his wife's behaviour over the last two days. First she had a terrible dream about his death and then she allowed herself to become scared out of her wits by a rabbit. Try as he might he couldn't fall asleep.

He heard the wall clock in the room strike twelve midnight and with some pride realized that he was one of the few people in the village who could afford such a luxury. The heat in the room was almost unbearable. Not a breath of air stirred, though the window was open. At about half past one Juse found his lids getting heavier and then finally he dozed off.

Suddenly, though, he was jolted awake by a fearsome scream. It was his wife. She had leapt out of the bed and was staring at her husband with a look of terror.

'The doll, the doll,' she shouted wildly. 'It came into my body. It came into my body.'

Those were the last sensible words that Juse heard from

her. Even as he watched her, all his senses alert, yet too shocked to do anything, she began to dance, oblivious of the fact that the cloth she wore around her body was falling to her feet.

It was the wild meaningless dance of a half naked woman who was and yet wasn't his wife. In the light of the moon which filtered through the open window she seemed like a marionette motivated by something other than her own self. She seemed in short, possessed.

For a few moments Juse was just rooted to his bed, watching the weird dance by his wife. No, a thing like this just couldn't happen to his Ran Menika of all people, who hadn't harmed a soul in all her life. But it was happening before his eyes in his very own bedroom. There was no mistaking her stupid, inane, disjointed movements, a hideous parody of a dance. He had seen something similar before when a relative of his had seemingly become possessed by a demon.

Something told Juse that the only remedy was a terrific shock to her system. So raising his hand he slapped her violently across her face. She ceased dancing, gazed at him with just an inkling of recognition and then realizing she was almost naked she bent down, retrieved her cloth and wrapped it round her body. Juse took hold of her hand and gently drew her to the bed. There was a vacant look in her eyes as she gazed towards the window and tears began to trickle down her cheeks. But she was once again, despite the vacant look, more or less, herself.

'What happened to you, Menika?' asked Juse gently as the trembling of her body ceased.

'I had a bad dream.'

'Again?'

'Yes . . .'

'What did you dream?'

But Menika was silent as though reluctant to recall her experience.

'What did you dream?' asked Juse again.

Menika spoke at last with difficulty. 'I dreamt that I was walking alone through our village. In the distance . . . I saw, I saw a cloth doll. It was made of cloth but yet, but yet, it was alive, and it was hideous to look at. It came walking fast, fast, right towards me and then it entered into my body and I screamed. I don't know what happened after that.'

Juse was silent for a few moments, as though collecting his thoughts. Finally he said very quietly, 'Don't you know that you danced before me just a few minutes ago, half naked?'

'No,' said Ran Menika, listlessly. 'I don't know.'

From that moment Juse wondered whether he would have to consult a Kattadiya or sorcerer, one of those who had mastered the art of exorcism, apart from many other accomplishments such as producing charms and talismans. But before he made a final decision he decided to wait another day and see whether the phenomenon happened again.

Juse's worst fears were to be confirmed and, unfortunately, the children were witnesses on the second occasion when their mother rose from her bed possessed by a demon power and began her strange and tortured performance. Very soon everybody in the village knew of what was taking place in the house of Juse. Many were secretly glad and hoped that it would not be easy to find a cure for the stricken woman. Prema and Marthelis, in particular, gloated over the fact that Ran Menika was ill.

'I hope she dances for the rest of her life,' said Prema to her husband when she received the good news.

Marthelis chuckled. 'Our Juse will have to spend a lot of money if he wants to cure his Menika,' he said, 'there are not many Kattadiyas as good as Malhamy.'

Prema agreed. 'I think we had better go tomorrow and pay him,' she said.

Marthelis didn't reply immediately. Money was

always a problem. 'Do you think we can afford the thirty rupees?' he said at last.

'Don't worry,' said Prema. 'I've sold my old pair of earrings.'

Marthelis was shocked. 'What!' he exclaimed. 'Your only pair of earrings?'

'Yes,' said Prema. 'It was worth the sacrifice.'

As Marthelis looked at the large bony features of his wife's face, embittered and hardened by suffering, he knew better than to argue the point.

Meanwhile Juse Appuhamy acted quickly. He journeyed by bus to a village about sixty miles away from his own where he knew of a famous sorcerer called Siyadoris who was said to be even better than Malhamy, though not quite so affluent.

Now Siyadoris, unlike Malhamy, was a thin, fair complexioned man with sunken cheeks and deep set thoughtful eyes. He was well known as a sorcerer who never used his knowledge of the occult to do evil. He lived in a humble little mud hut with a cadjan roof, bordering the main road, and the only other occupant was a youth about twenty-three years in age, who he called his Golea (pupil). This Golea assisted him in all his exorcism ceremonies. When Siyadoris heard Juse's story he was deeply concerned.

'Your wife does seem possessed by a demon,' he said, as he squatted on his veranda, listening to the details. 'But first let us chew on the beetle leaf. It will help us to think clearly.'

Juse accepted the beetle leaf that he was offered and Siyadoris continued. 'I can come to your house in about three days time,' he said, 'but meanwhile I want you to set up two altars made of tender coconut palms. In one of them you must put, on the night of the ceremony, offerings of rice and fruit and flowers. This will be the offering to the Deviyos (deities) who will help me in my efforts to drive the demon out. On the other altar you must have the offerings to the demon, that is, rice, cakes, and meat. Also buy a cock-bird for the occasion just in case the demon expects a live offering.'

When Juse returned home that day he felt much easier in his mind. He had done all he could think of and it now remained for Siyadoris to drive out the demon who had brought misfortune on Menika. On the night of the ceremony, well illuminated by a petromax lamp, Ran Menika was laid on a mat in the garden, her head resting on a pillow, while Siyadoris commenced the overture to the ceremony.

Clad in a simple white banyan and a white sarong with a cylindrical drum slung from his shoulders, he walked up to the altar dedicated to the benevolent spirits or deities, joined his palms together and intoned with bowed head, 'May the blessings of the Deviyos (deities) attend this ceremony. May the demons be driven from the body of this sick woman.'

With these opening words he intoned a few more verses in praise to the benevolent deities and then only began the ceremony proper. Returning to the centre of the clearing in which Ran Menika lay he beat the first clear rhythm on his drum. The rhythm was taken up on a much smaller drum by a local assistant whom he had hired for the occasion. Thus bass and treble drums combined to produce the first weird rhythms of the Yak Natum (Devil Dance).

As the weird, yet deeply melodious, throb of the drums was heard, someone burst through the crowd of villagers who had gathered to watch the ceremony, and with a great leap commenced to dance. This was the sorcerer's Golea or pupil who wore on his head a hideous wooden mask. Huge black eye-balls jutted out of the mask, painted garishly in red. From a gaping cavern of a mouth flanked by fierce looking tusks, white teeth projected. The nose was curved like the beak of a hawk.

Above the head of the mask slender cobras, beautifully carved, wound their way upwards till their puffed hoods met in the centre. A white banyan, flouncing red skirt and white stockings from thighs to ankles completed the ensemble of the dancer.

Ran Menika meanwhile, lay on the mat, a sheet covering her up to the shoulders. Her lips seemed bloodless in the bluish light from the lamp and damp wisps of hair straggled over her face. Her eyes had sunk deep in their sockets and were gazing blankly at the dancer. A few solicitous relatives sat by her side fanning her with folded newspapers. These were the women, who, fortunately for Juse, had taken things over when they realized that Ran Menika was in no condition to attend to her daily work.

The dancer continued leaping to the rhythm of the drums. In one hand he held a glowing faggot which he waved about his body creating intricate lines of light as he danced. At intervals he threw some inflammable powder on the torch and great tongues of flame leapt skywards, flushing the darkness of the trees for an instant with amber.

At about two o'clock in the morning Ran Menika, who hitherto had been on her mat, gazing fixedly at the dancer, as though mesmerized by his movements, suddenly came alive. She leapt up from her mat, flung the sheet that covered her, aside, and stared with bloodshot eyes at the dancer.

Siyadoris, who as master of ceremonies had been watching everything, increased the tempo of his rhythm. Faster and faster he beat the drum until the tempo became a frenzy. The dancer became a whirling mass of movement, so fast that one could barely distinguish the outlines of his body.

Ran Menika, meanwhile began to tremble. She looked terror stricken at the crowd around her and tried to escape but immediately her relatives held her arms.

Suddenly her body heaved. She struggled violently before collapsing in a swoon.

The dancer, too, at this moment was galvanized into a final burst of movement which he kept up for almost ten minutes. Then spent he too heeled over. While he was still on the floor in his hideous mask, Siyadoris advanced towards him.

'Who are you?' he asked the fallen dancer in a tone of authority.

'I am Kalu Kumara,' said the dancer, in a voice which seemed peculiarly high-pitched.

'Kalu Kumara, the Black Prince, himself.'

The onlookers gasped as they heard the reply. Kalu Kumara, they knew, was a demon of great power who generally tormented women. But Siyadoris was by no means awed. He was truly master of the situation.

'Have you left the woman?'

'Yes,' said the high pitched voice, 'but only for a moment.'

'And now you possess the body of my golea?'

'Yes.'

'Leave him, too. Leave the vicinity of the woman for good.'

'No. I will not leave.'

'Leave him immediately,' shouted Siyadoris.

'No, no,' said the voice, its high-pitched tone becoming almost a shriek. 'I will not leave till you have given me an offering.'

'What offering do you want? We have laid out rice, cakes and flesh for you on your altar. What more do you want?

'I want a live offering.'

'Will a cock-bird suffice?'

For a moment there was silence, as dancer and sorcerer gazed at each other, one on the ground and the other standing menacingly above him. Finally the high-pitched voice said, 'A young cock-bird will suffice.'

'If we offer you a cock-bird,' said the sorcerer, 'what sign will you give us that you've left the vicinity of the woman for good.'

'I will tear a branch off the Jak Tree in this garden.'

The sorcerer gave a sign to Juse who had bought a young cock-bird for this eventuality. The bird was given to the dancer who with both hands held it aloft by the neck. The crowd surged closer. There was a moment of silence and then a collective gasp of horror as the dancer tore the bird's neck apart with his powerful hands, and dropped it on the ground. Someone picked up the bouncing cock-bird with the severed spinal column and took it to the altar of the demon.

A few minutes later there was an ear splitting sound and a huge branch of a Jak Tree in the garden crashed down to earth. The villagers scurried to avoid it. Meanwhile, the dancer too had fallen into a swoon and lay limply, limbs stretched out on the sand. The sorcerer sprinkled some water on his face and body and recovering, he rose slowly and pulled off the mask that he wore.

Ran Menika, too, had risen from her mat and from that moment onwards she began talking to Juse Appuhamy and all those who surrounded her as though nothing had happened. Among the many onlookers there were two people who were bitterly disappointed and furious at the successful outcome of the ceremony – Prema and her husband Marthelis.

Neither Juse nor his wife suspected the evil role that their neighbours had played in this grim affair. But when a week later Prema was found dead on her mat one morning by her husband, with a look of terror in her staring eyes, they began to wonder. It is a common belief in villages that when a person harnesses the aid of a demon, he or she runs the risk of death at the hands of this same demon, should their sinister purpose fail.

White Lady of the Hohenzollerns

Clyde Clarke

The Royal Palace in Berlin was ablaze with light. Before the dressing-table in her boudoir the Queen smiled at her reflection in the mirror. She was wearing a gown of ivory brocade embroidered in silver that she had secretly ordered from her native Hanover. Opening a silver-bound casket, she lifted glittering jewels and let them slip through her fingers, joyously, as a child might play with running water. To her they represented buried hopes and vanished dreams, and tonight she was to wear them again after many years. There was the diadem she had worn as the bride of Frederick William I, the diamond necklace her brother had sent at the birth of her first child, and the bracelet her husband had clasped upon her arm when at last, after fervent prayers and long waiting, their son, the future Frederick the Great, was born.

She rose and surveyed herself in the long Venetian mirror and was almost happy. Then Princess Ulrica came in.

'Gracious, mama,' she exclaimed, 'you look as if

Heaven and all its stars had fallen upon you. You are beautiful! Did our most Royal King and father command you to appear tonight in those lovely jewels?'

'Hush, child! You know how the King despises ornaments and luxuries. If he could see me he would die with rage.'

'No, sweet mamma, he would calculate how many giant soldiers he could hire for his personal Guard for the price of this necklace, or how many miles of military roads he could build with this diadem.'

'Don't speak of the King, child! Think of other things, of whom you will command to dance with you at the ball this evening. Your father will soon be thinking of a prince for you, for he intends you to be a Queen.'

'I will marry whom I please,' the little Princess said haughtily, 'and I shall wear diamonds every day if I wish to. I will not be miserable as poor brother Frederick is.'

'If your father commands, you must obey – as we all do,' Sophia sighed, kissing her daughter lightly on the cheek.

They went into the ante-room, and at that moment Poellnitz, the Grand Chamberlain at the Court of King Frederick the First, threw open the doors and announced that the guests were assembled.

As they followed the Grand Chamberlain through the crowd of richly dressed women and men covered with stars and orders, Sophia managed to whisper to Ulrica: 'The King has commanded us to be merry tonight. And take care, child, Frederick has spies everywhere. When you speak to Poellnitz, remember that he repeats every word to the King.'

After making the grand tour of the *salons* the Queen seated herself at a card-table with the Margrafin Maria Dorothea and the English and French Ambassadors. Never had she been more gracious, more queenly. Behind her chair stood two maids of honour. She turned to them now and then to give some order or to send them to look after the young princesses, who were dancing in the next *salon*.

Suddenly the music ceased. The May evening seemed very still. An ominous silence oppressed the room. Then, from the other wing of the palace came the sound of loud knocking – hammer blows resounding in slow, solemn rhythm.

The Duke of Holstein spoke to General Schwerin, so that the Queen might hear: 'Is the King at work in his carpentry shop? I thought he could not leave his chair.'

'They say he has worked all day at his carpentering,' the General replied. 'He thinks his gout will be better and his arms and legs will be less stiff if he uses them.'

The Queen tried to smile and go on with the game. She turned to Poellnitz who was standing near: 'Why does the music stop? Do have them play on. It is so much more cheerful.'

She played her cards absently, as the music started again. Then she turned to one of her maids of honour: 'Have the princesses come to me as soon as the dance is over,' she commanded, her face grave.

But beforc the command could be obeyed, the Princess Amelia, pale and horrified, rushed to her mother, greatly agitated.

'My dear child, what is wrong?' the Queen cried.

'The Lady in White!' Amelia whispered, her voice trembling. 'I saw her as I looked out the window. She was moving among the lilac bushes!'

The Queen turned pale. She rose instantly and in another moment all were standing. In the tomb-like stillness that fell over the rooms they could hear the rhythmic beat of the hammer in the other wing of the palace. A faint perfume of lilacs was in the air.

The Grand Chamberlain came very softly to the Queen's side. He bowed. 'Your Majesty, command me!' he said, his voice a trifle unsteady.

'Has anyone else seen "The Lady in White"?' she asked, anxiously.

'Yes, Your Majesty. Several of the sentries have seen the spectre, but not in this part of the palace. The figure was seen floating – '

'Where?' she whispered. 'Floating where? Tell me.'

'In the gardens and around the corridors of the other wing of the palace.'

The Queen recovered herself quickly: 'I command that the dance proceed!' She was still very pale, but she turned to soothe Princess Amelia. 'It is nothing, child, it is but a myth. Go back to your dancing and be gay. Remember, we are commanded by the King to be happy tonight.'

Amelia went away reluctantly with a young margrave who had accompanied her, and the Queen talked in whispers to General Schwerin.

The English Ambassador was curious, and he asked the French Ambassador, in a low voice: 'The Lady in White? Who is she? I do not understand.'

'It is the legendary spectre that has haunted the ruling family of Prussia for centuries,' the French Ambassador whispered. 'It always portends the death of a member of the Imperial family. If it wears white gloves, it means a woman is to die; if black gloves, it means the death of a man. It is said always to appear before the death of a Royal personage.'

As the music started again the Queen resumed her seat at the card-table and calmly arranged her cards. 'Let us play,' she said.

In the wing of the palace occupied by the King, there was silence. Frederick William sat alone in his bare room. Slowly he raised himself from his chair and extended his arms.

'They think I am suffering, chained to my chair!' he cried. 'But I have no pain tonight. The work has cured the pain!' He stretched his arms and moved his fingers gleefully.

'They think that the doors of the Royal vault will soon open to receive my corpse. But Frederick William will not die! My son shall not reign! This weak, riotous youth, this dreamer! Prussia has no need of this sentimental boy, who finds the tones of his flute sweeter than the sounds of trumpets and drums! Never shall Prussia be ruled by a dreaming poet!'

His breath came fast. He was trembling with rage. 'Bah! the fool has said that Voltaire was as great as a king – yes, greater than the kings anointed by the Pope! A fool shall not govern Prussia. The King will live!'

Worn out by this outburst, he sank into his chair again, murmuring: 'They think I shall die, but I shall be well. I have commanded Sophia to give a ball that the world could see that the Queen and my daughters are gay and happy!'

He called the servant who awaited his pleasure in the adjoining room and commanded him: 'Call together the gentlemen who compose my Tobacco Club, and arrange everything for a meeting of that august body!'

'But those gentlemen, Your Majesty, are at the Queen's ball,' the servant said, astonished.

'Then go for them. Bring them quickly. Poellnitz must come, and Eckert, and Baron von Goltz and Hacke, Duke of Holstein, and General Schwerin. Quick! In ten minutes they must all be here, but,' he cautioned, raising a shaking finger, 'let no one know why he is sent for. Only whisper to each one that he is commanded to come to me. Tell him he must tell no one where he is going. I will not have the Queen's ball disturbed. She must be happy tonight! Go!'

In ten minutes six gentlemen, their faces very pale, stood in the King's ante-chamber.

'What does this sudden summons mean?' they asked each other anxiously. No one knew.

The servant entered the King's room. His Majesty, dressed in the full uniform of his Guard, sat at a round table, on which the pipes and the mugs filled with foaming beer were already placed. He had condescended to fill a pipe with his own hands, and was on the point of lighting it at a nearby candle.

'Sire,' the servant said, 'the gentlemen are waiting in the ante-room.'

'Do they know why I have sent for them?' the King asked, blowing a cloud of smoke from his mouth.

'Your Majesty forbade me to tell them.'

'Well, go now and tell them I am more furiously angry today than you have ever seen me, that I am standing by the door with my crutch, and that I command them to come singly into my presence.'

'What is the matter? Why is the King so angry? What orders do you bring from His Majesty?' the men questioned the servant in anxious whispers.

The servant assumed a terrified expression as he replied: 'His Majesty has never been so outrageously angry. Woe unto him over whom the cloud bursts. He commands that each you enter the room alone. Go now! For heaven's sake do not keep the King waiting. I fear for what may happen to you!'

The men looked at each other in consternation. No one wished to be first to encounter the King's rage.

The Grand Chamberlain, bowing to the Duke of Holstein, said: 'Your Grace has precedence.'

The Duke winced. 'No,' he said, 'you are well aware that His Majesty does not regard Court etiquette on these occasions, and would be most indignant if we paid any attention to it. Let us not displease him. Go first yourself, my dear friend.'

'Not I, Your Grace. I would not dare to take precedence in this group. The King would be angry with me. If you decline the honour, it is due to General Schwerin.'

'Gentlemen,' interrupted the servant, 'His Majesty will become impatient and then more angry.'

'But, my God, who will dare go first?' Count von Goltz cried.

'I will,' said Councillor Eckert. 'I owe everything to His Majesty, I will place my life at his service.' He braced himself, and with firm steps went to the door and opened it.

His companions saw the King's eyes flash as he raised his crutch over the head of his favourite, and then the door closed. Though they heard no sound, they waited anxiously.

Poellnitz spoke to the servant in faltering tones: 'Against which of us is the anger of the King directed? Is it I?'

'Alas, I do not know,' the servant replied. 'Let the next one enter. His Majesty must not be kept waiting.'

Poellnitz stepped boldly to the door, and as he entered they saw the King standing in threatening attitude inside the door. Each time this scene was repeated, and then General Schwerin, the last of the six, went in to the King's presence.

This time the King was not standing at the door. He lay in his arm-chair, laughing until the tears rolled down his withered cheeks.

'The joke succeeded to perfection,' he said, exultantly. 'Even you, Schwerin, who never knew fear on the battlefield, are trembling with fear.'

The General tried to smile: 'Yes, Sire, a shot is a trifling thing compared with a flash from your eyes. I have no fear of death, I only fear the displeasure of my sovereign.'

'Give me your hand, Schwerin,' the old monarch said. 'You are a brave fellow. And now, gentlemen, away with all constraint and etiquette. We will suppose the King to be at the ball. I am only your companion, Frederick William. I will now proceed to the opening of the

Tobacco Club. Tell your very best guardroom jokes. Make me laugh!'

The big empty room was lighted by but four tallow candles, for the King would tolerate nothing beyond bare necessities, and the four streaks of light seemed pale and sickly in the blue smoke that filled the air.

'Light more candles,' the King commanded his man-in-waiting. 'Our Tobacco Club must present a festive appearance tonight so that the contrast between it and the ball be not too great.' Then he spoke to the Grand Chamberlain: 'Tell me, Poellnitz, is the Queen's ball a brilliant one? The Queen – is she gay, and are the princesses dancing merrily?'

'I have never witnessed a more magnificent spectacle, Sire, nor has Her Majesty ever been more beautiful. I had no idea she possessed such priceless jewels.'

The King's face set in its accustomed hard lines. 'Fill the glasses, Jochen,' he said to the valet. Then a harsh laugh escaped his lips. 'So she has put on her jewels, has she? They are taking advantage of my absence. They think I am writhing on a bed of pain.'

Poellnitz put down his mug and smiled. 'The Queen has good reason for being happy tonight, for Your Majesty is not ill. You have worked all day in your carpentering shop. In the ballroom above the music we could hear the blows of your hammer.'

Frederick took a long draught of beer, and the lid snapped loudly as he banged the mug on the table. 'I should not be surprised if Frederick had clandestinely come over to this ball,' he said. 'He thinks to govern Prussia with his book-learning and his poems. A dreaming scholar can never be a good king. He who wields pen and fiddle-bow instead of a sword and sceptre, will never be a good general.'

Poellnitz set down his mug quietly and said quickly, in soothing tones: 'Your Majesty forgets that this is a sitting of the Tobacco Club and not of the State Council. Let us be gay as the others are gay tonight. Your pipe is out and your mug is empty, Sire!'

'True,' said Frederick. 'Fill my mug, Jochen, I shall drink to the health of him who first overcame fear and dared to enter this room. Who was it? I have forgotten. You are all cowards in my presence. Raise your glasses! Drink!'

'The toast is to the Privy Councillor von Eckert, Sire,' said Count Hacke with an ironical smile.

'He entered the chamber as he goes into battle,' Poellnitz laughed, 'in the spirit in which he took leave of all the fine breweries and artfully constructed non-smoke chimneys which he built. He marched courageously into the Royal presence.' The King's favourite was far from popular with the other officers.

Eckert's face was pale in the flickering light, and he scowled at Poellnitz, as the other men laughed heartily.

'Really, your wit this evening is dazzling, Poellnitz,' he said. 'I am charmed with your pleasantries.'

'Silence!' Frederick commanded. 'No more of this raillery.'

Suddenly the door opened and the King's valet appeared.

'Your Majesty,' he said, 'your orders have been obeyed. The White Salon is ready. The last work of your hands has been placed there for your inspection. The paint is quite dry.'

'Illumine the White Salon!' Frederick cried, struggling to his feet and throwing his mug on the table. 'Jochen, give me your arm!'

In the grand ball-room the music went on without pause at the Queen's demand. The May air was soft and the scent of lilacs drifted through the open windows. The face of the Queen was pale but very sweet under the glittering diadem, and she tried to smile as she played her cards.

Suddenly the Princess Sophia Dorothea, who stood nearby, gave a low cry of terror and fell back into the arms of a maid of honour. 'The King!' she whispered. 'My God, the King!'

In the corridor, approaching the doorway, they saw Frederick, his eyes flashing, his limbs trembling. Supported by his valets, he came slowly towards the room.

The Queen whispered to the attendant behind her: 'Remove my long ear-rings and the necklace quickly!' Then she calmly played a queen on the table before her. The French Ambassador played a king.

'Lost!' she said, trying to smile. 'So must the Queen ever be lost when the King comes.'

Frederick fixed his blazing eyes upon her and called her name. A hush fell over the room. She rose instantly and went to him, a faint smile on her pale face.

'Ah, my husband,' she said, 'what a pleasant surprise you have prepared for us! It is most amiable of Your Majesty to honour this feast with your presence.'

The King grasped her arm savagely and his voice was harsh: 'It is necessary in the midst of earthly pleasures to be reminded of the fleeting vanity of earthly things. I am come to administer this medicine to your vain and sin-sick soul. Come with me! All of you. Follow me! Let none remain behind!'

In vain the Queen pleaded with Frederick to tell her his plan. She could only walk tremblingly at his side and go with him. She knew not where.

The King kept his eyes steadily before him. His face was set and hard. He did not speak. The bejewelled ladies and gentlemen of his Court followed the Royal pair in a long, glittering procession. No one dared to disobey the King's orders. Though it looked like a wedding procession, the courtiers and their ladies felt as if they were marching towards their doom.

The Queen looked anxiously from side to side, anticipating some new terror as the long parade passed through the flower-decked dressing-rooms, through the brilliantly lighted ante-chamber, on through the endless corridors and up the long staircase, until at last they reached the door of the White Salon, which Frederick had built and adorned.

At the King's command the doors were thrown open and he led Sophia into the room.

She gave a cry of horror: *'Two coffins! Your Majesty – what does this mean?'*

'Yes, two coffins, mine and yours. I have made them with my own hands. I finished them tonight – while you revelled. In these coffins we will soon rest and all earthly vanity and glory will be at an end. No one will then fear my glances or my crutch. No one will admire the glittering jewels of the Queen. Dust will return to dust and the King and Queen will be nothing more than food for worms.'

Under the crystal chandeliers the lights glared in the marble whiteness of the room. For a moment no one moved or breathed.

Then Sophia summoned her courage and spoke softly: 'Not so, my King! The dust of common mortals will be scattered in every direction by the hand of Time. But from our dust history will build enduring monuments!'

As she spoke the Queen seemed endowed with fresh beauty. She needed no royal diadem, no gleaming jewels to enhance her queenly bearing. She was the wife of the King of Prussia, the sister of the King of England, the mother of the future King of the Prussian Empire.

Her composure angered Frederick. With a trembling hand he pointed to the statues of his ancestors that adorned the room. His tone was imperious, terrifying: 'So, then, let my ancestors see how well we will look in our coffins! The world knows that jewels become you and that I am a fine fellow in my uniform, but let us try our coffins!'

The Queen faltered: 'Oh, my King – '

'Do not waste precious time – you have wasted enough at the card-table this evening. See if you can take your place with grace and dignity in this coffin I have made for you with my own hands. Lay yourself in your coffin, Sophia, that I may see a picture of you that you can never behold. I have brought you here that we may try our coffins.'

'This is a cruel jest, Frederick!' There was a tremor in her voice, but she turned to one of her maids of honour and said: 'Duchess, give me your hand. I am very weary, and for a time I shall rest in peace upon this bed.'

As the Duchess took her trembling hand, the Queen lifted the skirt of her royal robe slightly and stepped over the edge of the coffin. Proudly erect she stood for a moment and then, with dainty grace, she stooped and stretched her body until with closed eyes she lay still and calm in the white coffin.

The rudely made coffin creaked and groaned. A murmur of horror came from the richly attired company.

The King stood looking on, his features set in cruel lines. After a few moments Sophia opened her eyes and looked up at him. His eyes avoided hers and he stared at the floor.

Slowly the Queen arose, very pale, but with her imperial dignity unbent. The Duchess held out a hand to assist her, but she declined it saying: 'Kings and queens must leave their coffins by their own strength and greatness, sustained by their deeds alone.'

With these words she stepped over the edge of the coffin and bowing profoundly to the King, said: 'Your Majesty, it is your turn now.'

The King looked at her darkly and stepped awkwardly into his coffin. He called some of his courtiers to assist him in lying down. 'Here I will soon sleep,' he said.

Sophia reached her hand to him. 'May that time be far removed, my King,' she said.

At that moment the awed silence of the room was

broken by loud piercing cries and the sound of hastening feet in the ante-chamber.

Frederick sat bolt upright in his coffin, a look of terror in his drawn face: 'What is it? What has happened? I demand to know!'

The major-domo stepped forward with shaking limbs: 'Your Majesty, the sentries in the corridor have seen the figure of a tall woman clad in white – she passed the whole length of the corridor and entered this room!'

'The Lady in White!' cried Frederick, falling as if broken to pieces in his coffin. The courtiers recoiled and the ladies stood paralyzed with amazed horror. Only the Queen was calm.

Frederick suddenly sat up in his coffin and asked in a creaking voice: 'Did she wear white gloves or black?'

For a moment no one spoke. A deep silence pervaded the room. The scent of lilacs drifted in from the palace gardens.

At last the major-domo dared to break the silence: 'She wore black gloves, Your Majesty.'

'Black! That means I am to die,' Frederick cried. 'Help me from this coffin! You will put me back soon enough!'

As morning dawned, Her Majesty, the Queen, stood at the window of her apartment and looked out into the mist of the new May day. White lilacs hung in pallid clusters from bending boughs. Birds twittered softly among the leaves. Ghostly swans swam placidly, skirting the water-lilies on the border of the lake.

Beyond all that she could see with her eyes was the castle at Rheinsberg, where the Prince Royal was sleeping peacefully, his flute on the table at his bedside.

In his bare room across the misty garden the King lay dying. She knew that the time was at hand when Frederick William II, afterwards known as Frederick the Great, was to ascend the throne of Prussia.